About the Author

Ruth Ward is the younger, better looking sister of the author Mark Hayden. Until recently, she lived abroad and worked for a mysterious organisation whose name and purpose have never been clear.

When she returned to Britain, Ruth was at a loose end and volunteered to write a cosy mystery featuring some of the characters from her brother's King's Watch universe.

Ruth lives in north Lancashire with her cat, Wombat.

Also by Ruth Ward

The Caffè Milano English Village Mysteries
Featuring Bridget and Lucy
Available from Paw Pres

Murder Within Tent
Extra Shot of Murder

Murder Within Tent

A Caffè Milano English Village Mystery

Ruth Ward

PAW PRESS

www.pawpress.co.uk

Originally published in eBook 2022.
Revised and re-published 01 December 2024

www.pawpress.co.uk

www.katiebirks.co.uk

ISBN-13: 978-1-914145-06-3
ISBN-10: 1-914145-06-2

***

To Volunteers Everywhere

Who all make a huge difference to their communities. You are the unsung heroes of life.

Publisher's Note

If you would like to see more maps, character lists and other information about the world of Byford, they can be found on the Paw Press website. This book was originally written in 2022, but the action takes place some time between the Brexit Referendum and the Coronavirus Pandemic.

www.pawpress.co.uk

MURDER WITHIN TENT

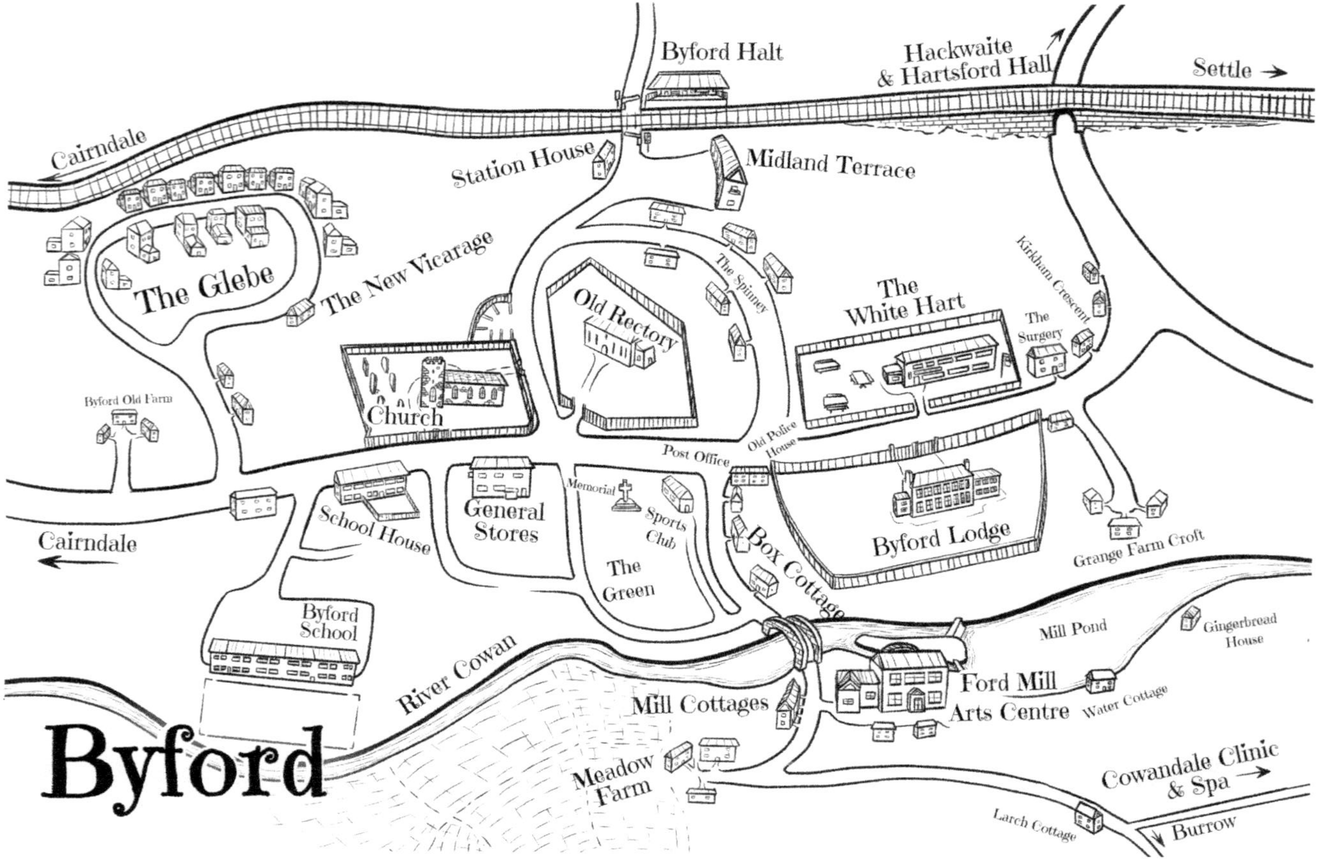
Byford
Byford Halt
Hackwaite
& Hartsford Hall
Settle
Cairndale
Station House
Midland Terrace
The Glebe
The New Vicarage
Church
Old Rectory
The Spinney
The White Hart
The Surgery
Kirkham Crescent
Byford Old Farm
Post Office
Old Police House
Byford Lodge
Grange Farm Croft
Cairndale
School House
General Stores
Memorial
Sports Club
The Green
Box Cottage
Byford School
River Cowan
Mill Pond
Gingerbread House
Ford Mill
Arts Centre
Water Cottage
Mill Cottages
Meadow Farm
Cowandale Clinic
& Spa
Larch Cottage
Burrow

Chapter 1

'On your marks.'

'Get set.'

'Bake!'

The audience gave a spontaneous round of applause and the game was afoot: the Byford Mayfest Bake Off had begun.

The five competitors started weighing and measuring ingredients, the helpers started running around, the hosts smiled encouragingly, and one of the judges frantically checked her phone.

As soon as no one was looking, the *other* judge slipped into the tent. Well, having arrived late, she wasn't going to waltz in and have everyone staring at her like the last time, was she? And Bridget had the feeling that once they saw what she was wearing, they'd be staring at her soon enough anyway.

She scuttled round the outside of the workstations and stopped dead, then took two steps back. One of the poor sods taking part in the competition was doing so on a workbench *made from coffins*. That's right: under the plain wooden worktop, the station was actually a stack of caskets. *Cool,* thought Bridget. *I must suggest that to Lucy for the Cairndale refurbishment.* And then a much darker thought hit her: *How in the name of Jesus did they come by that many coffins? And are they all empty?*

With a shudder, she sidestepped a helper carrying a bucket of water and joined Lucy at the front of the tent. Lucy was many things to Bridget: her friend, her boss, her occasional tormentor and, for today, her fellow judge. Bridget smiled, but Lucy didn't.

'Where've you been,' hissed Lucy. 'I've been trying to get through to you for ages.'

'Sorry, Luce. Train was late and it rattled so much I couldn't text properly, and then I had to quick march down from the station. I'm here now, aren't I?' She paused and said what was really worrying her. 'You didn't think I'd bail on you, did you? You know I wouldn't do that.'

Lucy was still angry. Angry enough to say, 'I know you wouldn't do it *deliberately*, but …'

It was like a slap in the face: that Bridget's *issues* (as other people called them) might lead her to neglecting her duty.

Lucy recoiled and went red. 'I'm sorry, Bridge. I didn't mean it that way. You know me better than that.' She took a deep breath. 'You're here, the competition's begun, and now we're ready to rock. You can leave your coat over there.'

'Do I have to?'

Lucy frowned. 'Yes. Is that an apron sticking out the bottom of your coat?'

Bridget was mortified, and she had a bad feeling that this wouldn't be the last time today. She slowly unbuttoned her vintage greatcoat and revealed her choice of outfit for their first social event in the country village of Byford.

Lucy's eyes immediately flicked from Bridget's dress to the judging table, and Bridget knew that Lucy wasn't looking at the distinctly home-made trophy of a wooden spoon embedded into a plinth.

'You told me I couldn't wear black today,' pleaded Bridget.

'I know, but you didn't have to wear the tablecloth!'

It was true: the judging table was covered with a blue gingham tablecloth that could have been cut from the same bolt of fabric as Bridget's dress.

'Why?' was all Lucy could muster. She, of course, looked smart in a green dress from some designer label's petite range.

Bridget sighed. 'As far as I could see last time we came here, everyone wears Barbour jackets and walking shoes. No way am I wearing that, so I went on this cottagecore website to look for recommendations.'

'Cottagecore?' said Lucy weakly. 'They won't care what you wear, so long as you're nice to them and you're not too honest about their baking.'

'They're all norms on the outside, but that's just a front. Underneath, they're all demonspawn.'

Lucy gave her a dead eyed stare. 'You should fit right in then.'

'I will never fit in here.'

'Whatever. Look, the hosts are coming.'

'At least it's got long sleeves,' mumbled Bridget, mostly to herself. Lucy would never, ever criticise Bridget's tattoos, but Bridget wasn't ready to share them with the locals just yet. She was scared they'd burn her as a witch, or worse still they'd ask her to join in their secret coven and sacrifice goats. Actually, the goat sacrifice might not be a bad idea.

Lucy gave Bridget's arm a squeeze, right where the skull and roses tattoo was hidden by the gingham sleeve: it was Lucy's way of saying *We're a team*. Bridget breathed out and got ready for the onslaught.

While the hosts made their way over to them, Bridget scanned the tent to see if any of the three people she'd previously spoken to in Byford were here. This was her second visit to the village, and her first had taken place some weeks ago. It had been fleeting and scary. Were they here? No, was the answer. Or not yet. She had, however, spied on one of the competitors during that first, brief, visit to the village, and was not looking forward to making her further acquaintance.

She could also guess at the identity of one of the hosts: the dog collar was a dead giveaway, and it wasn't like the spiked dog collar Bridget saved for party nights, either, and would have enjoyed wearing today because it might have stopped them talking to her. Nothing like a bit of bondage gear to give yourself a nice cordon sanitaire. Emphasis on the *sanitaire*.

Lucy made the introductions. 'This is Marjorie Lutworth, chair of the Mayfest Committee, and this is the Reverend Deborah Giddings. Ladies, this is Bridget Gorrigan, my operations manager and friend. Mostly friend, though.'

'Call me *Jorie*,' said Marjorie as she leaned forwards to shake hands.

'And it's Deborah, not *Reverend*,' added the vicar.

'Nice to meet you both,' said Bridget. 'Sorry I'm a bit late, but I had to catch the train.'

'Aah,' said Call-me-Jorie knowingly. 'You're from Liverpool, by your accent. Like Paul Hollywood himself.'

Bridget was thirty-six years old, and ever since the day she'd first left her home city on a family holiday, she knew the brutal truth: open your mouth in England, and everyone judges you. Even the *actual* Paul Hollywood, the celebrity baking judge off the telly, probably found the same thing.

For Lucy's sake, Bridget bit back a savage response and played the ball, not the woman. 'Paul Hollywood's from the Wirral, not Liverpool, but close enough.'

The Reverend Deborah slid in smoothly. 'And I'm sure you'll be a much better judge than he is.'

'I'm sure,' added Jorie. 'Here's a copy of the programme. We'll make a start with our grand tour in a minute, shall we? You're going to meet an awful lot of new people today, and it can get quite confusing. It's one of the things that makes a village like ours seem cliquish – we all know each other.' Jorie added a smile that bordered on the patronising and continued, 'Don't worry, just act as if you've known us all for years. No one expects you to remember all the names straight away.'

Bridget accepted the printed sheet and tried to calm down. At least neither of the women had mentioned her dress. 'How was it before I got here?' she asked Lucy.

Her friend grimaced. 'I didn't get away from the Mill until ten minutes before the start, so I only just beat you. It's all signed, though; we take over on Monday.'

'Monday? You're joking, aren't you?'

'I wish I was. The administrators said they'd pull the plug on Miller's Rest regardless, so I had to sign up there and then. I got an extra ten per cent off the fittings, though. And they finally threw in the kitchen as part of the lease.'

'Mina will love that when she finds out. If she finds out.'

Lucy's eyes softened in sympathy. 'Are you okay about the Mill?'

Bridget blew out some air. 'Yeah. I'm fine really. I've come to terms with it, but I'm not so keen on Monday. A couple of weeks would have been better.'

'I'll pick you up bright and early Monday morning,' said Lucy. 'I'd better check my phone before we start and see if Tom has messaged.'

Lucy went to her bag, which was sitting on the cloakroom table behind them. Bridget would *never* have left her bag there, especially if it was a Di Sanuto like Lucy's. You can't be too careful, even in the countryside. Lucy's boyfriend – partner – was a copper, and a senior one. That wouldn't stop people robbing her, though.

Lucy finished messaging and left her phone next to the bag; Bridget tried not to wince at the risk her friend was taking and asked, 'Any news about Granddad Morton?'

'No change. Tom sends his love and says good luck for today.'

That was Tom Morton all over. Thoughtful. Too thoughtful, sometimes. Tom had had some bad news during the week: his grandfather had fallen badly and broken his hip. Tom was devoted to the old man and had gone back to Yorkshire for the weekend.

Bridget looked down at the folded programme. On the front was a rather accomplished line drawing of a picnic (probably nicked off the internet) and the title:

The Byford Mayfest Bake Off
Sponsored by Caffè Milano

And that was how Bridget Gorrigan, Goth of Garston, came to be judging a baking competition in the middle of the Westmorland countryside. Her company – Lucy's company – was about to take over the lease on a coffee shop up the road, and this was part of the price.

Bridget loved to look on the dark side in public (someone had to), but at least they had been spared the actual May Day celebration, which had taken place last weekend. Thankfully, Lucy had been at a massive wedding, so the Bake Off competition had been put back a week.

Bridget turned the page and looked at the introduction. Rather than perform three challenges like they did on the TV version, the competitors had to complete one compulsory decorated bake in an hour, then produce a full afternoon tea at four o'clock, and the presented tea had to include certain prescribed elements, one of which also had to be baked in the tent. Call-me-Jorie and Rev Deb had been round to the competitors' houses yesterday to make sure that pre-made bakes were indeed *made* and not *bought*.

Lucy was fiddling with her dress, patted it, then handed Bridget a

Caffè Milano name badge with her name on it. Lucy was big on branding. 'Let's get it over with.'

The hosts came back, and Jorie said, 'Shall we begin?'

As they set off across the tent, Bridget's underskirt gave an unsettling swish. Hopefully no one heard. Jorie extended a regal arm to push them towards the second bench down. Hmm. What was she hiding? Why didn't she want them to start at the first one?

Bench Two was occupied by a woman already hard at work. She wore jeans, a loose shirt and looked almost normal by country standards.

'Maria, this is Lucia Berardi and Bridget Gorrigan. Ladies, this is Maria.'

Bridget twitched. Lucy had told her not to argue, but if she were addressed as a lady again, she might not last the afternoon. And then it got worse.

'I guessed,' said Maria. 'The name badges were a clue. You're the Caffè Milano girls, aren't you?'

Bridget's mouth was open to say *I'm not a girl*, but Lucy cut her off.

'That's us,' said Lucy. 'But call me Lucy, unless you speak Italian. What will you be serving?'

Now that Maria had looked up, Bridget could see she was older than she'd first thought and must be over … sixty? Maybe the country air really was good for you. Maria had a series of laminated recipe cards in front of her. This, Bridget approved of. Lamination was a Good Thing because you can wipe laminated cards clean. Maria handed Lucy a copy of her menu, and while Lucy studied it, Bridget leaned over to check Maria's hygiene. There were no finger marks, stains or spills on any of the jars or Tupperware. Also Good. Perhaps Bridget would grow into Maria one day. Yeah. Right.

'Flapjack and millionaire's shortbread, then soda bread for the sandwiches, Yorkshire tea loaf, scones, profiteroles and cupcakes,' said Lucy. 'Mmm. I'm getting hungry already.'

This was not good enough. Maria was letting the side down here. You could be laminated and adventurous. Of course you could. It was time to let her know.

'You've played it safe, haven't you?' she said.

'Every recipe is tried and tested,' Maria responded.

This might be true, but Bridget would be the judge of that. 'Well, all I can say is that every element needs to be perfect.'

Maria rocked back a fraction. That had told her.

'Shall we move on?' said Jorie.

Chapter 2

Bridget recognised the competitor at Bench Three and wondered if it would be mutual. Bridget had nicknamed her the Valkyrie in her head, on account of the height, the long blonde hair and the toned body. It might be early May, but out in the countryside, it was not warm by any means. Perhaps Anya Calvert would work up a sweat – she was definitely dressed for the gym, not for a picnic.

When Jorie made the introductions, Anya had a brave stab at welcoming them to her workstation in Italian. It was the price Lucy paid for being in the newspapers: she was easy to Google. Lucy rattled off something in return and accepted the (unlaminated) menu.

Since Bridget's first trip to Byford, she'd been doing her own version of due diligence. Lucy and their now honeymooning financial adviser had been looking at cash flows and footfall, but Bridget had spent the past three weeks looking at the humans who would cross the threshold and hand over the cash. The ones she could find online, anyway.

Bridget had seen Anya Calvert and her little daughter in the shop, and now Bridget knew that Anya was married to a tech millionaire called Dominic, she could understand why the village Valkyrie had the time to always look so *groomed*. Bridget's impression of wealth was reinforced when Anya pointed to the judges' cloakroom table and said to Lucy, 'I see you've brought one of your mother's creations. You could induce a serious case of bag envy in the village.'

'They only come out on special occasions,' said Lucy.

Anya stared at Bridget's dress, then at Bridget herself, until it clicked. *Damn. She's remembered me.*

'You're looking … different. Different from when we met in the shop.'

Before Bridget could say anything that they'd both regret, Lucy hurriedly changed the subject. 'You're going for cannoli? Brave. Is anyone else risking a deep fat fryer?'

Bridget looked down to examine the Valkyrie's hygiene: satisfactory, but more effort could have been made to sterilise the bench. She looked up. 'A deep fat fryer in here? I hope you've got a fire extinguisher handy.'

It was clear that this hadn't crossed Anya's mind. She looked at the helpers in the background and shouted, 'Dom!'

A man wearing co-ordinating athletic wear rushed over. The yellow rubber gloves were not a good look on him, but Bridget forgave that. The helpers had a lot of work to do – washing up and providing water when you're in a tent is a bigger challenge than actually doing the baking.

'Yes?' said Dominic.

'When you bring the fryer, can you bring the extinguisher?'

'Of course.'

'So long as it's a wet chemical extinguisher,' said Bridget. 'Anything else would be ... interesting.'

There was another machine already on the bench, whirring away. Bridget saw it as a gauntlet thrown down. 'Show me your ice cream recipe,' she demanded.

Anya's mouth opened to object, then she remembered that this was a competition and handed over the sheet. Bridget studied it and asked, 'Did you follow this *exactly*?'

Anya wiped her forehead with the back of her hand. 'Yes.'

A voice from the crowd piped up. 'With extra rum, knowing Dom!'

'Well, it looked a bit mean,' said Anya defensively.

Bridget returned the recipe and for the first time channelled Paul Hollywood. 'We'll see, shall we?'

Anya's mouth dropped open slightly and her eyes bulged.

'We'll let you get on,' said Lucy hurriedly, physically dragging Bridget away.

Bridget normally lashed out when people touched her unexpectedly. It was a sign of how much she loved Lucy that she didn't mind. 'Go easy, Bridge,' hissed Lucy. 'We don't want to alienate people like Anya.'

'Just putting her in her place,' said Bridget. 'And we don't want the tent to burn down, do we?'

Lucy sighed. 'No, we don't. I wonder who's next?'

Rev Deb had been hanging back so far and letting Jorie make the introductions, but she decided to muscle in for Bench Four. 'This is one of the amazing team at St Peter's School,' the vicar announced. 'Millie Easterby.'

Millie Easterby did not look amazing. What she looked was worried. She was soft and mousey and slightly confused by the ingredients.

'Millie stepped in at the last minute,' said Rev Deb. 'I call that very brave, and some of her menu is gluten-free. How's it going?'

'Good, thanks,' said Millie. She looked at Lucy and Bridget. 'The gluten-free part is for one of the children in my class. Baking's not really my thing, but, you know, it's for the village.'

'Is the village that hungry?' said Bridget mildly.

Instead of flinching back, Millie held her gaze. 'You have no idea … Bridget, is it? The appetites of Byford can be insatiable.'

Who rattled your cage? thought Bridget. *Looks like I'm not the only one who's got the measure of the locals.*

Millie blinked. 'And there's an Easterby on every honour board or trophy in Byford,' she added. 'I thought I'd give it a go.'

Easterby. She'd heard that name on her first visit but couldn't remember the context. The teacher looked like more of a fighter than Bridget had given her credit for at first, so Bridget said, 'We'll let you get the hang of it then we'll come back.'

She didn't know why, but she added, 'Good luck.'

Jorie and Rev Deb almost raced to Bench Five, the first male competitor. Jorie beat the vicar to it by a nose, and instead of introducing him, she said, 'Off to a good start, Perry?'

Please don't tell me he's the local Eligible Bachelor, thought Bridget. There was nothing wrong with him to look at, she supposed. In his forties, with sandy hair and blue eyes. Oh. The T-shirt. *Bakers have nice buns.* It was automatic. She couldn't help it, and she checked out the goods. He did have nice buns.

He gave the hosts a warm smile and said, 'All under control.' And when he smiled at Lucy, the smile was even warmer. 'Ms Berardi. Lovely to meet you in person, but I won't shake hands. Bit doughy.'

Of course. Unless Byford was overrun with Peregrines, this would be Perry Lockwood, estate manager to Edwin Duke. Lucy and Perry had been negotiating the lease electronically for a fortnight, and now here he was in the flesh. Buns and all.

'It's Lucy, please. And this is my right-hand woman, Bridget. She'll be in charge at the Byford branch.'

Rev Deb and Jorie exchanged a look. This conversation was not one they were keen to encourage for some reason. 'Are the boys not spectating?' asked Jorie.

'Colonel Shepherd picked them up and took them to rugby. They'll be back for the judging. If they're not in hospital.'

Bridget had heard of Colonel Shepherd – he was the senior stipendiary magistrate at Cairndale court. 'Good for a search warrant, so long as you've got your ducks in a row,' had been the verdict from one of the detectives who frequented the Cairndale branch of Caffè Milano, which was also Bridget's home at the moment. Well, the upstairs flat was where she lived, but it was being refurbished, so she spent most of her time working.

Perry's menu was ... robust. No dainties here, except for the macarons with home-made cherry jam, a point she made to Perry. He looked down. 'Family favourite,' he said. 'I got special dispensation to include last year's jam.'

There was definitely a story there. Maybe later. And now it was time for Bridget to ask the question she'd been dying to ask since she first arrived. With a flourish, she lifted the cloth from the front of Perry's workstation. 'Would someone like to explain why Perry is baking on top of a stack of empty coffins. They are empty, aren't they?'

Lucy snorted, Call-me-Jorie winced and Rev Deb turned puce. It didn't match her light blue clerical blouse. The only one who thought it was funny was Perry. 'It's amazing what you can rustle up in a small village like ours.'

He pointed to the group of spectators. 'Ask Mike. He supplied the coffins, and don't worry. I may have been devoted to Lisa, but she's safely in the churchyard. Having her spirit with me is enough.'

Oh. That explained a lot, including the macarons being *family favourites* and a magistrate looking after his children. It was up to Bridget to navigate this particular conversational swamp, so she said, 'And I hope she keeps an eye on the oven while your back's turned. Who's Mike, by the way?'

The man Perry had indicated was grinning all over his face, and Perry raised his voice. 'There he is. Michael Mason: dairy farmer and rural entrepreneur. No scheme too small or too dodgy, is it Mike?'

'I resent that,' said Mike. 'Micro businesses are the future of the countryside economy, and Elysian Meadow Joinery is in the ramparts.'

'Vanguard, Mike,' said Perry. 'They're in the vanguard.'

Mike was going to come back on that, but Rev Deb stepped in front of him and said, 'Just one more to go, then we'll have a cup of tea, shall we?'

As they walked back towards Bench One, Jorie muttered under her breath. It sounded like *Brace yourselves,* and Bridget wondered just how much of a threat the good-looking, dark-haired man could possibly be.

When Rev Deb said, 'And this is Feargal Hulme,' Bridget knew exactly why they needed to brace themselves. With a fixed smile on her face, the vicar continued, 'Feargal, this is …'

'I know who they are and what they're doing here,' he said, with a mild Irish accent. 'So long as we stick to baking, we'll get on fine. Isn't that right, Miss White?'

Ouch! Lucy's father was Gary White, and Lucy had mostly been Lucia White-Berardi until her father was arrested. How would Lucy handle it? Would Bridget have to step in and play Bad Judge?

Lucy answered it with a smile. 'So long as your menu is better than your business plan, you'll be fine, Feargal,' she said.

Feargal blinked, then his chest heaved with a laugh, and a very muscular chest it was too, from what could be seen underneath the full-length Miller's Rest Tea Room branded apron. 'Touché, Lucy. You'll allow me "Lucy"?'

'Of course. Show Bridget your menu.'

'There you go,' said Feargal.

Bridget stared blankly at the paper and took a moment. Feargal Hulme was the reason they had bought the lease at Ford Mill, because his business, the Miller's Rest Tea Room, had gone into administration last week, and had been failing for quite a while. Bridget could forgive his little jibe at Lucy. With a laugh like that, Bridget could forgive a lot of things.

She drew breath and focused on the competition, studying the menu carefully. 'Another one with a portion of gluten-free? I know you're not a teacher, so …?'

Feargal could at least multitask. He carried on mixing and said, 'As it happens, I am a teacher. Or was. Looks like I'll have to go back to it now.' He looked up and stared at Bench Four. 'When I was with Millie, we used to bake together in the evenings sometimes. I got used to making the occasional gluten-free batch for Aidan. With there being only four teachers at the school, he's been in Millie's class for three years now.'

'Did you ever bake for Miller's Rest?' asked Bridget. Sometimes it was good to take the Irish bull by the horns.

'Only towards the end. You do anything to save your baby. Not that I can do much cooking where I am now. The kitchen at Midland Terrace isn't like the one at School House.'

Again the lingering glance at Millie's workstation. Bridget hoped for Feargal's sake that his bakes weren't as bitter as the man who made them. She returned the menu, and Feargal smiled again.

'Is it right you're keeping on Kat Chester?' he asked.

It was no secret, so Bridget said, 'Yes.'

'Then fair play to you. I hope you make a go of it, girls.'

Somehow, being called a *girl* by an Irish hunk who was younger than Bridget didn't seem to be such a problem, even if he did look more at Lucy than her.

'Tea, I think,' said Jorie.

Chapter 3

'That was awkward,' said Lucy as they crossed to one of the support tables after their conversation with Feargal Hulme. 'Then again, I think he's more cut up about the collapse of his marriage than his business.'

'He was married to Millie Easterby?'

'Mmm. Edwin Duke told me. He didn't go into details, but when Millie kicked him out of their dream home, she also withdrew her guarantee with one of the banks or something financial. It was downhill all the way from there.'

A smooth-looking man was in charge of refreshments for volunteers and judges. Rev Deb introduced him as, 'Our amazing headteacher, Nathan Frost. St Peter's is graded Outstanding and is oversubscribed thanks to him.'

'Which I couldn't have achieved without the awesome Millie Easterby and our amazing chair of governors,' he responded. *Pass the sick bag*, thought Bridget.

'Here,' he continued. 'Four teas, all without sugar, which is over there. I'd have entered myself, but for some reason all my bakes come out like rock buns.'

The four women took their tea to a quiet corner. 'What do you think?' asked Rev Deb.

'About what?' replied Bridget.

'About who's going to win, of course.'

'Perry,' said Bridget. 'Any man who can cook on a stack of coffins gets my vote.'

'Millie for me,' said the vicar. 'She's got the lightest of touches.'

'I reckon Anya's in with a chance,' said Lucy. 'If she can nail the cannoli, she'll blow your socks off. They're exquisite.'

'It will be Maria,' said Jorie with some finality. 'She's secretary of the Women's Institute and she's won more WI rosettes than she'll admit to.'

'Will you excuse us,' said Lucy. 'We need a word with Edwin.'

They walked towards the group of new spectators who had arrived now that the time for the first judging was getting close. One of them was the Sacrificial Victim, also known as the May Queen, complete with white dress and floral crown. 'Do you think she's still a virgin?' asked Bridget.

'Shh!' hissed Lucy. 'That's Jasmine Chester. Kat's little sister.'

A figure detached himself and came over. As far as Bridget could tell from her internet searches, Edwin Duke owned more land and property in Byford than anyone else, and one of his businesses was Ford Mill, where Bridget would be heading on Monday – the coffee shop was in the old spinning room on the ground floor.

Edwin Duke was on his own today: no sign of his unlikely wife, Lady Felicia, a point which Bridget made after they'd said hello. 'She's bringing Violet and Grace back from Baby Ballet in Cairndale. Won't be long.'

The group of three had been stepping away from the crowd, and when Lucy was satisfied that no one could overhear, she stood on her toes and hissed into Duke's ear. 'You could have told me that Feargal Hulme was a competitor! I was mortified. And his ex-wife, too.'

Duke found this amusing. 'Why spoil the surprise? And you can't get away from people in a village. You have to find a way of living with them. If you don't want to see your ex in the White Hart or the coffee shop, you have to move.' Duke looked at the row of bakers. 'Which Feargal might well have to when he gets the rental agreement from Perry.' Duke turned back. 'I let him live rent-free at Number Four Midland Terrace while he tried to salvage the business.'

Lucy and Bridget frowned. That was both generous and harsh. Duke smiled to change the subject. 'I hear the documents are all signed. Are you looking forward to it?'

Lucy smiled back. 'We are. It's a shame we've got to close for a couple of days, but that … that *thing* just won't do. I'm hoping the engineer can come to install the new machine on Tuesday. I don't want to disturb Perry while he's baking, but you will remind him of the vacant possession clause, won't you?'

Duke was taken aback for a second. Lucy might be short, friendly and female, but she was no pushover. She probably got that from her father.

'Of course,' said Duke. 'We'd better get back.'

Jorie was talking to a tall, slightly stooped man who had been organising the helpers during the baking. 'This is my husband, Vaughan.'

He gave them a quick handshake and said, 'Nice to meet you, girls, but I've got to dash. The bloody hosepipe from the Institute keeps coming apart.'

'And we'd better see how they're getting on,' said Jorie. 'After a time check. Can you see Deborah? Her pulpit voice is much louder than mine.'

There was no sign of Rev Deb, so Jorie told the competitors that there was half an hour remaining, and then they circulated round the benches again. Deborah reappeared, breathless, and said that she'd had to pick something up from School House for Millie. Bridget thought that was unfair, but there you go.

The compulsory part of the competition was "Two contrasting traybakes", and all the competitors bar Anya were on the decoration stage. Anya had indeed worked up a sweat, and her blonde braid was starting to unravel. 'Amazing how time runs away from you,' was her only comment.

They left the bakers to finish uninterrupted for the last ten minutes, and Bridget's day got a whole lot worse when a lad grasping a weird contraption which held his phone came over. Lad? He was a man in his early twenties with a substantial, new-looking leather jacket that would have suited Feargal Hulme much better. Not that Bridget was making comparisons or anything.

Rev Deb said, 'This is Bradley Nicol from the *Lancashire Mercury*.'

Bridget narrowed her eyes and frowned. 'I've heard of you,' she told him. 'Why haven't you been into our Cairndale branch yet? You're based there, aren't you?'

Nicol was completely wrong-footed and stammered out, 'Erm. Sorry. I'm, err, I do a lot of work at the courts, so Rhona's place is closer, and I've sort of …'

He trailed off before he could comment on the quality of Rhona's coffee compared to Caffè Milano. Bridget sniffed. Her opinion of their rivals in Cairndale was not something she wanted to air in front of witnesses or to have on record.

Nicol was nothing if not persistent, though. 'Talking of your business, Ms Berardi, congratulations on the new venture at the Mill. I wondered if I could do a double feature? Write about the Bake Off and interview you as a woman entrepreneur. Get some pictures …'

Lucy smiled. Bridget did not, and said, 'How are Lucy's business skills related to her sex, Mr Nicol? And would you be interviewing her if it wasn't for the hen party spread in *Celebrity Enquirer*?'

The vicar stepped forwards. 'Give Brad a break, Bridget. We very much want him to cover the Bake Off and if he has something else to go with it, the editor is far more likely to print it.'

'Of course,' said Lucy. 'I'd love to do an interview, but not today. Can it wait until we've moved in?' She paused. 'And Bridget's right – we'll lose the gender angle, shall we?'

'Great,' said Nicol. 'I'll start by getting pictures of the judges and the hosts while it's quiet, if that's okay.'

It was not okay with Bridget, because that would mean posing behind the judging table, and everyone would see that her dress matched the tablecloth. She didn't argue, though. Lucy had backed her, and it was time to do as she was told.

Nicol fussed and bothered until he had the pictures, then Jorie looked at her watch and gave the one-minute warning. The tent fell completely quiet as the bakers furiously primped and neatened their work, or in Anya's case they tried to unblock a piping nozzle.

'Time! Step away from the traybakes and get ready for first judgement,' said Rev Deb. She paused, then added, 'Not to be confused with the Last Judgement.'

'I'll bet her sermons are a barrel of laughs,' murmured Lucy.

There was a short hiatus while the crowd gathered round the judges, their phones at the ready. Bridget recognised Jackie Chester from the village shop, standing next to her daughter, the May Queen. Jackie's other daughter, Kat, was holding the fort at the Mill on what would be the last day of trading for Miller's Rest. On the other side of Jasmine was one of those men of average height and average build who can disappear into the background, especially with three women like Jackie, Kat and Jasmine in the house. He must be Chris Chester, and Bridget was about to look away until he met her gaze with a penetrating look. Chris might not stand out, but he certainly knew what was going on.

Two tweenage boys were now here, still in their rugby kit and watching their father, Perry Lockwood. The thick-set man behind them must be Colonel Shepherd. Maybe he was their late mother's father.

Jorie drew a bingo ball from a bag, and said in a loud voice, 'Number Four. Millie, if you could be first to approach the gingham altar?'

Millie had put a selection of her bakes on a platter and carried it on a tray that also held a rack of coloured test tubes containing her novelty element. She had explained that her Neapolitan tray bake went much better with a shot of almond liqueur.

Millie looked pale and none too steady on her feet as she crossed the gap to the judging table. She stopped ten feet away, drew a breath and tried to take another step. With a groan of pain, she staggered, dropped her tray and collapsed onto the grass.

'Millie!' said Feargal, and he was the first to rush to the writhing form of Millie Easterby, followed by a woman from the crowd. Bridget, who was the nearest at the judging table, stepped forwards and planted herself as a barrier.

Feargal dropped to his knees and tried to grab his ex-wife out of desperation to do *something*. Millie was gripping her stomach and gasping terribly. Her eyes were open and she was screaming inside. Bridget stopped and bit her lip, her mind dredging up what had happened in Giuseppi's that Sunday. *Not again, please God.*

The woman who'd come over pushed Feargal roughly aside and put her fingers on Millie's neck in a very medical way. 'Is someone calling an ambulance!' she shouted in a Scottish accent. 'And someone get the defibrillator from the Institute!'

Bridget felt for her pocket. Empty. She looked up, and at least three people had phones clamped to their ears, including Bradley Nicol, who was the first to get through to the control room. He began giving details in a clear, even voice despite the panic in his eyes. Bridget looked down again.

Millie Easterby's face was turning a horrible red colour, and her eyeballs had rolled up out of sight. It was happening very quickly.

'Give them some room! Some air!' shouted Deborah using her pulpit voice. Bridget saw the look of devastation on Feargal's face and backed away. Right away. Millie was going to die in agony and die very soon. Bridget knew that, and she knew that there was nothing she or anyone else could do about it. She did not want to be a spectator to that.

She backed away and bumped into something solid. She wheeled round and found herself looking at Colonel Shepherd's back. He had his phone to his ear, but he wasn't looking at Millie, and he hadn't dialled 999. Bridget was about to apologise, but Shepherd had barely noticed her as he waited for his call to go through.

'Ross, it's Will Shepherd,' he said curtly. 'I'm at the Bake Off on Byford Green. There's a serious problem. Young woman's collapsed. Seriously ill, and I don't think she's going to survive … No. She's called Millie Easterby.' Shepherd took a deep breath. 'I've seen this before, Allister, and I'd send the area car and have the cavalry on standby … No, I'm not overreacting, I …'

Whatever Shepherd was going to say next was drowned out by a cry from Feargal. 'For God's sake, save her!'

'Defibrillator here!' cried someone, and the crowd parted to let him through.

Shepherd had turned round, and he suddenly realised that Bridget was next to him. 'Looks bad,' he said into his phone. 'This doesn't look like illness, Ross. It looks like —'

'Cyanide,' said Bridget.

Shepherd frowned. 'Did you hear that? … She's right, though … Good.' He took a deep breath. 'You should know that one of the witnesses is Lucia Berardi. Yes, Tom Morton's girlfriend … is he? Right. I'll keep an eye out.' He disconnected the call and took in Bridget, her outfit and her name badge. 'How do you know about cyanide, Miss Gorrigan?'

'I just do. Was that Commander Ross? Good.'

'Hang in there, Millie,' said the Scottish woman. 'Keep going.'

Colonel Shepherd put his phone in his pocket and stepped back, away from the crowd and towards the entrance. Bridget was the only one who noticed, and she was the only one who saw Shepherd stop a woman from leaving the tent, gently barring her way and pointing to the chairs along the side.

Behind the wall of people, the drama played itself out as the clock counted down the last minutes of Millie's life. The defibrillator was unpacked, and the Scottish medic was getting ready to deploy it when Bridget heard the sirens coming. The local first responders tried the defibrillator once before two police officers ran in, and they had already given up when the ambulance got there. The only thing the paramedics could do was pronounce Millicent Easterby officially dead.

Chapter 4

The police took charge, and Bridget edged round the crowd to be with Lucy. 'Are you going to tell Tom?' she whispered.

'He's taking his grandma to afternoon visiting. I don't want to disturb him because there's nothing he can do. Later is soon enough to find out about this.' She gestured towards Feargal, who was being helped up by Perry Lockwood and the vicar. 'What do you think happened, Bridge?'

Bridget put her mouth next to Lucy's ear. 'Cyanide poisoning. Will Shepherd called Ross 'cos he saw it too. We might be here a while.'

The senior officer in charge was Sergeant Ryan Marsh (a Caffè Milano regular), and he was talking into his radio. His junior colleague was stopping people leaving the tent, and the crowd backed away from the entrance and the judging area, huddling together in shock. CID arrived next, and Bridget saw another familiar face.

Detective Sergeant Liz Swindlehurst was formidable, fair and around forty. If Anya Calvert looked like a TV Valkyrie, Liz Swindlehurst had the power and lungs to sing the role in an opera. Liz frowned and pointed to a spare table, telling the PC to move it outside for some reason.

Liz was joined by the most junior of the Cairndale detectives, DC Barney Smith. Bridget saw more of him than any of the others because the coffee run was at the top of the trainee detective's job description. She smiled reflexively. Barney had that effect on you, even in the presence of death. Liz gave him some orders and stood back to let the paramedics leave. Their work here was done.

It took Liz Swindlehurst two minutes to realise that things were soon going to get out of hand. She stood by the entrance to the tent and filled her chest with air. 'If I could have your attention, please!' She paused, then carried on at a slightly less stadium-filling volume. 'I don't want to keep you here one minute longer than I have to. As soon as we've got ourselves sorted, we'll ask you to form a queue. Officers will take your details and check your bags on the way out, if that's okay with you. We'll ask some of you to wait in the Institute so that we can take statements.'

She breathed in and out. 'This is a terrible thing. Please do *not* post any pictures on social media. It's really not worth it. What I will ask you to do is take a note of our Community Policing upload link. Please send any pictures or videos to that address. It's the same one we use for dashcam footage. Thank you. If those of you with children could go first, that would be great.'

Bridget saw one mother slap her child's hand as he reached for an abandoned cake. Not surprising. Those not in complete shock were beginning to realise that this was not a medical emergency: at the very least it was a suspicious death. No one would be taking home their bakes, even if they'd wanted to, and Bridget suspected that all cake-related items would be staying in the tent until Tracey and her team of crime scene technicians got here.

Four more uniformed police officers arrived, and DS Liz Swindlehurst quickly gave them orders. Their arrival allowed her, Barney and Ryan to set up outside. Another police sergeant marshalled the queue, and the tent finally began to empty. Some were eager to be gone, and others like Lucy and Bridget were reluctant to push in. Except Brad Nicol. He'd barely waited until the children had gone before he rushed out. *Humph,* she thought. *I wonder how long it'll take for this to get on the* Lancashire Mercury *website.*

Everyone sat or stood in silence, and Bridget watched the village depart with shock and fear written on its collective face. 'Our turn,' she said to Lucy. They were about to leave when their way was barred by another agent of the forces of law and order, and she was just as formidable as Liz Swindlehurst.

Tracey Kenyon was, in her own words, 'the best crime scene manager north of Calais'. She was also the grumpiest. Bridget had heard her moaning about her non-existent love life on a regular basis to anyone in Caffè Milano who would listen, and now Bridget had a front row seat for her professional performance.

'Please tell me this is an April Fool!' Tracey began. 'Please do not tell me I have to deal with a tent full of food that's had a whole village dancing the highland fling in it since dawn.'

From outside the tent, Liz was the only one to respond. 'You love it really, Tracey. Think of the overtime.'

'Which I will spend drowning my sorrows.' Tracey, as yet

unencumbered by protective clothing, took a look round and let her eyes rest first on Bridget and then on Lucy. 'If you're here, Lucy, where's the Sheriff?' she asked, using DCI Morton's nickname.

'York,' said Lucy. 'Family emergency.' Tracey grunted and retreated outside; Bridget and Lucy followed her.

Bridget went to Liz, and Lucy went to Barney. Bridget hadn't brought a bag, so she emptied the pockets of her greatcoat. Liz took a quick glance and typed into her Lancashire & Westmorland Constabulary tablet computer. 'Do you know your phone number, Bridget?'

Bridget did know her number and rattled it off. Liz finished typing and sighed. 'This is just my luck: the one person I'd want to be making the coffees is a witness. Is it right what they said? You two are taking over the Miller's Rest?'

Bridget nodded and was about to say something when Barney interrupted. 'Sarge? This was in Miss Berardi's bag, and she says she's never seen it before.'

The junior detective had a glass container in his gloved hand, the size and shape of a spice jar. It was half full of a clear liquid, and Barney was holding it at arm's length.

'Tracey!' said Liz. 'Over here!'

The crime scene manager's protective suit had reached her ample waist and Tracey was trying to get it over. Her complaints about *short* suits needing to be *large* round the middle were another feature of her conversation. No wonder she rarely made it past a first date. She waddled over and said, 'What now?'

'Do you have a quick test for cyanide?'

'Yes. What the fuck for?'

'This. You haven't seen the … deceased yet. It's a strong possibility.'

Tracey looked incredulously at the jar, at Lucy and finally at Liz. 'Do you know how unlikely that is? If you're not down a gold mine or in a metal plating workshop, cyanide is rarer than hen's teeth. We only carry the test kit in case of industrial accident.'

'Even so,' said Liz.

Tracey sighed. 'Dave! Bring an evidence bag over here will you.'

When the minion had handed over a plastic bag, which Barney wrote on, Tracey stormed off muttering to herself.

The detective sergeant shifted in her seat and blinked at Lucy.

'What's going on, miss?'

Lucy was red in the face, and her curly brown hair was starting to collapse and frizz at the same time. 'I honestly don't know, Liz. Really and truly. I have never seen that jar before. Ever.'

Liz looked at Bridget. 'Do you know anything?'

Bridget folded her arms. 'Other than seeing dozens of similar jars lined up on the benches during the Bake Off, no I don't, alright? This has nothing to do with Lucy.'

Liz held her hands open. 'No one's saying it does, Bridget. We're just checking. It's just routine.'

'Holy shit!' came Tracey's voice from the back of her van. They all turned to look, and Tracey waved Liz over. Liz quick marched to the van and bent her head. Tracey's voice didn't have a quiet setting, and Bridget heard her announce, 'There are traces of cyanide.'

Bridget found herself saying, 'Test it for amygdalin.' This was rapidly turning into a nightmare.

Tracey frowned. 'Remind me what that is again.'

'It's a cyanogenic glycoside.'

'Oh. Hmm.'

'Care to enlighten us mundane folk?' said Liz rather tartly.

Bridget left Tracey to answer that one.

'It's a chemical, Sarge. Basically, it's a chemical that turns into cyanide and sugar when you eat it. I have no idea how you test for it.'

'And how do you know this, Ms Gorrigan?' asked Liz with studied politeness.

Lucy butted in, her face a white mask. 'Bridget knows stuff like that. Alright?'

'Thanks, Tracey,' said Liz. 'If you could action that one.' The crime scene manager nodded and replaced the bottle in its evidence bag. Liz turned back to Lucy. 'Ms Berardi, I think we need to take a formal statement from you at the station.'

'Right.'

Liz continued, 'DS Les Gartside is on his way back from Barrow, and he'll conduct the interview with Commander Ross. It shouldn't be me because … well, because. Barney? Could you sort out a vehicle to take Ms Berardi back to Cairndale?'

'Yes, Sarge.'

Bridget wasn't having this. She was *not* going to let this happen to

Lucy, and she needed some extra fire-power. She turned to Liz. 'In Tom's absence, what about Mina's fiancé? … I mean husband. Conrad Clarke's in the security services, isn't he? He knows the area. Can't he come and take over?'

'He's on his honeymoon,' said Liz flatly.

'From what I've heard, he owes Tom Morton favours,' countered Bridget. 'He might come back from his honeymoon if he thinks Lucy is in trouble.'

Liz was already shaking her head. 'We have a new saying in our clan … Sorry, I mean *in my father's family*. We say, "May your problems never be so bad that Conrad Clarke is the solution." Seriously, Bridget, you don't want him on the case.' She stood back. 'I'll let you have a minute with Ms Berardi.' Then the detective raised her eyebrows and nodded. Bridget got the message, and Liz walked off.

'I'll call your uncle Paul,' said Bridget. 'He'll know what to do.'

'I'm fine,' said Lucy. 'And Paul's not a criminal lawyer. No one can do anything unless they arrest me, and I don't want to be arrested. I know what to say and what not to say.'

'I'll tell him anyway. Don't try to stop me. Listen, I saw you put your phone next to your bag when I got here. Have you put your hand in your bag since then? To get a tissue? Anything?'

Lucy thought for a second. 'No … No, I haven't.'

Bridget sighed. 'That's good. Your prints won't be on it, then, and you haven't got any gloves in there?'

Lucy tried to smile. 'I'm not you, Bridget. I don't carry around disposable gloves. Or sanitiser.' She shook her head. 'Look, you might have to take over at the Mill.'

Her friend was right. Whether or not Lucy was actually arrested, there was a good chance that Bridget would be left on her own, one solitary Goth against the village. She swallowed hard. 'Can't we postpone? Given the circumstances?'

Lucy shook her head with a grim smile. 'Does Edwin Duke strike you as a man who'd let murder get in the way of running his business?'

Bridget had no answer to that. 'What about Lilianna? She could do it.'

Lucy came closer. 'Not only do we need her in Cairndale, *you're* the operations manager. This is why I chose you, Bridge.'

'But they'll never accept me! Not after seeing me today, and Anya remembered the last time, too.'

'As soon as you rock up, they'll quail before you. Just remember: they're more scared of you than you are of them.'

When Bridget had no answer to that, Lucy raised her voice. 'Liz? Do you need to search my car?'

'A quick look. That's all,' replied the detective sergeant. 'But one of the team will drive you, Lucy.'

'Fine. Take the keys out of my bag, and give them to Bridget when you've finished with the car. She'll drive it back to Cairndale.'

'Will I?' said Bridget with alarm bells ringing in her voice. This did not sound good.

'Yes you will. And you'll love it, and you'll be waiting for me in the flat with the Merry Mersey special. Got that?'

'Yeah. Right. Gotcha.'

A uniformed officer whom Bridget didn't recognise was walking over, probably drafted in from the police stations in Lancaster or Morecambe.

Lucy stood up and sighed. 'How did we get here, Bridge? How did we end up in this place?'

Chapter 5

Three and a half Weeks Earlier.

The figure swept across the market square, black coat skimming above the cobbles and black skirts swishing. Her black boots crunched heavily on the stones as if they'd crush anything that got in their way, and when the figure arrived at the cross, the woman's black-gloved hand lowered her hood and black hair cascaded out. She scanned the market square and shook her head. *Bloody Lucy's always late,* she thought to herself. Unlike Lucy, Bridget was *never* late.

She lifted her phone and put it in selfie mode to check her make-up. She peered at the screen and pouted. On the one hand, choosing deep purple lipstick completed the look, but on the other, it was a total swine to keep looking fresh. Okay for now, though. A loud blast on a car horn made her look up, and there was Lucy, heading into the square at way too fast a speed for a girl whose boyfriend was a copper.

The gleaming, bright red brand-new car circled the Market Cross and Lucy lowered the window. 'What do you think?'

'Very you, Lucy,' said Bridget. 'What is it? Some sort of Mini?'

'Mini Countryman. Since when did you care about cars?'

'I don't. I was just checking. For later.'

Lucy gave the day's first eye-roll and said, 'Get in. We're late.'

'No, girl, *you're* late,' said Bridget, stressing her Liverpool accent and making the point clear. Bridget *always* made the point clear.

Point made, she swept round to the passenger side and packed herself and all her outfit into the front seat. Lucy drove off the second the door closed, and well before Bridget had fastened her seat belt. Bridget let Lucy concentrate on driving for a minute while she took in the equally gleaming interior. Nice. And the seats were comfy, too.

They turned left onto the main road and crossed the River Cowan. Both of them glanced at the gleaming menace of Cairndale Division Police HQ, where Lucy's boyfriend was head of CID, and from where a distressing number of Bridget's customers now came. Bridget liked

Tom Morton. He was a totally sound bloke. Not just that, he was good for Lucy. What Bridget didn't like was the constant stream of other bizzies who came into the café.

There were so many of them that Bridget had put blue lights on two of the tables so everyone knew where they belonged. The coppers probably thought that patronising the Cairndale coffee shop was expected of them now that Lucy's company, Caffè Milano, had taken it over. Only Lucy wasn't there every day, was she?

Caffè Milano had bought the Cairndale coffee shop a few weeks ago, and Bridget had been parachuted in to turn the gloomy Formica hole into a caffeinated paradise, and she'd barely begun, so today's outing was totally unexpected. Why had Lucy summoned her for an *exciting escape* this morning and urged her to call in extra staff for cover? They had arrived at the traffic lights, and Bridget was about to put the question into words when Lucy stabbed the display panel with her finger and reactivated the satnav.

'Turn right onto Lune Road,' said the polite female voice. And with that, Bridget frowned, because as far as she knew, this road only led into the Rivers development, a series of expensive family homes. They passed straight through the identikit executive houses and emerged on the other side. As soon as the road sign signalled a change in the speed limit, Lucy put her foot down, and Bridget spoke up.

'Why are we here?' she asked, trying to keep the petulance out of her voice.

'Because this is where the satnav sent us.' Lucy spared her friend a glance. 'You didn't want a philosophical answer, did you?'

Bridget twisted round to watch the small town of Cairndale and its slender promise of civilisation disappear behind the car. They were heading into enemy territory, now. They were going … into the countryside.

She considered crossing herself for protection against the forces of rural darkness, until the car launched itself into space and bounced down with a thump of the tyres and a slam on the brakes that threw her into the steel embrace of the seat belt.

'Careful!'

'I did not see that coming,' said Lucy, in awe at the height of the humpbacked bridge which had nearly killed them.

'I'm not surprised you didn't see it,' said Bridget. 'Can you not raise the seat? You can barely see over the wheel.'

Lucy drove into a car park next to the bridge, spinning the wheel violently and sending the back of the Mini Countryman drifting dangerously towards a barge moored on the water. She skidded to a halt and started to pump the lever that would raise the driver's seat. Presumably Tom had driven it last.

'This must be the Lancaster Canal,' Lucy observed, as if she hadn't nearly wiped them out ten seconds ago. 'I wonder how far you can get on a barge? Kendal? Windermere? Scotland?'

Bridget's eyes bugged out in disbelief. 'A barge? We're on the road to nowhere and now you want to get on a barge? And you still haven't told me how your last car ended up in the Manchester Ship Canal.'

The satnav caught up with Lucy's deviation into the car park. *'Turn left onto Byford Lane,'* it announced.

'We're not on the road to nowhere,' said Lucy, ignoring the reference to the drowned Skoda. 'We're on the road to Byford, and that proves it.'

Before Bridget could vent any more stress, they were back on the lane, and then they were facing a T-junction whose sign offered a smorgasbord of options. To the left was *Cairndale, Avoiding Bridge*. They were definitely taking that route home on the way back. If they survived.

Three different signs pointed right: one white, one brown and one red. The white sign was standard issue and gave the distances – *Byford 4, Hackthwaite 8*. Lucy pointed at the two other signs and said, 'That's where we're going.'

Bridget stared at the options on the brown and red signs. 'The prison? Why? Is that where your dad is?'

'Only if he becomes gender-fluid. It's a women's prison.'

Gary White was the least gender-fluid person you'd be likely to meet, so where were they going? And why did HM Prison Cairndale ring a bell?

'Ford Mill Arts Centre,' announced Lucy. 'Have a look in my bag. There's a printout on top.'

Bridget bent down and felt under her skirts as Lucy pulled out of the junction and set off on the road to Byford. *'Follow Byford Old Road for four point seven miles,'* said Flick, the voice of the satnav.

Bridget extracted Lucy's bag and admired it for half a second.

Lucy's mother was a world-famous designer of handbags, and Lucy had run a shop selling them before she decided to become the new Starbucks. Yes, the bag was gorgeous, but that was nothing new. Bridget found the papers and unfolded them, and the first was a printout of a flyer from the arts centre, specifically the craft centre section.

Bridget skimmed down the paper and saw that visitors could spend their time and money at *Turn the Paige Bookbinders and Printmakers* (were they even a thing anymore?), *Fine Jewellery by Aurora Valenti, Penny's Papercraft, Holly Oak Wood* … and onwards via textile art (please no), furniture upcycling (an even bigger no), plain old *Esther Thornfield Artist,* and then finally something that Bridget could get her polished black nails into. 'I like the sound of Wiccan Weaving! Can we go there first? And hopefully last.'

Lucy gave an eye-roll. Bridget knew that. She didn't need to see it to know.

'No,' said Lucy with way too much relish. 'She's on maternity leave.'

'Don't fancy the rest much. I'll wander lonely as a cloud along the river, shall I, while you spend some more of your money.'

'We're not shopping! Well, we are, but not at the Craft Centre. Turn the page …'

'Was that a joke? 'Cos it wasn't that funny.'

When Lucy said nothing, Bridget turned the page, and there she found something much less colourful but much more interesting. *Invitation to Tender for the Lease of Coffee Shop Premises at Ford Mill Arts Centre, Byford, Cairndale,* it said at the top.

'No! We can't be going there.'

'Why not?'

'Because I've dressed for a trip out, not a business meeting! Turn round *now*.'

'Can't turn round here.'

'They'll all think I'm mental if I turn up like this.'

'No they won't. If you don't fancy it, stay in the car.'

'Vaffanculo,' said Bridget. She had insisted that Lucy teach her a selection of Italian swear-words as soon as she realised that Lucy was fully bilingual. This was one of the stronger ones. 'I'll be the Dark Angel sitting on your shoulder, then.'

'Great. Now have a proper look at the paperwork.'

Bridget grunted and got stuck in. According to the documents, Ford Mill Arts Centre was a combined gallery, craft retail and performance space in an old mill by the River Cowan, just outside Byford. Part of the ground floor was leased to a café, and that lease was being surrendered. No wonder Lucy was dragging them out here – opportunities like this didn't come along very often.

It was a leap, but if they got it, this would be the fourth branch of Caffè Milano. The first, in Southport, was doing well, but the second and third were still being refurbished, and Bridget was having to manage the ice cream business from over an hour away. She had every confidence in the girl she'd trained up to capture the Italian essences in Giuseppi's Gelati, but it would only take one accident with the proportions to ruin the good name that Bridget had spent years creating.

A fourth coffee shop was a lot to take on, and Bridget was coming to the point where loyalty to her friend was being stretched. Bridget knew ice cream. It was all she'd ever wanted to do: make the best ice cream in Lancashire. And then Lucy had breezed into the gelateria, and things had never been the same since. With a sigh, Bridget looked more closely at the tender document.

There was a good footfall in the building as a whole, but clearly not enough for the café to be a going concern, or they wouldn't be surrendering the lease. And then Bridget saw how much the owners wanted in rent. To make enough to turn a profit, sales would have to be very good. Perhaps the existing leaseholder was surrendering the lease in order to pitch a lower offer.

She turned to the second page and suddenly remembered why HMP Cairndale was so familiar: Mina Desai.

Lucy had turned Bridget's life upside down, no question, but Lucy's own life had been torn apart last year when her father had been sent to jail, more or less forcing Lucy to leave Cheshire. Since then, as well as a new business and a new man, Lucy had also picked up new friends, some of whom were a little … unusual. It was those friends who had led to Lucy appearing in the national papers and (allegedly) to the car/canal incident.

Chief among those friends was Mina Desai, who was almost unique in being shorter than Lucy, and who was also a former accountant.

Former because you aren't allowed to practise accountancy when you've done time in jail for money laundering. That didn't stop Mina from being Lucy's financial adviser, though.

Lucy had gone with Mina and Mina's even richer friends on a hen party last weekend – and one of those friends was famous enough to get her picture in the papers, along with the rest of the Hens. Lucy couldn't deny that part of the weekend, but she had been totally unforthcoming on what happened later, especially when it came to the car … Bridget would get it out of Lucy one day, and there was still the wedding to look forward to in a couple of weeks.

Back to business. Mina had done some preliminary calculations which led to a big number in a big circle at the bottom: *ROI 8%*. Bridget was trying to remember what ROI was when she was pitched forwards into the seat belt again.

Chapter 6

Instinctively, Bridget dropped the paper and slammed her hands on the dashboard. She looked up and she was eye to eye with death in the shape of hundreds of sharp spikes sticking out of a huge green engine of mass destruction.

The spikes were about two metres from the front of their car, and behind the spikes was a red tractor, almost the same colour as the Mini. *How is that even allowed?* thought Bridget.

'Idiot!' said Lucy, reaching for the button to lower the window and shout at the tractor driver.

It was time to intervene. Bridget reached out and put her hand on Lucy's arm. 'We're not in Milan, Luce. You need to back up, and you need to stick to English. You need not to call the farmer a *figlio di puttana,* even if he is one.'

'But he is!'

'And he has a tractor with a ... spiky thingy on it! You've only had this car two days. You don't want to upset these people.'

Lucy muttered something and reversed into a gate. The tractor roared its engine and bounced past, gobbets of mud shaking themselves free from the monstrous rear tyres and landing on the pristine paintwork of the Mini. As the tractor cab drew level, Bridget saw the bald driver lift his fingers from the wheel in acknowledgement of his victory. Or in thanks for their letting him pass. One or the other. She left the printout in the footwell and focused on the road ahead.

The next two miles passed without incident, and Bridget was starting to relax until they came to a sign ahead. Bridget almost missed it. 'Look!' she said.

'So what? Byford welcomes ... Oh. *Byford Welcomes Careful Drinkers.* I like that.'

They passed the sign, and whoever had changed *Drivers* to *Drinkers* had done a most professional job. Out here in the sticks, it was probably called Local Colour. They must be very bored in Byford.

Lucy drove slowly past houses, mostly big and set back from the road. Bridget craned her neck to get an overview of the village, but Byford didn't offer any vistas, revealing itself slowly, one house at a time.

There was a final, tight bend and then they were in the middle of the village. Here, at least, Byford opened itself to scrutiny by flaunting its village green. Instead of following Flick's injunction to *'Keep straight on'*, Lucy pulled in to the kerb on the right.

'Why have we stopped?'

'Reconnaissance. Intelligence gathering.'

'Eh?'

'We're going into the shop. Come on.'

'I can't go in there looking like this! Do you know what they're like out here?'

Lucy was losing patience or, what was worse, she looked excited. 'You should have thought of that.'

'And you should have told me we were going undercover. I'd have worn a dirndl.'

'And you still wouldn't fit in. Just own it, Bridget. Be loud and proud. That's what you're always telling everyone else.'

Yet again, Lucy was one step ahead of Bridget. Her friend had boxed her into a corner, and short of acting like an *actual* teenager, Bridget had no choice but to front it out. With a bit of luck, she'd never have to come here again.

She eased herself out of the Mini and took a good look round. Just behind them was St Peter's CE Primary School, complete with small children running around at playtime. On the other side of the road was the looming grey shape of St Peter's Church itself. Bridget squinted at the noticeboard outside the gateway. Was that a woman's name as vicar? Yes, it was.

The through road continued off to the right, with a smaller road circling the green and giving access to the Byford Institute Sports Club. The Institute was too far away to see what sort of sports were played there. Foxhunting? Burning of Wicker Men? Both were popular in the country, she'd heard. Oh, and cricket. What did that idiot call it? *The smack of leather on willow.* To Bridget, that sounded like something which Willow and her consenting friend got up to in the bedroom, not a sport to be played in public.

'What are you gawping at?' said Lucy.

It was Bridget's turn to blush, and she turned from thoughts of Willow and her potential peccadilloes towards the cottages clustered around the green and beyond. 'Why are some cottages blue and some mucky grey?'

'How the hell should I know? Come on, we're being watched.'

'There's always someone watching you out here,' said Bridget darkly as she turned to face Byford General Stores.

A sprightly looking old man was standing outside the shop door clutching a folded newspaper and a loaf of bread. He'd been staring at them, totally unembarrassed, as if the girls were a free attraction. When Lucy moved towards the shop, he started heading for the road with a smile. 'Morning,' he said.

'Morning!' Lucy trilled back. Bridget opted for a smile. If he heard her voice, he'd know she was a Scouser. Did they hunt Scousers out here? She'd rather not find out.

On the way through the door, Lucy hissed, 'I'll keep them talking, you look for clues.' Then she headed over to the counter, leaving Bridget behind.

Clues? What was she on about? Clues to what? Bridget turned right and headed down the aisle of tinned and preserved goods. Other than clues to the natives' diet (a mixture of soup and baked beans, apparently), there was nothing of interest, so she listened in to the conversation.

There were two women in the shop already, a customer leaning on the counter and a member of staff. The woman in charge of the till was in her forties, sporting a green apron and possessed of incredibly wild hair. It was brown, with hints of grey, and either she was a natural source of static electricity or she had long ago given up trying to tame the explosion of curls, twists and frizz. When she saw that Lucy was coming over, she gave a warm smile that travelled up her face and appeared behind the enormous black-framed glasses.

'Hi,' said Lucy. 'We were looking for the Ford Mill Arts Centre.'

Bridget cringed inside: she was constitutionally incapable of being a damsel in distress, but somehow Lucy could turn it on whenever she wanted. Perhaps that was why Lucy always had men running round after her.

The shop assistant pointed the way they'd been heading. 'Just carry on down the road and turn right at the end of the green. There's a signpost. You can't miss it.'

'Oh,' said Lucy. 'Is it in walking distance?'

The customer who'd been leaning on the counter straightened up. Goodness, she was tall. Almost freakishly tall. And very well groomed. From the gleaming trekking shoes to the glossy blonde hair, she stood out as a woman who had time to get dressed in the mornings. Even when visiting the shop. 'It depends how fast you walk,' she said to Lucy. 'And whether you're wearing heels. Are you going for anything special?'

Lucy gave another guileless smile. Sometimes that girl had more front than Blackpool. 'We'd heard it was a good outlet for artists.'

The tall woman gave a bland smile, but the shopkeeper jumped straight in. 'You need to speak to Louis, then. Can't miss him. Just look for the outrageous floral shirts. Ooh, that reminds me, Anya, are you going to Barbados again this year?'

The tall woman – now pegged as Anya – ignored the question and said, 'You've just missed one of the artists. He could have told you all about it.'

'If you didn't mind missing lunch. He does go on a bit. And then a bit more.'

'That's because you encourage him, Jackie.'

So, the old man who still read newspapers (were there a lot of them out here?) was an artist of some sort. Probably painted cows or something.

Bridget had successfully navigated the chilled cabinets (stuffed with a huge range of vacuum-packed local meat products. Lancashire Haggis, anyone?). She turned round the final corner, where she found the sweets aisle, a noticeboard and a small child. The little girl couldn't have been more than three or four and could only reach the bottom shelf, but she was rooting round the bargain confectionery like a seasoned veteran of the January sales.

Bridget tried not to step on the child and focused instead on the noticeboard, losing track of the conversation at the counter until she heard the inevitable question – from the shopkeeper rather than the Valkyrie. 'Weren't you in *Celebrity Enquirer* last week? At Aintree races?'

How was Lucy going to get out of that one, eh? The price of fame can be high. Lucy might have got her picture in the papers next to the stunningly beautiful (and rich) Tara Doyle, but *Lucia Berardi* was only one click away from *Lucy White* and the news of her father's imprisonment.

While Lucy was flannelling for an answer, the little girl gave a cry of delight and pulled out a hideously bright chemical blue lollipop. Bridget pegged the colour as a triarylmethane dye, FCF No 1 probably. The sort of thing she'd never dream of putting in the ice cream.

The child peeled off the wrapper and started to lick it, and then she suddenly realised that she wasn't alone and stopped to stare at Bridget, her tongue stuck to the revolting sweet.

'Grace!' said Anya to the child. 'What have I told you about opening things? Bring it here. Now.'

The child toddled over to her mother, craning her neck to see all the way up to Anya's face. 'Mummy, that lady has black lips, like I get with the lolly. Has she been eating lollies?'

The shopkeeper's hand flew to her mouth, suppressing a huge grin. Anya looked horrified and swept her arm down like a fairground crane to whisk up her child and dispossess her of the lollipop. She put the sweet on the counter and fished a pound coin out of her pocket. 'Sorry,' she said to Bridget and exited the shop just as Grace started screaming.

Bridget joined Lucy at the counter, where Jackie was trying not to corpse with laughter. 'Would you like a free lollipop? Only slightly used?'

Bridget bared her teeth in what was technically a smile, but one that she hoped came over as feral. From the look on Jackie's face, it had worked.

'Thanks for your time,' said Lucy. 'See you again soon.'

Chapter 7

Outside the shop, Bridget paused to look round again. A couple of cars passed, and an old lady emerged from one of the cottages. There was no other sign of life. 'They're all mad,' she said to Lucy.

'If you will dress up when we're on business, you're going to get comments. No skin off my nose.'

'I didn't mind the girl. It was the other two: the Valkyrie and the Queen of Randomness and Over-sharing. If they weren't mad before, living here has driven them insane. I'm telling you.'

'Shut up and get in the car.'

They got in and fastened their seat belts. 'There's more,' said Bridget. 'They actually want to have a human sacrifice.'

Lucy paused, giving her the *please explain* look that she used whenever Bridget 'went off on one'.

Being a Goth wasn't like being a Freemason. There isn't an oath and a set of rules to go with the outfits. Many of Bridget's sisters in black were covered in Kabbalistic sigils and practised ritual magic. Not Bridget. As a Catholic and a scientist, she was instinctively averse to *pagan* mumbo jumbo.

On the other hand, she was very much a lapsed Catholic and these days pretty much a lapsed scientist. Neither had offered her much comfort in her hour of need, and when Natalie had told her that there were spirits who'd support her, she'd been willing to give it a go. Shame the spirits hadn't been there for Nat.

'It was on the noticeboard,' she told Lucy. 'They actually want to have a May Queen. A young girl has to wear white and be paraded round the village on the back of a cart. It's paganism. Thank God it's been cancelled.'

Lucy hesitated, like she always did when Bridget mentioned things to do with religion. Or magic, for some reason. It was almost like Lucy wanted to tell her some dark secret and that it was never the right moment to do so. It looked like now was not the right moment either, and Lucy gave the start button a decisive stab. She engaged Drive and pulled out. 'Why has it been cancelled? Lack of local virgins?'

'No. Something to do with it being linked to a baking competition and not having a sponsor, so no human sacrifice of Jasmine Chester. It was in the minutes of the Byford Mayfest Committee meeting on the shop noticeboard. There's more, but I lost the will to live.'

'It seems like a very friendly place to me. Don't forget, I grew up in a village.'

'No you did not. You grew up in a palace in Milan and then a mansion in Cheshire. You may be slumming it now, but you no more grew up in a village than I did.'

Lucy didn't deny the Cheshire mansion. 'It wasn't a palace in Milan. It was a villa.'

'Same difference. What do you think the Cowandale Clinic is? Is that where they lock up the locals at the full moon?'

Lucy jerked the wheel fractionally. 'What do you mean?'

'Where you've just turned. The sign said we're headed to Ford Mill Arts Centre and also the Cowandale Clinic & Spa.'

Lucy sighed, almost with relief. 'I've heard of the CCS. Some of the older wives went there. It's a very, very discreet cosmetic surgery clinic. One of the best outside London, according to the Evil Stepmother.'

Lucy's father, before his arrest, had been a sports agent. His clients had included the current England football captain. There were lots of other household names, too, if your household liked football. Bridget did not like football.

An agent like Gary White looks after every aspect of their clients' lives, including finding cosmetic surgeons for their wives, because, you know, when those girls reach thirty, they need to start running to stand still.

Lucy slowed right down as they approached another bridge, this one much older and less precipitous than the canal bridge which had nearly wiped them out. As they crested the rise, Bridget looked left and over the River Cowan, up to where it had been dammed to give Byford Mill its water and energy supply.

Lucy crawled towards the Ford Mill entrance, a turning to the left. Opposite this was a run of four utilitarian cottages, no doubt built for the workers and no doubt now occupied by retired artists. As you'd expect, the four cottages had been knocked into two less modest dwellings.

The entrance to the mill site was flanked by twin signboards. On the left, a substantial, permanent board had the Ford Mill name and logo at the top. The arts centre logo was very abstract and, well, arty; Bridget could barely distinguish a sketch of the mill and a pair of theatrical masks. Underneath the header sign were four additional boards announcing the *Cowan Theatre,* the *Dukes Gallery,* the *Byford Craft Community,* something called *Elysian Meadow Joinery* and finally the *Miller's Rest Café.* The Miller would not be resting for much longer if Lucy had her way.

On the right of the entrance was a blank board for shows and exhibitions. Currently featured in the Dukes Gallery was *Just the Earth: an exploration of skyless landscapes* by Dave Hughes, and coming soon was *Kiss Me Kate* performed by Cairndale Light Opera. Bridget was not planning to buy tickets.

Bridget looked at the old building, a four storey stone factory that presumably once churned out cloth or cotton or something. 'What on earth is a mill doing out here in the middle of nowhere?' she asked.

'I asked Tom the same thing.'

'And how is a solicitor-turned copper an expert on industrial archaeology?'

'He's a man and therefore stuffed with useless information of all kinds.'

Bridget reflected on this and found it to be true. In the case of most men she'd encountered, the useless information mostly manifested itself in knowledge of sports, though many of them could also add something truly niche. On one memorable occasion when she used to have a social life, she'd been jaw-droppingly bored by an insight into the Goodyear welting process for men's shoes.

'And?'

'The spinning and weaving technology was developed before reliable steam engines and railways to move the coal about. Apparently. So the early mills were built near water power. That's why there's a smaller mill here and that monstrosity in Cairndale. Tom looked it up and said that Ford Mill – this place – added boilers when it was rebuilt.'

'Fair enough.'

Lucy drove towards the imposing square lump of stone that constituted the main mill and found a space in the small car park at the front. As well as the huge mill, they were surrounded by a range of mismatched buildings that could have been a litter of puppies clinging to their mother. Some were stone, like mother, others were brick or concrete; some looked to be in use and others abandoned. Beyond this cluster, a sign pointed to the main car park. It certainly had the capacity to welcome a big crowd.

'Do you have an appointment?' asked Bridget. 'Or is this another undercover reconnaissance mission, you know, given that your mugshot's been in the papers.'

'Ouch!' said Lucy. 'Bit less of the *mugshot*, please.'

Bridget flushed. It was one of the reasons she went for the heaviest foundation: anything to cover up the tendency of her pale skin to go red. 'Sorry.'

Lucy touched her tiny fingers to Bridget's well-padded shoulder. 'No, it's me. This could be a big break, Bridge.' She withdrew her hand and picked her phone out of the cupholder. 'We've got an appointment with Mr Edwin Duke at eleven thirty, and I was in a hurry to get here before then so we could evaluate the customer experience.'

Lucy had degrees in business studies (from Milan and Manchester), but Bridget didn't hold it against her. Lucy didn't spout rubbish like *evaluate the customer experience* very often. With a grin, Lucy grabbed the keys and pushed open her door. Bridget sighed and followed.

The entrance to the Mill was new, a glass box with pitched glass roof about the size and shape of Granddad Gorrigan's greenhouse, not that Bridget's grandfather ran to smoked glass and automatic doors. Beyond the grand entrance, a lot of money had been spent turning a Georgian factory into the foyer of a cutting-edge arts centre. Out here? How? Why? Did the Arts Council of Great Britain have *that* much money to spare, or did the owner know someone?

Stairs directly opposite led up to the Dukes Gallery and the Byford Craft Community, and the foyer was equipped with a small ticket booth, lots of artfully arranged seating and imposing doors under a sign saying *Auditorium*. The walls were painted an artistic black and covered with posters from past performances. Bridget was a bit short-sighted and had to squint, but she reckoned that there was an eclectic mix of crowd-pleasing musicals, stand-up comedy and avant-garde theatre, the whole thing seasoned with dance. What she couldn't see anywhere was music. Odd.

'Lucy …'

'Shh. Quick.'

Bridget's arm was grabbed and dragged left, towards an opening that led to the Miller's Rest Café.

'Where's the fire?' whispered Bridget.

'Floral Shirt!' hissed Lucy.

'You what?'

'Morning!' said Lucy brightly, beaming a smile at the girl behind the counter. If Bridget had tried that, the poor girl would no doubt have fainted, because the barista looked anything but focused on *The Customer Experience*. In fact, she looked like her dog had just died. Bridget let Lucy try to breathe new life into the staff and looked round for a table.

There were only a few people at this hour, some couples next to the full-height windows and a group of women on the comfy sofas at the back. Bridget headed for a spare table by the window.

The designer had opted to keep the original high ceilings of the old spinning room, along with the cast iron supports, now suitably distressed. Atmospheric.

Did it work? Yes, because as well as the ageing Victorian features, modern fittings of a high quality had been installed, and they looked scrupulously clean. Good. Bridget liked things to be clean.

When she got to her chosen table, she bent from the waist to check the surface – you can only check if a table is *really* clean by looking at an angle of thirty degrees, and her hand had already reached into her bag for the anti-bac wipes. *No you don't!* she told herself. *Not today. That would not go down well with the current management.* She sniffed. It would do.

She settled herself on to the chair (unpadded wood. Hmm) and looked out of the window. Wow. That was impressive.

She was looking upstream, towards the millpond, and she had a view of the mill race, where water bubbled towards her before dropping on to the steadily rotating wheel in a scene that couldn't have changed in two hundred years, for all that the modern double glazing blocked out the sound. She fumbled in her bag, not for wipes but for her glasses to get a better look at the whole thing.

'What are you looking at?' said Lucy. 'And budge up, will you?'

Lucy plonked down the heavily laden tray with an *oomph* and started distributing the goods.

'Did you get the Look?' asked Bridget.

'Yeah. She knew she'd seen me before, but couldn't work out where.'

'What was that rubbish about floral shirts?'

Lucy looked blank, then blinked. 'Camp bloke in a floral shirt. Must be the artistic director, Louis Young.'

Lucy had pronounced the *s* in *Louis*, and Bridget had to correct her. 'It's pronounced *Louis*. The French way. According to Jackie.'

'Jackie who?'

'Woman who runs the shop. Weren't you listening? Oops, looks like the barista knows exactly who you are now.'

'Eh?'

'There's a middle-aged guy talking to her and pointing at us. Now she's frowning. Poor girl.'

Lucy was resisting the urge to turn round and gawp. 'Why would she be frowning?' she hissed.

'Because she thinks we're gonna put her out of a job, that's why. Here we go. He's coming over.'

Chapter 8

Bridget sat up straighter. Lucy finally gave in to curiosity and swivelled round, putting on a smile. The man was probably in his forties, with vanishing hair and a spreading middle. He wore a sumptuous pink shirt that must have cost a packet, but no tie or jacket. What he did have on was one of those waxed jacket things, like Mina Desai's fiancé always wore. He paused to grab a chair and came over. It was time to stand up.

The man put down his chair at a safe distance and smiled at them both as if he meant it. 'Good morning. I'm Edwin Duke.' He turned to look at Lucy. 'And you're Lucy Berardi, I presume.'

Lucy stepped forwards to shake hands. 'That's me. Nice to meet you. This is my operations manager, Bridget Gorrigan.'

Bridget didn't like shaking hands much, especially with total strangers who wore countryside coats. You never knew where their hands had been or what they'd touched. The old, pre-Lucy Bridget would have hung back and smiled or something, but the new Bridget took the man's hand firmly in hers. 'Pleased to meet you,' she said.

Duke had taken in her outfit, her hair and her make-up, and all he said was, 'Welcome to Byford. We'll finish our coffee here and then go somewhere quieter, shall we?' He paused and looked at the groaning tray. 'You didn't get one of those for me, did you, because Kat's bringing one over.'

It was Lucy's turn to be flustered, so Bridget did what her grandmother had told her to do: tell the truth and shame the Devil. 'God no,' she said. 'That's all for us. We like to try out the goods.'

If Bridget's grandmother were still here, Bridget would no doubt have got a clip round the ear for only wanting to tell the truth when it was likely to embarrass someone. Duke's eyebrows raised a millimetre. 'Don't blame you. I certainly would.'

He retrieved his chair and waited until Bridget and Lucy were seated, then he smiled again, and this time there was a challenge in his eyes. 'Don't let me stop you.'

'Err, I don't think—' began Lucy.

'Thanks,' said Bridget, cutting across her. She picked up the branded espresso cup and sniffed, then she slurped, then she sucked in air. 'Well, I can tell you one thing: they're not buying their coffee from Lavazza no more. I think I'll pass on the cappuccino, Luce, that milk looks too hot and too thin.'

She replaced the cup and sat back. Lucy was holding her head in her hands. She did that a lot when Bridget was around. If Duke was impressed or appalled by her performance, he was giving nothing away. Instead, he turned and waved the barista over, who brought him his Americano as if she were waiting on him at his ancestral home.

Bridget was no expert on the local accents. Even so, Duke didn't *sound* like he came from here, nor was his voice generic public school posh, so she recalibrated the *ancestral home* idea. The barista, complete with Miller's Rest apron, placed the coffee down. Bridget had thought that the floor was raised behind the counter, but no. The girl, who looked to be in her early twenties, really was very tall. Bridget could see that her name tag did indeed say *Kat*, but it also gave her surname.

'Hi,' said Bridget. 'Have we just met your mum in the shop or are there Chesters all over the place out here?'

Kat could have taken offence. She didn't, she just rolled her eyes. 'What did she say this time?'

'She didn't say anything!' said Lucy, desperate to move the conversation on.

'Thanks, Kat,' said Duke. It was designed to be both polite and to get rid of the girl. Kat Chester could take a hint and returned to the counter with a nod.

Bridget must have had an effect on Duke because he sniffed his coffee and put it down untouched. He looked from Bridget to Lucy. 'What do you think of the place?' Bridget folded her hands in her lap. It was time to be quiet because this was Lucy's show now.

'Nice,' said Lucy. 'I love the way it's been refurbished. The website said six years ago.'

'That's right. I bought what was left of the Easterby Estate and moved here eight years ago. We focused on the Lodge at first, then when we'd moved in there, we started work on the Mill.'

Ooh, there's so much to unpack there, thought Bridget. The way Duke had moved from *I* to *we*, the way he implied that he'd picked up a sledgehammer and knocked down the walls himself. Unlike Lucy, Bridget hadn't had the luxury of Googling Mr Duke in advance, so she wondered what card her friend would play next. Unfortunately, instead of asking about the *we*, Lucy went for the boring option.

'You only lease out the coffee shop. The other businesses are owned by Dukes of Derbyshire.'

Bridget couldn't help it. 'You're actually the Duke of Derbyshire? I thought that was whatshisname? Stanley?'

Duke – *The* Duke? – found this amusing. 'Sorry, Bridget. Edward Stanley is the Earl of Derby.'

'Oh yeah. Knowsley Safari Park and all that. Sorry, erm … do you prefer Edwin?'

'Only my wife calls me that. Most people call me Duke, but I don't object to Ed or Eddie. My grandfather thought it would be amusing to call the family business Dukes of Derbyshire, which is where I'm from.' His eyes flicked from Bridget to Lucy and back again. 'In case your boss hasn't told you, Dukes of Derbyshire is in the extractive business, and if you want someone with a title, you'll have to wait until you meet my wife.'

Before Bridget could move on to the way more interesting topic of Duke's marriage (and he was definitely not an Ed), the man himself stood up. 'Shall we adjourn to the office?'

Bridget looked at the unsampled cakes and was tempted to take one for later. Better not.

Instead of leading them to the foyer, Duke took them to a side door and out to the car park. Lucy attempted to get back to business by matching his stride and asking about the leases again; Bridget was content to float behind them.

'That's right, Lucy. Louis runs the other businesses at the Mill, and normally you'd be dealing with my estate manager, Perry Lockwood, but he had some sort of school emergency this morning. Saves a bit of time anyway, because I'd still have wanted to cast my eye over you in person.'

Bridget did not like that? 'Oh yes? And what do you reckon now that you've sized us up?'

'I reckon that you know your coffee, Bridget. And I've done as much due diligence on Lucy's business as she's done on mine. This is the estate office. We're upstairs because the ground floor has chronic damp.'

It was one of the puppy buildings, made of stone and substantial in its own right. A modern door was set in to the side, complete with security panel. Duke held it open and Bridget followed Lucy up the steep stairs.

The estate office could have been anywhere, so thoroughly modernised had it been. Even the high ceiling had been sacrificed for a clean roof and efficient lighting. There was no reception as such, just three desks, one of which was almost empty, and a table that had been borrowed or stolen from the Miller's Rest across the road. At least the estate office had bought some proper chairs.

'Perry has a part-time assistant,' said Duke, 'though as you can see, not today. Please, have a seat.'

They gathered round, and Duke draped his coat on the back of the chair. 'There's been a change since Perry put out the tender document, I'm afraid. Last week the Miller's Rest went into administration. Shame.'

No wonder Kat Chester looked upset: she was going to be out of a job even sooner.

Having paused to let this sink in, Duke continued, 'I had a word with the administrators and convinced them to keep trading for now, and they were delighted when I offered to transfer Kat's employment to the Estate. The other staff have had to go.' He paused. 'Except Feargal.'

'The owner?' said Lucy.

'Former owner. He now works part-time for minimum wage, and that was one of the reasons I suggested you come over today: I knew he wouldn't be here.'

'Awkward,' said Lucy. 'Obviously, this changes things. If Miller's Rest couldn't make a go of it at this rent …'

And that was why Lucy was the boss: not only was she rich to start with, she had no shame when it came to talking about money.

Duke smiled back. 'The failure of Miller's Rest has more to do with the business skills of Feargal Hulme than it does with the level of rent.'

'Mmm,' said Lucy. 'Fixtures and fittings?'

'The lease is on vacant possession, so all those belong to the Miller's Rest.'

Lucy nodded thoughtfully. 'The footfall at the Mill would plummet if the café closed, wouldn't it? That would be a disaster.'

Duke's face said that it would. His words were more measured. 'Running a coffee shop is not something the estate office is equipped for, certainly.'

Lucy played her next card. 'If we could buy the fixtures and fittings from the administrator, we'd be in a position to move quickly. Can any of the other bidders do that?'

Duke ignored the question, so clearly they couldn't. 'This is an excellent long-term proposition for someone,' he declared.

Before Lucy could say any more, the outside door banged open and a woman's light footsteps pattered up the stairs. Duke didn't look entirely happy at the sound, one he clearly recognised, because he stood up in anticipation of the woman's arrival.

Chapter 9

The woman who emerged into the office was clearly used to making an entrance because she paused with her hand on the rail and let them get a good look at her, just as she was getting a good look at them.

The woman's glossy black leggings were adorned with giant spider webs and paired with a long T-shirt featuring Albert Einstein. They made a loud statement, as did the bird's-nest hair, and it took Bridget a second to twig: it was all an *act*. The clothes said *rebel,* but none of that outfit had been bought from a stall at a music festival. Oh no, like the hair, the clothes had been artfully and expensively chosen for maximum impact.

'My wife, Lady Felicia,' said Duke. 'She's the one with the title.'

Mrs Duke stepped forwards. 'God, Edwin, how many times have I told you? It's *Fliss*! You must be Lucia Berardi. Nice to meet you.'

Lucy shook hands and introduced Bridget. 'I *love* your boots,' said Fliss. 'Has Edwin not offered you refreshments?'

Her husband didn't quail in front of his younger, titled wife, but he did shake his head ever so slightly. 'We met in the Miller's Rest and came over to talk in private.'

'And I shall leave you to talk in private, once I've asked the question.'

Fliss – Lady Fliss? – rested her hand on the back of Lucy's chair; the nails were as exquisitely manicured as the rest of her outfit. 'I bet he hasn't even mentioned it yet,' she declared.

Edwin Duke was not someone Bridget wanted to play poker against. If he was bothered by his wife sticking her nose in his business, there was no sign of it on his face. Maybe they'd have words later. 'I was just getting round to it,' he said mildly. 'You do realise that there's a long way to go before anything is signed.'

Fliss made a sour face. Her hair had been dyed black with maroon highlights and then carefully teased to frame her pixie face. The sour expression did nothing for it. 'Tell me about it, Edwin. I had to wait long enough for the theatre, didn't I?'

Bridget shuffled away from the table and got a better look at the oversized Albert Einstein T-shirt. Underneath the great man were the words *Let There Be Life. Nope,* thought Bridget, *not a flipping clue.* There was, however, a clue in Fliss's last statement: the theatre was her baby.

Duke didn't respond at first, so Fliss piled on the pressure. 'Time really is of the essence, Edwin. If we want the May Day celebrations to go ahead …'

'And we do,' said Duke, smiling at his wife and turning back to the Caffè Milano team. 'The Miller's Rest was going to sponsor Byford's Mayfest celebrations, and they're only a few weeks away.'

'Can't you step in, erm, Fliss?' asked Bridget.

Fliss gave her a dazzling smile. 'We have to be careful with what we sponsor in the village. We're doing the Harvest Festival and Anya Calvert is doing the Christmas Fayre.'

Oh, so that's how it is, thought Bridget. *Fliss and Anya are the rival queen bees.* She frowned. 'Isn't the May festival over the bank holiday weekend?'

Fliss's hand flew to her mouth. 'Of course! Your wedding! I'm sorry.' She looked at Lucy's fingers and frowned when she didn't see an engagement ring.

Lucy laughed. 'Not yet. If ever. *Celebrity Enquirer* are in such deep shit about that. It wasn't *my* hen party, it was Mina's. They are going to have to seriously grovel to avoid being cursed, but yes, I will be at *a* wedding over that weekend, even if I'm a bridesmaid this time and not the bride.'

'All weekend?'

'From Friday to Tuesday. We're getting the full Indian. With added cricket.'

'Cricket!' said Bridget. 'You didn't say nothing about cricket, Luce.'

Fliss waved that comment away and said, 'Fine. We'll hold the May Day celebrations on the Sunday and the Bake Off on the following Saturday. The seventh. How about that?'

There was a pause while Lucy wondered how to ask *How much?* without sounding cheap and Bridget wondered how to ask *Are you serious?* without losing them the contract.

'Good,' said Fliss with another smile. 'I'll leave you to it. Don't forget that Violet has a play date with Martha tonight.'

'You mean that you have a Prosecco date with Martha's mother,' responded Duke. 'I won't forget to pick you up.'

'Nice to meet you,' said Fliss. 'Hope it all works out.' She cast a lingering, envious glance at Lucy's handbag. 'See you later.'

When she turned to go down the stairs, the back of her shirt explained the front: *Let There Be Life* was a dramatic performance of some sort, and it had been premiered at the Cowan Theatre.

The outside door closed, and Lucy spoke before Edwin Duke could say anything. 'How much?'

'Feargal was going to pay seven hundred pounds,' said Duke in an even, flat voice.

'Charitable status?'

'Yes.'

'Then I'll pay a thousand. If we get to be the judges.'

This time Duke raised both eyebrows. 'Up to you. Right, shall we get back to business?'

Bridget and Lucy didn't talk on the way out of the estate office – Lucy because she was thinking, and Bridget because it wasn't her place to comment on the deal which Duke had finally offered. She was itching to comment on having to judge a *baking competition*, though. Time enough for that.

'We need Mina's input,' declared Lucy when they were outside. 'I'll message her the new figures.' She paused, sent the message, then unlocked the car. By the time they'd fastened their seat belts, Mina was FaceTiming them.

'This is only just acceptable,' she said.

'And hello to you, too,' responded Lucy. 'Bridget's here. See?' She passed over the phone, and Bridget saw the distinctive, diminutive face of Mina Desai.

Bridget and Mina had some things in common – trauma and loss, for example; when Mina got spliced to Conrad Clarke, she would be writing *widow* in the status box of the register. And there were some things which marked them apart: Bridget had never been in prison for one. There were other, more obvious, differences, but to Bridget, Mina's Indian heritage actually brought them closer together. Their upbringing made them both outsiders in the worlds they'd chosen to dwell in.

'Hello, Bridget. Couldn't you have got Lucy to knock another hundred a month off the rent?'

'Hey! How is that down to me! You haven't heard about the sweetener she's thrown in yet.'

Mina frowned, and some of her lustrous black hair slipped from behind her ears. Mina was looking directly into her phone's camera, and Bridget's lips twitched a little as the angle shifted. If Mina needed to look at something away from the screen, she would move the phone to make sure that her nose was never in profile. We all have our vanities.

'There is a thousand pounds here for goodwill,' said Mina.

Lucy tried to grab the phone back. No way. Mina needed to hear this. 'You could say that,' said Bridget. 'You could also say that she has bribed the owner's wife by sponsoring the Bake Off competition. And she wants me to judge it with her.'

'Excuse me? Did you just say—'

'Oy!' said Lucy. The seat belt's anchor snapped into action and stopped her reaching any further.

'Yup. Lucy thinks it will help win over the angry yokels.'

Mina blinked. *That girl has the most gorgeous eyelashes. Helps draw your gaze away from the nose. And the scars on the jawline.* 'I think that's an excellent idea! One of the reasons people accepted me in Clerkswell is because I helped start the women's cricket team.'

'I used to like you,' said Bridget. 'You're supposed to be on my side.' She brought the phone closer to her face. 'And when you went to Manchester for your hen party, did you try to fit in by making friends with the stripper, eh?'

Mina lifted her head, her nose taking on the outline of an eagle's sharp beak. 'Pass the phone to Lucy, please, Bridget.' Then she blinked and grinned. 'No comment.'

Bridget allowed Lucy to take the phone, and her friend said, 'Look, this is only a starting point, Mina. I don't think they'll move on the rent, but there's plenty we can get them to include. Especially the kitchen. You have to see it to believe it.'

'The kitchen?'

'It's huge, and because of the way they've converted the mill, it's no use to anyone but the café. They've put the lift shaft and stairs next to it, so the only internal access is through the Spinning Room. I reckon we can get it if we hold out.'

Mina looked intrigued, a particularly Indian mixture of curiosity and disdain. 'How will you function without it? And why would you want it?'

'Without it, we could move the serving area and install under-counter dishwashers. Easy. But if we had it, think of the potential for expansion! We could start a bakery in there.'

Mina's head rocked from side to side, the camera keeping track as it did so. 'Up to you. Now, they've listed the existing coffee machine in the fixtures and fittings. You've put a star next to it.'

'Obviously we're getting a new one, but I won't tell them to take it out until the eleventh hour.'

'Good. This seems like a sound basis for negotiation. Who are you going to send in to manage it? Surely not Bridget ...?'

There was devilment in Mina's voice, and a challenge that Bridget couldn't resist. She snatched the phone back and said, 'And why not, eh? I'll wear a hazmat suit and have the place sorted in no time.'

'Why would you need protective clothing? The tender says nothing about decontamination.'

'This is the countryside,' declared Bridget. 'You never know what you might catch out here.'

Mina waved a hand. 'I used to think like that. You'll soon get used to it, and before you know it, you'll be moving out there.'

Bridget snorted. 'Like hell I will. Ten pounds says I'll finish at the Mill and be back in Cairndale.'

'You're on. Now you must excuse me, I have a team to manage.'

'A team of what?'

'Caterers. Dressmakers. Jewellers. Marquee erectors. Bridesmaids. Priests. The list is endless! Good luck, Lucy.'

When the call ended, Lucy screwed up her nose at Bridget. 'That was mean. Trying to get Mina to nix the Bake Off was sneaky.'

'Hey! All's fair in love and baking. What other chance have I got to talk you out of it?' Bridget thought for a moment. 'Why can't Lili do it? She'd put the fear of God into them.'

Lucy smiled and opened her palms. 'Lilianna is perfect to take over in Cairndale, and you need to see and be seen by the village. You'll thank me in the long run.'

'Like hell I will. Now stop winding me up and take me back to civilisation.'

'Turn up there,' said Bridget as they approached the heart of the village again after crossing the river.

Lucy was driving more slowly than she had during their arrival and near-death experience with the spiky tractor, so she had time to ask, 'Why?'

'Signpost said Byford Halt. I want to see how far the village is from the station. If you go ahead with this deal, I'm gonna be using that train a lot.'

Lucy indicated to turn, and while they waited for a van to pass, Bridget looked around. The shop and village green were on their left now, and on their right was the church on one corner and facing it on the other was a big house. A very big house.

The twin stone gateposts sported a brass plaque each, and now that she was wearing her glasses, Bridget could read the name of the house: *The Old Rectory*. The other plaque said that Calvert Developments were based here. As in Anya Calvert presumably.

Lucy turned and drove up Church Lane. No wonder Fliss Duke and Anya Calvert were the Queen Bees of Byford – Fliss lived in the Lodge, home of the former squires, and Anya lived in the Old Rectory, displacing the vicar. Bridget smiled to herself. *Game on*, she thought.

The car accelerated, and in a few seconds Lucy had to slam on the brakes: they had arrived at Byford Halt, the tiny unmanned railway station that served the village. They were lucky here: throughout most of Britain not one in a hundred villages still had access to trains.

'You really do need to get a car,' said Lucy, executing a three-point turn in front of the station. 'This is ridiculous.'

Bridget gave a *humph*. Lucy took it to mean that Bridget didn't have any money and said, 'I know you haven't been on a decent salary for very long, but we've got outlets in three places now, and we're looking at a fourth. When I get Mina to check the new numbers for the Ford Mill contract, I'll ask her about leasing a company car for you.'

What Bridget had actually meant by *humph* was that she hadn't driven for years and it was one of the many things she was trying to avoid. She'd passed her test at eighteen, but in the eighteen years since that day, she'd never owned a car of her own and she hadn't driven one for the last twelve. She sighed. Like a lot of things, she supposed she'd have to give it a go, but only when forced to.

Lucy drove back down the hill towards the village and said, 'Are you going to come back before the Bake Off?'

'Why should I? Are you sure we're ready to take this on, Luce? It's a big barn of a place in the middle of nowhere. One of us would have to be on site pretty much full-time. Maybe you and Tom could buy a proper house out here. It's only ten minutes from Cairndale police station.'

Lucy halted at the junction. 'Maybe. I don't know. He's doing alright in CID, but he's still on a year's secondment. He doesn't know whether he wants it or not, and Commander Ross doesn't know whether or not he wants Tom.'

'He'd be a fool if he didn't. They all rate Tom, you know. I haven't heard a single bad word about Sheriff Morton from any of the detectives, not even when I'm earwigging.'

There was a gentle toot on the horn from behind them, and Lucy took her foot off the brake to turn right and head back towards Cairndale and civilisation (hopefully avoiding the canal bridge). 'We'll see, eh?' she said.

Bridget folded her arms. Byford was a lovely village, but it was *in the countryside*. Goths with Scouse accents weren't exactly in their native element here. Perhaps if Bridget bribed Mina, their financial adviser would advise Lucy to avoid the Mill. But how do you bribe the woman who has everything and is about to get married to the man of her dreams? Bridget shuddered. She'd only met Mina's fiancé a couple of times, and Conrad Clarke was most definitely not the man of *Bridget's* dreams. Nightmares, maybe. She sighed and put her trust in the gods and spirits she sometimes believed in. If Bridget was meant to go into the jungle, then what would be would be.

At least Bridget would be safe out here: one of the items on the parish council minutes was a police report. According to Sergeant Ryan Marsh (who Bridget really liked, and not just because he was a fellow Liverpudlian), there had been *no* reported crime in Byford during the last year. *No crime!* How was that possible?

Chapter 10

Three and a Half Weeks Later

Downstream from the village of Byford, the River Cowan grows broader and becomes tidal as it passes through the small town of Cairndale, where the third branch of Caffè Milano nestles in a corner of Market Square, squeezed between the library and a branch of Boots the Chemist. The signage from the previous tenants still dominated the front of the café, apart from a red poster in the window: *Now a branch of Caffè Milano.*

It had been a busy day there, made busier by the extra police officers drafted in to help. Lilianna, the assistant manager, had filled takeout cup after takeout cup, and had even got her husband to raid the supermarket for extra pastries. If the supermarket had known where they were going, they wouldn't have been happy about the unlicensed resale, but the detectives at Cairndale nick weren't interested in a little off-the-cuff profiteering. They were just glad to have something to line their stomachs.

The café was in a three-storey Victorian building and had a good-sized apron in front of it. Lilianna's husband was now busy stacking the tables and chaining up the chairs ahead of closing, and inside, his wife was cleaning down the counter. Upstairs in the flat, Bridget was praying for Tom Morton to hurry up and get back from York.

The previous owners of the building hadn't let out the flat for years, preferring to use the middle floor as storage. Work was under way to refurbish the apartment, but there was a long way to go, and they'd started with the most urgent job: the bathroom.

Before she'd moved in, Bridget had ensured that everything had been cleaned by professionals, who'd worked for two days under her meticulous supervision, and although the living room was bare of carpet and curtains, and the walls had several different patterns of half-peeled wallpaper, it was clean. In a corner of the high-ceilinged space, a chain store sofa sat in front of a charity shop coffee table, and on the coffee table was the alternative first aid kit.

Lucy had been dropped off half an hour ago after being interviewed by CID, and Bridget had the emergency kit all ready: two glass dishes, two spoons and two cartons of Giuseppi's *Break-up Special* ice cream. Lucy said it was the most comforting food known to woman. And when Lucy had come in, she had dropped her bag on the couch and headed straight for the battered sideboard where one of her many gifts to Bridget was hidden: an unmarked bottle of Nonno Berardi's home-made grappa. Strictly illegal and unlicensed, but as Italian as the espresso served downstairs.

Lucy was on her third and final glass of Milanese anaesthetic when both girls got a message from Tom Morton: *Here. Getting coffee.*

'At last,' muttered Bridget under her breath. She pushed off the couch and offered a hand up to Lucy. 'Time to go, Luce. Your prince will be here shortly.'

'I know! And I need the loo.'

Lucy weaved towards the bathroom, and Bridget went to let Tom into her flat, buzzing him through the outside door and smoothing down her dress as she waited. *I really should have got changed,* she thought. *Damn car.* Tom climbed the steep stairs from the backyard with all the energy of a man who's been dragged away from hospital visiting to deal with the aftermath of a murder. Not that he'd be in charge of the investigation.

Bridget forced herself to get ready for a kiss. She hated social kissing so much that she sometimes thought about moving to Japan. There was a lot to like about that country, if the TV were to be believed: no handshakes, no social kissing. Immaculately clean public transport ...

'Bridget?' said Tom, opting to take a slurp of his coffee rather than go for a kiss. Then again, Tom had known her a long time now. Instead, he asked, 'Why are you dressed like that?' Tom might be a perfect gentleman with a high level of emotional intelligence, but he'd gone to a posh school, and you can take the schoolboy out of the school, but ...

'Don't you start,' said Bridget. 'How was Commander Ross?'

'Fine.'

'Really? I didn't think Ross did *fine*.'

Tom pushed back his floppy hair. 'He called me in to tell me that he'd stake his career on Lucy having nothing to do with Millie

Easterby's death, and he'll make sure the team gets the message. I said the same about you.'

'Good. It's about time there were a few bizzies with common sense. Present company excepted, of course.'

She stepped through to the sitting room, and Tom looked at the coffee table. With a smooth movement, he hid the bottle of grappa and picked up Lucy's handbag.

'How's your granddad?' asked Bridget.

'No change. How's Lucy?'

'Relaxed. Told me that Les Gartside had been professional, courteous and thorough. And it helped that Lucy usually sees the good in people. A police interview room is much less scary if you think the police are there to serve justice and not plant their feet on the necks of the working class.'

Tom paused to show he'd heard her but wasn't rising to the bait today. 'How many grappas has she had?'

'Doesn't matter,' said Lucy from the doorway. 'I'm not driving 'cos I've given my car to Bridget, and she's discovered something: she quite likes automatics. Never driven one before today.'

Tom strode across the floor, his leather-soled shoes cracking loudly off the boards and booming back from the walls. He took Lucy in his arms, and she sagged with relief, murmuring something that Bridget couldn't hear into his chest.

He held her for a moment, then gently disengaged. 'Did Les Gartside give you anything to eat?' he asked her.

'Lucy was just telling me how much she'd love a curry,' said Bridget. 'I'll message Ranjiv and put an order in, shall I? At this time of night, you'll be back home well before it goes cold.'

The Jewel in the Crown was just across the square, and it was by far the best takeout option in Cairndale. 'Please,' said Tom. 'When shall we pick the car up?'

Bridget's fingers got working on the takeaway order, and Lucy answered the question about the car. 'We're not picking it up,' she said, 'and I'll tell you why.'

Tom waited, then realised that the alcohol had slowed Lucy's brain down quite a bit. Or brought out her inner diva. Or both, probably. 'Go on.'

'Because we've got it! I signed the lease on the Mill coffee shop today, and we take over on Monday. Or Bridget does, to be *exactement*.'

'Food's ordered,' said Bridget. 'Fifteen minutes.' Tom heard the subtext: *Get her outside for some fresh air before she decides we need more grappa*.

'Can't you give Bridget a lift on Monday morning?' said Tom.

'Aah. We have a *prrrroblem*,' said Lucy, mangling her voice into a Scottish accent.

'Give over,' said Bridget. 'You mean *I* have a flippin' problem.' She stared at Tom. 'As well as being gentle with her, your Commander Ross told Lucy that it would be "for the best" if she avoided Byford for a bit. Sounds like it was an offer she couldn't refuse, so muggins here is on her own.'

'You'll be fine,' said Lucy airily.

'I know I'll be fine,' said Bridget. 'I'd be even finer if I had another pair of hands, thank you.'

Tom gave Lucy her bag and dropped her phone inside. 'Coat?' he said, more to Bridget than Lucy. Bridget shook her head, and Tom steered Lucy towards the stairs. Thank goodness she wasn't wearing heels.

Bridget went over and wrapped Lucy in a hug. There were some people she *did* hug. When necessary. 'You take care, yeah?'

'I'll be fine!' said Lucy. She burped. 'Though I could murder a curry. Oops.'

'Thanks, Bridget,' said Tom. 'Thank you very much.'

They were halfway down the stairs when Lucy unleashed her parting shot. 'Look after my car! And don't wear that dress on Monday.'

'That was harsh,' said Tom. He steadied Lucy with one hand and opened the door with the other, and clearly wasn't used to the flat's acoustics because he added, 'She didn't look that bad.'

'She looked awful,' said Lucy. 'But that's not the point. She needs to be in Caffè Milano colours on Monday.'

Tom let the door close behind him, and Bridget heaved a sigh of relief. She didn't begrudge Lucy's dramatic response to what had happened. After all, Lucy had been found with the alleged poison in her handbag and then been dragged off by the cops. And they'd both been there when the life left Millie Easterby.

'Sod that,' she told the echoing space. She went over to the table and picked up her shot glass, the level barely below what Lucy had poured her. Bridget downed the smooth spirit in one and winced as it burned through her insides. 'Whoa, kid. That was something else. Woo. Gets me every time.'

She wasn't talking to herself, of course. Still less was she talking to the empty room. She was talking to Natalie. Just because Natalie was ashes in the Mersey, there was no reason to stop talking to her. Not while she lived on in Bridget.

'You'd fit right in out there, Nat,' she told her friend. 'They'd see the pretty girl with blue eyes and they'd open their arms for you.'

The bare bulbs high in the room turned the picture windows into mirrors, and Bridget caught sight of herself. *Shit.* The night-time punters would be rolling into the market square soon, and Bridget did not want to feature on Twitter wearing a tablecloth. She killed the lights and did what she usually did in the evenings: retreated up to her bedroom where the windows faced the alley and weren't overlooked by anyone.

It was Lilianna's day off tomorrow, and Sunday was always busy. Good. It would tire her out and stop her thinking about what was coming on Monday.

She poured herself another grappa and went upstairs to wrestle with the zip on that bloody dress. Good job Lucy had been too stunned to ask how much it had cost.

There was a reception committee waiting for Bridget at Ford Mill on Monday morning. 'They're up early,' she muttered to herself as she drove Lucy's car carefully past the sign announcing that the whole building was closed for two days.

There had been no reprieve phone call on Sunday, just a message to say that everything was in place and wishing her luck. *You're a professional,* Bridget told herself. *You can do this.*

She carried onwards into the small car park and chose a spot near to the side door: less distance to carry the stuff that way. She sighed and climbed out of the vehicle with as much dignity as she could muster – it was designed more for someone of Lucy's build than hers.

The May sunshine of Saturday had given way to clouds, and with the regularity of clockwork, it would rain later. *That's North Lancashire for you,* she thought. Although Liverpool was very much in Lancashire, this part of the county had fifty per cent more rain a year. She knew that because she'd looked it up and it wasn't an urban legend. Rural legend. Whatever.

Three men waited for her at the main entrance to the Mill. She had no problem with men waiting for her (not enough of that happened in her opinion), but she would have preferred it if her woman were there, too; there was no sign of Kat Chester, their only employee out here in darkest Byford.

'Morning, Bridget,' said Perry Lockwood.

The land agent of the Byford Estate was no longer wearing his *Bakers have nice buns* T-shirt, and it had been replaced by a dress shirt with no tie. His voice was neither sad nor overly bright, just professional and welcoming. 'Have you met Louis and Amos?'

He indicated the mismatched couple to his right. The shorter, slighter one had to be Louis because there was a floral shirt clearly visible under his open puffer jacket. The other one was altogether bigger, stronger and looked indigenous to Byford even if he wasn't. His waxed jacket looked like it was so old it might be a family heirloom, and the boots were made for hard and dirty work.

She didn't enjoy it, but Bridget stuck out her hand to greet Louis. He looked like he was going to give her a kiss (not going to happen) but settled for a handshake. 'I'm Louis Young, in case you hadn't guessed. It's *lovely* to have you here.' His voice was sing-song and musical, and definitely camp. Not stage camp, but camp nonetheless. 'This is my husband, Amos Ayre. He works for Mike the Milk.'

Amos shook her hand, keeping his strength in reserve. They were real worker's hands, though. No doubt about that. He saw the look on Bridget's face and said, 'Welcome to Byford. I work for Mike Mason. Louis is the only person who calls him *Mike the Milk*. It winds him up no end.'

'Is there no Lucy?' said Louis, scanning the car park. 'I'm dying to meet her.'

Bridget could guess why: Lucy's connections to the world of celebrity opened a lot of doors, but they didn't always let the right people in. 'Not today,' said Bridget cheerfully. 'Where's Kat?'

Perry had stood back and watched so far. A very reserved man, it seemed, and not the sort to gossip. Unlike Louis, who declared, 'Kat is *not* a morning person. Expect her at ten. On the other hand, the poor girl has no social life, so she's happy to work late.' He paused. 'Just consider me your HR manager.'

'Shall we go inside before it rains?' said Perry.

They'd been standing to the side of the glass entrance, and as soon as they moved in front of it, the automatic doors slid back. Perry led the way and moved into letting agent mode. 'This entrance was Lady Felicia's idea, but it's a bit of a pain, to be honest. I'll run through the alarm systems later, but there'll be nights when you're last in, so you need to know how to get out when you've lowered the metal shutters here. Paperwork's all ready.'

Several sheets of paper had been set out on the counter of the box office and weighted down with keys. Louis and Amos stood back, and Perry pointed to the blank signature box at the bottom. A pen had materialised from somewhere and he offered it to Bridget. 'This is to sign for receipt of the keys, for the furniture sold by the administrators and for the possession of the coffee shop.'

Bridget couldn't help it. She looked over her shoulder for Lucy: this was her big day, not Bridget's. Lucy would insist on someone taking a picture and putting it on Instagram. Lucy would have people messaging enquiries. Her phone pinged, and she checked the ID: Lucy. Spooky. 'One moment,' she said.

Lucy's message was as typically Lucy as her untameable brown curls: *Thinking of you, Mistress of the Mill. You've got this, Bridge. Don't forget to check the place before you sign anything. Love you. XXX.*

'Shall we have a look first?' Bridget suggested. 'Just to make sure.'

'Aah. Hmm,' said Perry. 'About that.'

Bridget's fingers stopped halfway to the zip of her coat. 'What?'

'Feargal was in no fit state to clear out after Saturday,' he replied, 'so Amos and I set to. I didn't realise that the coffee machine was plumbed in when we pulled it out. There was a bit of a leak. Well, a lot of a leak. Sorry.'

'Tell me you're joking, Perry.'

'My fault really,' said Amos uncomfortably. 'I'm more used to milking machines than coffee machines. There wasn't much water damage. Perry said that the new machine isn't coming until tomorrow, and there's an emergency plumber due at eleven.'

The three men stood in a line, like guilty schoolboys. Bridget folded her arms (which wasn't easy with the coat stretched over her chest). 'What time's afternoon milking?'

'Four o'clock,' said Amos with a frown.

'Then you've got seven hours and forty-five minutes to get the place sorted.'

She unzipped her coat and shrugged it off. Louis didn't stay guilty for very long when he saw her arms. 'That is some serious ink, Bridget.'

On her left arm was a complex Celtic triskele in blue. She'd had it for years and years, but most people stared at her right arm. In the broadest part was a skull, and growing out of the skull were red roses. She'd had that one done the day she'd walked out of the therapist's office for the last time.

Louis didn't know what to say about the skull and roses. Most people didn't. Instead of her ink, he pointed to her polo shirt. 'What a vivid colour. Very ... forceful. Not sure about the contrast collar, though.'

The new Caffè Milano uniform (which had recently replaced the original purple) was a bright and vivid red with black collar and black logo on the chest. On the reverse, it proclaimed Bridget as *Senior Barista*. Lucy had wanted it to say *Boss*. Not having that.

'Blame Herbert Kilpin,' said Bridget, turning and walking towards the archway of the Spinning Room. She'd have preferred her coffee shop to be sealed off, but she could see why Duke's architect had left it open.

The guilty schoolboys (and Louis) followed behind. 'Who's Herbert Kilpin?' said Louis. 'A very angry designer?'

'No. He was the founder of AC Milan. It's Lucy's tribute to her Italian heritage.' *And her father, who used to play for them,* she added in her head. 'The red is for passion and the black is for the fear we inspire in our opponents. Show me the worst.'

Chapter 11

When she saw what Feargal Hulme's business had left behind, Bridget shook her head. 'Looks like we're gonna be busy,' she announced. Ugh. Even without the water damage, the removal of the old coffee machine had revealed things which should *not* be occurring in any environment where food was served. She handed Amos a selection of cleaning products and announced, 'Yours, I reckon.'

He accepted his task without a word and got on with it. She took one look at Louis's shirt and decided that she'd keep him in reserve for later. Perry walked round the room with her once before announcing that he had a meeting and disappeared. 'You can sign for the keys when you're ready,' was his parting shot.

Lilianna's husband arrived in his van at nine o'clock, having collected the new signage, menus and crockery. He and Amos carried them in, then the young Pole headed off to the coffee roasters in Warrington for the big order, leaving Bridget with a load of signs. She summoned Louis.

'You must be good at the display stuff,' she said.

'Must I?' said Louis. 'Is that because I'm gay, do you think?'

Amos snorted from behind the counter, then got back on his hands and knees.

'No,' said Bridget. 'It's because all the posters and artwork out there are immaculate, and I don't see anyone else doing it. I'll bet the gallery is just as organised.'

'You've found me out,' said Louis. 'I'll just go and get the ladder.'

'I'll get it. Where is it?' said Bridget. She'd need a ladder and hadn't seen one around.

'Downstairs. You don't want to meet Coffin Joe just yet.'

Bridget stopped. 'What?'

'I heard you putting your foot in it with Perry on Saturday about the coffins. That was before, you know, before what happened to Millie.' He sighed, as if he hadn't wanted to mention it. 'The coffin workshop is in the basement. Separate entrance, thankfully. Joe borrowed the steps last week. I won't be long.'

Unlike Louis, Kat Chester was more than happy to talk about the death of Millie Easterby, though she took her good time spelling it out.

Kat had dressed for hard work in an old pair of leggings and paint-splashed trainers. 'Am I late?' was her first question. 'I'm contracted from ten, and no one told me otherwise.'

Fair enough. Bridget had guessed at Medium for Kat's polo shirt and handed it over, along with the half-apron and a business card.

Kat looked from her new uniform to Bridget and said, 'No leather? No lace? Louis said we'd all have to wear steampunk when you took over.'

When Bridget didn't reply straight away, Kat got flustered, then blushed. 'It was a joke. I didn't believe him. Honestly.'

Looking at the gawky kid in front of her, whose full-length leggings barely covered her calves, Bridget couldn't get angry.

'Louis Young needs to wind his neck in before someone bites it. Welcome aboard, Kat. Text me your number and screenshot your bank details so I can get your wages sorted.'

Kat raised her eyebrows at the shirt (she wasn't the first new employee to do that), then stared at the card. 'Is it all still going ahead, then?'

Bridget misread the signals and said, 'Totally. Not going to let a bit of mess stop us. So long as we have water and power, we shall have coffee.' She tried a smile. 'And beans and milk, of course. They're coming later. Let's get unpacking, shall we?'

The plumber was early, and insisted the water be turned off. 'Can I fill the kettle first?' said Bridget. 'Do we have a kettle?'

'Upstairs,' announced Louis. 'We all deserve a break and there's a separate water supply.'

Bridget was last upstairs. She'd checked out the toilets, which were designed to accommodate an audience from the theatre, and found them wanting. It went onto her phone with the other items she'd need to talk to Perry about.

Louis's den was off a half-landing, and Kat was on her own inside. 'Louis's gone to get some milk from Mum. He always used to nick it from us. From Miller's Rest, I mean.'

'Hmm. We'll see about that.' She flopped into a chair. It was nice in here. Not an office, exactly, more of a study. 'Where's Amos?'

'Gone to see Mike and ask for a bit more time off. Won't be a problem.' Kat shuffled round to face Bridget properly. 'Is it true about Lucy?' she asked.

Bridget tried to keep her face straight. 'Is what true?'

'I heard she'd been arrested. That's why I assumed she wasn't here. Will you take over if she goes to prison?'

Bridget felt a surge of anger, enough to make her face match her shirt, but she controlled it. 'Who's saying that, Katherine?'

'It's Katarina, not Katherine, and don't call me that.' Point made, Kat looked at the empty room as if checking to see whether someone was hiding behind the armchairs. 'It's all over the village. Every WhatsApp group has someone who says it was Lucy.' She paused. 'I dunno about the Colonel, though. He doesn't do WhatsApp.'

'Why would Lucy murder Millie Easterby?' asked Bridget, appalled. 'Why would Lucy hurt someone she's only just met?'

Kat looked like, well, she looked like the Kat with the Cream. 'Is that what she told you? Look at this.'

She flicked through her phone and held it up. Bridget leaned forwards and saw a screenshot from Twitter. Must be a while ago because Lucy hadn't been on social media for ages. There was a man with his arm round two girls, both of whom were showing a lot of sweaty, sparkly flesh. Bridget sighed. They were much younger and very bright-eyed, but they were definitely Lucy and Millie. 'Where is this from?'

'Dunno who first found it, and it's been taken down now. It's from the guy in the middle's Twitter feed. He didn't explain it, but it was tagged at some nightclub in Manchester. I reckon that Millie stole him off Lucy and Lucy was getting her revenge.'

Bridget had never heard anything so improbable in her life. Ever. But it was no use trying to convince Kat, because Bridget didn't have any photographic evidence, did she, and we all know that the camera never lies, don't we?

Bridget took a moment to digest this, then took a deep breath. She could see what was coming next. Unless Tracey Kenyon found a forensic bombshell, Lucy would forever be tagged as Millie's killer. Bridget was not going to allow that. Oh no. The fact that Bridget would soon be *guilty by association* was neither here nor there. Bridget would be gone before long, but this would always be Lucy's business.

She smiled at Kat and asked, 'Is there a Ford Mill WhatsApp group?'

'Yeah. Course. There's two – one with the Dukes and Perry on it and one without.'

'Put me on both. Now.'

Kat was taken aback and moved away from Bridget's hard stare. 'Right. No problem. Whatever you say, Boss Bridget.'

'And I'm not the *boss*. That's Lucy, alright?'

Louis returned with the milk, and tea was distributed. Bit thin for Bridget's taste, but she could train him. She didn't say anything about the tea or about stealing milk in the future because Louis also had biscuits, and Bridget needed a biscuit desperately. This was her first working day for years when she hadn't been surrounded by cakes, pastries and chocolate. It was taking some getting used to.

'Right then,' said Louis. He held up his phone to display a neat photomontage – of Bridget.

She stared at herself in her habitual black layers, her Magenta outfit (from *The Rocky Horror Show*), in her Caffè Milano uniform, and, ultimate horror, in *that* dress. From Saturday. And in the most recent picture, she was eyeball to eyeball with Millie Easterby across the workbench. Louis turned the phone back to have another look himself, then clicked it closed. And smiled.

'What?' said Bridget. 'What are you going to say?'

'Me? Nothing. We have to see each other every day, Bridget. You'll tell me in your own good time why you love to dress up.'

And that's his idea of saying nothing? Bridget gave him her feral smile. 'If we're not going to talk about me, let's talk about you.'

'Nothing to say. I knew Fliss from the alternative theatre circuit. You know she had her own company, right?'

Bridget nodded. The Sinister Spinsters were – had been – good at self-promotion if nothing else.

Louis continued, 'When Fliss won the matrimonial lottery and convinced the Iron Duke to build an arts centre, naturally she picked me to run it.' He beamed a smile and dared Bridget to puncture his balloon of pride. She would, but not today, because she remembered where she'd heard the name *Easterby* before: Edwin Duke had bought

Ford Mill and Byford Lodge from the *Easterby Estate*.

Bridget treated herself to another biscuit. 'I'm guessing there was a connection between Millie and the Easterby Estate.'

'Oh yes. I don't know the ins and outs, though. One of the natives is your best guide to that sort of thing.'

As one, they turned to look at Kat.

'What?' said the girl. 'Don't look at me.'

'Didn't you grow up here?' asked Bridget, nonplussed.

'Yeah,' said Kat defensively. 'And Millie went to school here for a bit. She was years older than me, though. Then she went away and she came back when the old witch was ill.'

'What old witch.'

'Temperature Easterby. She was an old witch who lived in the Lodge and scared us all to death if we tried to get into the orchard by the millpond.'

'I think she means *Temperance* not *Temperature*,' said Louis. 'You can never tell with her.'

'Oy!' said Kat. 'Temperature or Temperance. They're both made up names, so what does it matter?'

Bridget did some maths in her head and tried to reconcile the dates and ages – she'd already seen online that Millie was thirty-two (so how did she know Lucy, who was four years younger?). If the Dukes had bought the Easterby Estate eight years ago … She gave up for now.

Amos appeared, a steaming mug in his hand. 'I've got until two o'clock,' he said.

'Thanks,' said Bridget. 'C'mon, Kat, we'll get back to it and leave Amos to finish the biscuits. Hopefully the plumber will be done by now.'

The plumber had finished, and the new brass fittings gleamed, ready for their union with the giant red monster machine which would be delivered tomorrow. 'Don't worry,' said the plumber. 'I've double checked, and that's the right-sized fitting for the model you're getting. I've even moved the waste trap six inches. That'll save the engineer calling me back out.'

'Excellent. Here, take these. Best I can do at the minute.'

Bridget offered him the first four vouchers from her book of freebies. The good book, the one with the free drink *and* free slice of cake.

'Cheers, love. I'm up and down Cowandale, so you'll be seeing me soon enough.' He grinned. 'Not poisoned, the cake, is it?'

'It can be. If I don't like you.'

'Err, right. You've got me number.'

Kat had been watching the exchange. 'I think he fancies you,' she observed. She looked down at Bridget's leggings. 'Some men go for big hips.' She looked up again with a smile. 'Are we allowed to make jokes about poisoning people? There's a really good one on the internet about a Frenchman and a batch of poisoned Viagra.'

Bridget stared at her only member of staff. 'No. I wish. And no. In that order. I need to make a call. You need to put all the crockery through the dishwasher, but only after you've messaged me that picture of Lucy and Millie.' Bridget left Kat to work out what she'd said and went outside.

Lucy answered on the first ring. 'How's it going?'

'Fine. Apart from the local cowhand causing a flood. All sorted now. Everything's under control, Lucy, so you don't need to worry about Caffè Milano. What you do need to worry about is why you didn't tell me about Millie Easterby and the fact that you knew her.'

'What! I didn't! I don't.'

'Have a look at WhatsApp.' Bridget thumbed through and forwarded the picture, then retrieved the call. 'Tell me I'm wrong.'

'You're wrong! If I was supposed to remember every time I got snapped in a club, I'd need Wikipedia for a memory.'

This is true, thought Bridget. Before her brother was murdered, Lucy had led an … interesting social life. And most of it had featured Manchester's more exclusive clubs. 'Do you at least recognise the bloke?'

'Oh. Yeah. He played for Trafford Rangers for a bit and they sold him to Arsenal. Disappeared without trace, in other words.'

A van bounced up the drive. It had *N.E.R.D.S* scrawled over the side in mock marker pen. 'Gotta go, Luce. Point of sale is here. Text me the name of the footballer, yeah?'

She disconnected and went to meet the driver, who looked nothing like a nerd. A bank robber trying for a change of career, yes, but a nerd, definitely not. Along with various graphics on the van extolling the virtues of North East Retail Data Systems, there was a small logo with the tag line: *Proud to work with ex-offenders*. Yep, the guy really was a bank robber. When he got out of the van, he cast his professional eye over Ford Mill.

'Morning, Dark Lady. Anything here worth nicking?' he asked.

'Some art, maybe.'

'Nah. Too much trouble to get rid of, and I've got no space left on me walls. Where are we this time, and have you sorted the VPN for me?' Before Bridget could answer, the driver/systems engineer/ex-bank robber looked over her shoulder and said, 'Morning, sir.'

Perry Lockwood was back. 'How d'you do. Did you want access to the Ford Mill network, Bridget?' he asked innocently. 'It's just that Lucy forgot to include it in the management agreement. I'm sure we can come to an arrangement.'

Bridget pointed the engineer towards the side door. 'Café's through there. Kat knows where the stuff needs to go.' And then, to Perry, she said 'Fine. We'll take a month at the same rate as Miller's Rest, then we'll negotiate properly, shall we?'

Perry laughed. 'Fair enough. I'll come inside and get your guy set up, unless you want me to send you the codes?'

'No. Might as well make yourself useful.' She dropped her voice. 'But whatever you do, don't tell him about the jewellery workshop upstairs, okay?'

'Why ever not?'

'Just don't, okay? Anything else?'

'I've had a message from Fliss.'

'I'm thrilled for you. I can't wait for the day when Honourable Ladies send me messages.'

Perry's mouth twitched in an involuntary tic. Had he been going to smile and then suppressed it? 'You should be careful what you wish for, Bridget, that's all I'm saying.'

'Are you not gonna say what she wanted, or are you gonna come over here every time her ladyship gets in touch?'

'I … erm.' He was flustered. Just a bit. 'Fliss is up at the spa.'

'Good for her. I take it she's not working a shift there?'

'She does Pilates or Yogalates or something. Anyway, she's friends with Niamh. Niamh Edwards, and Niamh runs the spa. Her husband, Bryn, runs the clinic.'

He looked lost again. 'You're not big on anecdotes, are you Perry?'

'Sorry?'

It had been years since Lisa died, and it looked like her husband's conversational skills had died with her. Bridget tried to fashion a reassuring smile. 'Go on, Perry. Was this Niamh asking about the murder or something?'

'God, no. I'm sure there's been a lot of that, but Fliss knows better than to gossip with me. No, Niamh was asking about the Miller's Rest quiz team.'

'There is no Miller's Rest anymore, never mind a quiz team. Where did they compete and who was in it?'

He gestured over the river. 'At the White Hart, and the team fluctuated. The last incarnation was Feargal, Millie, Fliss and me. We rarely won, but the point was to beat the spa team.'

'Quiz team? Me? You have to be kidding. I'd rather pluck hairs out of me legs with tweezers.'

He flinched back. She'd done it again, hadn't she? Returned kindness with sarcasm. 'I was just passing on a message, Bridget. I'll leave you in peace and go sort out the VPN access.'

'Thanks, Perry,' she called to his back. 'You're a lifesaver.'

He lifted his hand in acknowledgement but didn't turn around as he made his way into the Mill.

Chapter 12

Bridget's stomach was rumbling when the man from NERDS drove off and left her to it. 'I need to show you how the tills work, Kat,' she said, 'but me stomach thinks me throat's been cut. I think we should stop for lunch, only I've got no lunch. Are you going home, you two?'

Amos dropped his microfibre cloth into the bucket and nodded. 'See you in an hour, okay?'

Kat shrugged. 'Don't really do lunch. I'll grab a brew and catch up.'

'Catch up with what?'

'Insta. WhatsApp. My phone's been going mad for the last half an hour.'

Bridget had insisted that phones be placed in the kitchen during working hours, much to Kat's dismay. To get her own back, Kat had put her phone on vibrate, then left it on the large stainless steel draining board. Since then, it sounded like an army of insects was conducting a siege in the kitchen. If Kat did it again after lunch, Bridget was going to run the taps and fill the sink. That would weigh it down and make a slope; with any luck, Kat's phone would vibrate its way to a watery grave.

Bridget turned on her heel and looked around. No matter how hard she looked, there was still nothing to eat. 'What am I gonna do?' she said. Her blood sugar levels really were that low.

'Mum and Dad's, of course. Fresh sandwiches delivered every morning by Rodrigo.'

'Are they Mexican or something?'

'Ey? No. His name's Roderick and he comes from Carlisle. They're good. For a bought sandwich.'

Bridget grabbed her coat. She didn't really want to be seen in public, but needs must. She had planned to drive, but the rain had stopped. She tossed the car keys in her hand for a second. *I'll bet there's loads of eco warriors round here. If they see me driving to the shop for a butty, that'll be my card marked.* She sighed and shoved the keys in her pocket. Better get used to it.

She took a look at Mill Cottages as she exited the Mill site. She also huffed because she hadn't remembered the drive being *that* long on the way in. The cottages looked nice, and Perry's home seemed to be in good condition, considering it was inhabited by a widower and two boys. During one of the few pauses in preparation, she'd asked Kat about the late Lisa Lockwood.

'She was lovely,' Kat had said, staring into the distance. 'Died three years ago. I think. I was away. Cancer. I think she worked, but I don't know what at. The boys are okay. For boys.'

The cottages weren't far from the bridge, and Bridget paused to survey the river. Just down from the bridge was a sort of flat bit where it spread out. A path led to the water from both sides and she twigged: the ford! Byford! Well, there you go.

On the other side of the bridge, the road sloped up, with a fence on the left and two cottages on the right – Box Cottage and Rose Cottage. From what she remembered, Call-me-Jorie lived in Rose Cottage. It was immaculate. Fussy, but immaculate. To be expected, she supposed. Was it her, or was this hill a lot steeper than it had been this morning?

She stopped at the T-junction and peered right. There were more cottages on the river side of the road, and opposite them, she could see a car park and inn sign showing a big white deer. She filed it away for future reference and turned left.

Over the road was the high stone wall of the Old Rectory, and to her left was the village green. Part of her decision to walk had been the desire to see what was going on at the Bake Off tent, and she took out her glasses to get a better look.

'Good,' she announced. 'Still at it.'

They were. A scene-of-crime van, a marked police car and a grubby grey 4x4 were parked in front of the tent, and a white-suited figure emerged carrying an equipment box. Bridget nodded with satisfaction – the Commander was clearly leaving no rock bun unturned, even two days after the murder. She headed past the green and on to the shop.

She was going to wipe her feet on the mat outside when the door opened and out rushed Liz Swindlehurst, clutching a sandwich and three packets of Haribo. 'Oh, hi Bridget,' said the detective.

'Hi. Same idea as me. Minus the sweets.'

'Brain food,' said Liz. 'I'd have sent Barney, but he's taking yet another batch of samples to Preston. Means the SOCOs can focus on the important stuff.' She stepped away from the door (and from prying eyes). 'How's Lucy?'

'Fine. Has some helpful citizen shown you the picture of her and Millie Easterby?'

Liz frowned. 'Are you trying to get her in trouble?'

Bridget was of a height and almost of a size with Liz. She stood her ground and let her face do the talking for a second. 'Full disclosure, Liz. Full disclosure. Lucy had no idea the picture existed until I told her, and I can tell you know about it. Have you tracked down Diego from that picture yet?'

Liz shrugged. 'All the way to Naples. Someone's trying to talk to his agent because the club laughed when we called them. They thought we were journalists or internet prankers.'

'How's the rest of it going?'

Liz blinked a couple of times. She was in a difficult position here. Bridget could see that every copper's instinct was telling her not to discuss the case, but this was no ordinary case. Not only was Lucy her DCI's girlfriend, Bridget was her barista. You do not want to upset your barista.

'Early days,' said Liz. 'It doesn't help that Lucy is a witness …' She held up her hand when she saw Bridget about to bristle at her. 'I know, I know, but with her as a material witness, the Sheriff's right out of things, and there has to be a senior investigating officer. And the SIO has to have been a detective, and the Commander has never been a detective.'

This did not sound good to Bridget. 'So who's in charge, then?'

'Oh, believe me, Commander Ross is very much in charge. Unfortunately the official SIO is in Preston, so everything has to be signed off by him.'

'Can't he come up here? It's only forty minutes away.'

Liz gave her a look. 'What? And actually go face-to-face with Ross? Nah. It would be a brave man who did that. Much easier to stick to a desk and say *no more budget* from a safe distance.'

They shook their heads in mutual sympathy, and Liz smiled to dispel the gloom. 'What we're actually doing is collating statements and trying to put a timeline together. Forensics did a quick blood test yesterday and confirmed acute cyanosis and the presence of cyanide. Doctor Jepson's doing the postmortem today.'

Bridget shuddered. 'Don't you have to go to that?'

'Say what you like about the Commander, he would never delegate the difficult stuff. He's in charge and he's attending. Briefing tonight.' She sighed. 'How do you feel about saints, Bridget?'

What on earth was the woman on about? 'In what way? I haven't given much thought to saints since I prayed to St Charles Borromeo to lose weight, with him being the patron saint of diets. As you can see, it wasn't entirely successful.'

'Yeah, well, in my world we don't have a lot of saints. Trying to investigate a murder when the victim is a saint is not something I'm really equipped for, because who wants to murder a saint?'

'Roman emperors and Pagan kings, usually.'

'Sorry?'

'If you murder a saint, they become a Holy Martyr, and it was usually the ungodly heathens who did the martyring.'

'I'll take your word for it. See you later.'

Bridget frowned and watched Liz return to the green and the Bake Off tent. Something had given her an idea, but she was way too hungry to work it out.

She entered the shop, where a couple of men in hi-viz vests were browsing the crisp section, but there was no sign of Jackie Chester. Bridget went to the chiller and selected a cheese ploughman's. That should keep her going. She headed for the milk and smiled when she saw that, as well as offerings in plastic from Dales Dairies, there were actual glass bottles, with green laughing cows on them and the words *Mike's Milk* underneath. That could not be a coincidence. She picked up a bottle and examined it.

'You have to be kidding me!' she exclaimed.

'About what?'

She nearly dropped the bottle in fright. Where on earth had Jackie sprung from. 'Jesus, you gave me a fright! Is this really *unpasteurised* milk? Is that even legal?'

Jackie looked very, very uncomfortable. 'We're just storing it for a friend.'

Bridget replaced the bottle. 'If you say so.' She held out her hand. 'I'm Bridget Gorrigan, but you've probably guessed that.'

Jackie shook. 'I had guessed. Were you on business the last time you dropped in? When little Grace thought you'd been on the lollipops?'

Bridget gripped the sandwich so tightly that the plastic crinkled. Should she deny it? Should she pretend that the purple-lipped Goth who'd been here was someone else?

'I was on my way to a festival,' she lied.

'Nice,' said Jackie, as if it were nothing to her, when it clearly was. 'How's it going?'

'Great. So far. Can I ask you an honest question? In confidence?'

The shopkeeper took half a step back and drew out her answer. 'Yessss …'

'Is there any point in trying to get your daughter out of bed any earlier?'

Jackie laughed. 'No. Save yourself the heartache. We do. Chris and I gave up trying to change her years ago. She works hard enough when she's up, though.'

'She does. I'd better get back. With some *pasteurised* milk. I'll no doubt be seeing a fair bit of you.'

'We see a fair bit of most people. The ones who don't buy everything at ASDA, that is.'

'Good. Oh, and biscuits. What are Kat's favourites?'

'Custard creams. Or malted milk when she's been dumped. Get both to be on the safe side. You'll need the malted milk soon enough.'

Bridget left the shop feeling somehow more cheerful, a feeling that lasted halfway to the bridge. At that point, it started to rain again.

By four o'clock, there wasn't a lot left that Bridget could do without the coffee machine. The new premises were clean, the signage was in place and the tills were happily winking at them, desperate for sales to register. Time to go home, to Cairndale and to civilisation.

As she drove through the village, Bridget slowed down by the shop. Someone had said that Millie Easterby lived in *School House*, so where was it? She glanced right – nothing but the church – and nearly missed it. She was getting used to Lucy's automatic car, but sometimes forgot that the brakes could be … fierce. Ow! That *hurt*. The seat belt had caught her in a painful place, and insult was added to injury when a loud horn blared behind her.

'Calm down, calm down,' she muttered and pulled in to the side of the road. A large Mercedes roared past her and she scowled at the driver. After checking the road was clear, she took a good look at what she'd seen.

School House was where you'd expect it to be: in a corner of the school grounds. But that wasn't all, because School House was also the old school, complete with *Girls* and *Boys* carved over the entrances. Curtains were closed or blinds were down in every window and the house already looked deserted. How come Millie Easterby got to live there? Bridget had never heard of an ordinary teacher getting such a gorgeous-looking house as part of the job. When had the new school been built? She drummed her fingers on the steering wheel and realised that every hour that passed in Byford brought another question she couldn't answer. Or not on her own. She triple checked for tractors, vans or mad Mercedes drivers and got going again.

Lucy was on afternoon duty in Caffè Milano, Cairndale, serving the post-work crowd and training another young barista, this one a spotty lad who looked about twelve. Bridget had arranged for Lilianna to cover the morning shift so that Lucy could catch the slow train up from Garstang, where she and Tom were living in a short-term rental. Bridget went up to the spotty lad and said, 'I'm Bridget. Make me a double espresso.' He fled.

'What's got into you?' said Lucy with a frown. 'We can't afford to scare off the new recruits. We're going to need more soon.'

Bridget leaned on the counter. 'My caffeine levels are out of balance. I can't survive a whole day on tea. Unlike Tom. I need coffee and we need to talk.'

Lucy could make perfect coffee and talk at the same time. The portafilter was soon under the coffee machine's head while she talked, 'Tom's got to work overtime, for obvious reasons. As well as picking up Liz's caseload, he's having to stand in for the Commander at some meeting in Barrow. He's not due back till late. Do you fancy a pizza, because I think it's not just coffee you need? There you go.'

Bridget accepted the cup, and Lucy got on with serving one of the librarians who'd just come in. Bridget retreated to avoid him and realised that Lucy was right: she did need to eat something soon, and it was not going to be a Maltese pizza. This called for drastic measures. She downed the coffee and felt slightly better. 'I'm filthy. I need a shower first, then we're off to the carvery.'

'Are you serious? You are. Tom has said he'd rather die than eat in there.'

Sometimes Lucy couldn't help herself, and Bridget shook her head. 'The carvery has the highest food hygiene score in the area. Higher than that Michelin-starred place where Tom worships, and you can eat two meals at the carvery for less than the cost of one of Carl Christie's starters. We didn't all go to private school you know.'

Lucy took it on the chin, like she always did. 'You need food *and* a drink. I'll drive. See you down here at six.'

Chapter 13

'I'm having the beef,' said Lucy. 'It's amazing how one weekend in Clerkswell makes you long for the stuff.'

Mina Desai – or was it Mina Clarke now? Bridget hadn't bothered to ask, and Mina's married name wouldn't affect her status as a devout-ish Hindu, and beef had definitely been off the menu at her and Conrad's house during their wedding. 'Have you heard from her yet?'

'Total radio silence.' Lucy shrugged and picked up a tray.

They ate in silence for a good five minutes, then relaxed enough for Bridget to start running Lucy through the progress she'd made at Ford Mill and what the plans were for tomorrow. Bridget was about to broach the subject of Millie Easterby when Lucy asked the question that Bridget had been hoping to avoid. 'How was everyone? No pitchforks or wicker men?' she said with a cheeky Lucy smile.

'So long as I stick to the staff uniform and avoid black lace or blue gingham, I'll be fine. Just don't ask me to wear a waxed jacket.'

'Of course *you* were fine,' said Lucy with a frown. 'I was thinking more about the business. I'm worried that we're going to be accused of stepping into a dead woman's shoes. A lot of people still think of Miller's Rest as being as much hers as Feargal's.'

Bridget was mortified. Lucy didn't get it, did she? The waitress took their dessert order, and Bridget leaned forwards. 'We've got to do something,' she said urgently. 'As things stand, you're effectively excommunicated from the village. We can't have that, and it won't do me any good either. Or Tom.'

'Excommunicated! Haven't heard that for a while. I think Tom would say *persona non grata*.'

Bridget waited for the waitress to deposit her sticky toffee pudding (they didn't even pretend it was home-made, but they had a good supplier). She pointed her spoon at Lucy and said, 'I'm sure he would, but he's a Proddy Dog. His mother works for the flaming Archbishop of York for goodness' sake! You and me were brought up Catholics,

Lucy, and the Church punishes innocent people by *excommunicating* them, and that's what's happened to you. Tuck in.'

Lucy wasn't that interested in her cheesecake; she took a bite and left it. 'Sorry, I'm a bit tired. Don't you mean the Church punishes the *guilty*?'

'I know what I mean, girl.' She straightened herself up. 'I'm innocent, so why did the Priest threaten to excommunicate me, eh?' She softened again and leaned forwards. 'So what are we gonna do about it?'

'Nothing. They know who I am, they know who my father is and what he's done. They know about me being photographed with Tara Doyle, and the women mostly know my mother's handbags. What they don't know about is Tom. Yet. I won't do anything to get him in bother.'

'Drip, drip, drip,' said Bridget. 'Every day that they don't make an arrest, your name becomes more poisonous. They'll be calling you Amygdalin Berardi before long and sales of cake will plummet.'

'That is sooo tasteless. A bit like this cheesecake. I'm no happier about this than you are, Bridge, but what can we do?'

Bridget didn't answer straight away because there was still a pudding-shaped hole inside her. She polished off her plate and sat back. 'Get us an espresso martini and I'll tell you.'

They both knew that the coffee in here was rubbish (and the staff mostly knew they knew), but when it was drowned in Tia Maria and vodka, who cared?

'Cheers,' said Bridget. 'Thanks for this.' She took a sip and let it slide down. 'I saw Liz Swindlehurst coming out of the shop.'

'Don't tell me she gave anything away.'

'Of course not. Nothing that would get her in trouble. No, what she told me is that they're having real difficulty building a timeline out of the chaos in the tent. She also told me that the village has closed ranks and they're getting ready to canonise St Millicent Easterby of Byford. No one has a bad word to say about her.'

'So? Sounds about right. It's easy to be a saint when you have a good job and live in a nice house.'

'Hey!' said Bridget. 'That's my line.'

'I'm learning. So what if our victim was a saint?'

'No such thing as saints, only sinners with a coat of varnish. What we need to do is apply some paint stripper.'

Lucy was quiet. She swilled round the last of her one glass of Chardonnay and put it down. 'How?'

'You need to get as much as you can out of Tom, of course, and you need to go to the one person in Byford who can't turn you away.'

'Who? Perry Lockwood? Edwin Duke?'

'Give over, Lucy. You need to see the woman priest.'

'Vicar. They call them vicars.'

'Whatever. You need to be on her doorstep. You can do it.'

'I'm not sure I can.'

'Drip, drip, drip ...'

'Sod off.'

Lucy had once gone down on one knee (almost) and asked Bridget to take over as manager of the first Caffè Milano so that Lucy could go in search of the second. Bridget hadn't wanted to do it. She really didn't. What made Lucy *Lucy* was that she knew that Bridget might not have *wanted* it, but she *needed* it, and Lucy didn't take no for an answer until Bridget gave in. Ever since then, Bridget had worked on getting even, so when Lucy told her to *Sod off,* Bridget took it as Yes, and carried on regardless.

'If I know the way these types operate, she'll have been at the school today, spreading balm.'

Lucy took Bridget's cynicism in her stride. 'It's what they pay her for. If she's chair of governors, she'll also be talking to the head, trying to figure out what to do.'

'Precisely. Tomorrow she'll be in the church and visiting. You need to strike on Wednesday. The Commander can't object to you visiting the vicar, can he?'

Lucy looked dubious. 'I suppose not. I'll run it past Tom.'

'Run what past me?'

'Shit! How do you do that?'

If she hadn't seen it with her own eyes, Bridget wouldn't believe how Tom could sneak up on people. She wasn't sure which was weirder – the fact that he wouldn't admit it, or the fact that Lucy never jumped out of her skin. It wasn't that she knew he was coming, more that she knew as soon as he was *there*.

Lucy turned to let him kiss her, then said, 'Everything okay?'

'Sufficient unto the day,' he intoned. Tom had once been a solicitor, now a copper, and when he said things like that, Bridget reckoned he could have been a vicar. Nah. He was too useful to the world for that.

Tom looked really tired, and it would be cruel to make him stay. And probably counter-productive. 'I'll walk back,' said Bridget, gathering her things.

'Nonsense,' said Lucy. 'You'd only have to walk here in the morning. You need the car, remember?'

'Oh yeah. Forgot about that.'

'You drive Bridget back, and I'll meet you in the Market Square,' said Tom, turning to go.

On the short drive back to the Market Square, Lucy frowned at one point and said, 'I'm not saying I'll see the vicar, but I do need to deal with that journalist, Bradley Nicol.'

'Do you want me to scare him off?' asked Bridget.

'No need. I know how to deal with his sort. One of the useful things I learnt from my dad. Thanks, Bridget. Thanks for everything.'

They got out and Bridget took the keys. 'Don't thank me yet. Night, Lucy.'

Bridget waited until her friend was safely in Tom's car, then she got into the Mini. She didn't start the engine, but she did move the seat back, ready for action. Big day tomorrow.

The next morning, Kat Chester stood before the caffeine altar and shook her head. 'Wow. That's just … wow. You know that most customers drink tea, right?'

Bridget surveyed the newly installed four head coffee maker and conceded that, yes, it might not get the same amount of use as the one in Cairndale, but that wasn't the point. 'Which is why we've also changed the tea supplier. You cannot get a decent cup of tea from a catering wholesaler. I think we're ready, don't you?'

The girl looked nervous. She also looked smart in her new polo shirt and half-apron, and that was the main thing. Nerves would pass. 'Ready for what?' she said.

'Ready to tell the Millites that they can get a free coffee any time they want.'

'Millites?'

'Everyone who works here. We'll send out a message and see who crawls out of the woodwork. Do you think I'll get to meet Coffin Joe?'

Kat's nerves turned to uneasiness as she looked at the floor, underneath which Joe was presumably hard at work. 'Dunno. I haven't seen him for ages. It's a long way round from his entrance. The kids think he's a vampire.' The nerves vanished as she glanced at Bridget's tattoos. 'Aren't you into that stuff? Maybe you could get him to make you a coffin for your flat!'

Cheeky cow. On the other hand … 'We could have one in here. They seem very supportive of each other's businesses, so maybe we could mount an interactive display. Try before you die sort of thing.'

Kat blinked. 'You're winding me up again.'

'Am I? A selection of coffins might make a great attraction.'

Kat pouted and folded her arms. 'There's a load of your lot at ULIST. I'm surprised they haven't adopted you as their demon godmother.'

So was Bridget. 'Really?'

'Yeah. They mostly hang out at Spice Ireland on that road round the back of the ULIST building.'

'Figures.'

Cairndale's biggest employer had once been the cotton mill, followed by the various railways whose lines met there. The much-reduced engine sheds still echoed to the clang of hammer on iron (according to Barney Smith), and the biggest employer was still *based* in the giant mill, but the clatter of looms had been replaced by the clatter of keyboards at the University of Lancashire Institute of Science and Technology.

'Maybe I'll check it out,' said Bridget. The idea of going back to academia and finishing her PhD in the sterile sanctuary of the university instead of serving coffee in the unpasteurised countryside seemed suddenly very attractive.

Kat gave her a condescending smile. 'Lecturers aren't really welcome, and you're obviously too old to be a student.'

'Less of your lip, girl,' said Bridget, channelling her father. 'Go and send that invitation message, and don't take too long about it.'

Bridget fiddled with the settings on the machine until she was happy, then shouted through to the kitchen, where Kat, having been given permission to look at her phone was no doubt trying to cram in as much screen time as possible. 'Got a job for you!'

Kat returned, and Bridget could see that the oblong shape in the apron pocket wasn't an order pad. 'Phone. Away. Now.'

'God! You're worse than my mother. Right. What?'

'You're tall. You can tip the beans into the grinder, and careful. They're heavy and if you slip, you'll be picking up coffee beans for hours.'

'No need to rub it in,' said Kat.

'Rub what in?'

Kat carefully sliced open a corner of the plastic sack and got ready to lift. 'That I'm a freak and that you had to get a man's polo shirt to fit me.' The beans cascaded into the grinder in a controlled rush, and not one bounced onto the counter. 'There. Happy?'

Bridget's happiness was not dependent on successful stocking of the coffee grinder. At the same time, she recognised what she saw: the need for approval, the uncertainty, the shyness. 'Well done. Smooth. Put your hand at the bottom of the glass hopper. That's it. When the beans get down to that level, it's your job to fill it up again, and it's your last job at night, okay?'

'Right.'

Bridget looked at the doorway. No one was coming yet. 'This is a funny one, Kat, but usually we buy the whole business as a going concern, so we get the records and stuff. Not this time. Do you know if Feargal had a personnel file on you or anything like that?'

Kat's eyes flicked around and she shuffled her red Converse trainers. 'I was never in trouble. There was nothing to put in the file. You can ask him. Once he let me start at ten, I was never late again, and he never actually gave me a warning for it.'

'Easy, Kat. I'm just trying to save you a job, that's all. If he had a file, it would have all your certificates in one place. Save you having to get hold of them again.'

'Certificates? Like GCSEs and A Levels?' She looked worried again. 'You know I dropped out of Uni, right? Does that matter?'

'I didn't know and I don't care.' She paused. Was it time to share a little? Probably. 'I dropped out of Uni, too, so I'm the last person to throw stones in that house of glass.'

Kat squinted at her. 'So what's your real name? Or is there another Bridget Gorrigan who got a first at Imperial.'

Bloody hell! Bridget thought that all traces of her past life had been wiped from the internet. Just goes to show what a dedicated sleuth can uncover. 'No. That's me. It was a PhD I dropped out of.' To avoid the inevitable awkward follow-up, Bridget changed the subject and swore off sharing forever. 'When I asked about your personnel file, I meant your food hygiene certificates. Health and Safety. First Aid. That sort of thing.'

Kat looked relieved. 'Feargal handled all of that. He never saw the point of sending me on any courses. Thank God.'

Bridget shook her head and sighed. She was about to break it gently to her only employee that this wasn't good enough when a cheerful greeting saved her.

'Morning,' said Perry Lockwood. 'Do you do takeouts?'

'We do, but not today,' said Bridget. 'Are you off somewhere?'

'No, but my PA wanted to try the coffee and didn't want to come over in the rain.' He looked at the menu, thought for a moment and frowned. 'I'll have a cappuccino, please. Are those prices correct? They're nearly double what Feargal charged.'

'But they're more than twice as good. Coming up.'

She moved into position and waved for Kat to come closer. As she made the coffee, she talked through what she was doing, and when she looked up at the key moments, Kat was watching her intently. There was no sign that the girl thought she was being taught to suck eggs.

Bridget placed the drink in front of Perry and asked if he wanted chocolate or cinnamon on top.

'Cinnamon? Not sure if Byford is ready for cinnamon on its drinks. Chocolate please.'

Bridget held the chocolate shaker over the coffee. 'They said that Liverpool wasn't ready for the world's first intercity railway. It caught on in the end.' She drifted cocoa powder into zig-zag stripes and said, 'Have you got a minute?'

'Of course.'

Bridget made herself a cappuccino, repeating her running commentary. She was about to add the cinnamon when Louis appeared. 'Is this true about free tea and pastries?' he asked with a wink.

'No pastries today. Sorry. Tea was it? Kat will treat you to a pot of our unique Red Rose Lancashire tea, specially blended for Caffè Milano.'

Louis tilted his head. 'Isn't *Red Rose Lancashire* a bit of a tautology?'

Bridget paused. She might need this man's help soon. 'To distinguish it from Red Rose Tea of New Brunswick, Canada.'

She took her own drink and joined Perry at a window table. She angled herself to look away from the waterwheel because it was just too hypnotic, and said, 'What do you think?'

'I think you're right, actually. It is more than twice as good as Feargal's. Still expensive, though.' He raised the cup in a toast, then said, 'Have you come to ask about the PRS licence?'

Music was playing quietly in the background today, music that needed a Performing Rights Society licence if played in public. 'I thought we were covered by the Ford Mill licence?'

'Aah. The licence specifically mentions Miller's Rest Limited. We could add you …'

'For a small consideration. Yeah. I get the message.' She turned around. 'Kat! Kill the music.'

Perry thought this was funny. He had a weather-beaten sort of face, and his skin was sort of saggy, as if he'd lost weight. Not surprising, given his history. He had a nice smile, though: nice enough to convince Bridget this wasn't a day for messing around. 'Lucy is innocent. Well, she's innocent of murdering poor Millie Easterby.'

She left it hanging to see if he would challenge her. He didn't. Not directly. 'I hope my friends would be as upfront as you are about it. I've no reason to think otherwise, Bridget, and I certainly don't gossip.'

'Good. What can you tell me about the Easterby Estate. I know you came here after it was bought, but you must know a fair bit. After all, you're a director of it.'

He frowned. 'The no gossip rule applies even more in the case of my employers. What do you want to know that's not on the boards?'

'What boards?'

'The history of Ford Mill is told on display boards in the Dukes Gallery. Have you not been upstairs yet?'

Damn. Why didn't Kat tell her that? Because Kat probably hadn't been upstairs either. Except to the bookbinding and printmaking workshop, but that was another story. 'In case you hadn't noticed, I've been a bit preoccupied, Perry. Give me the headlines.'

'Have you come across the Earl of Morecambe Bay yet?'

Chapter 14

'I've heard of him. The Earl of Morecambe Bay owns Hartsford Hall, right? Lucy's boyfriend waxes lyrical about the restaurant there.'

Perry raised his eyebrows. 'They must pay detective chief inspectors very handsomely if he eats there. Well, the Malbranches – that's the earl's family – have been lords of Hackthwaite and Byford since the Norman Conquest or something. Or was it Richard the Second? Whatever. They owned most of the parishes of Byford, Over Byford and Nether Byford until they sold them after the Reformation. The new owner turned Byford Lodge into a proper squire's house and then his family sold the estate to Tobias Easterby in 1805. It was him who built the first Ford Mill.'

Perry paused to look around the room. 'Tobias's son was responsible for this upgrade, as he didn't call it. Tobias's great-grandson closed Ford Mill in the 1920s and left what remained of the estate to his infant daughter in the late 1930s. Temperance sold it to Edwin eight years ago when she moved out of the Lodge and into School House.' He blinked. 'It doesn't say this on the boards, but the estate was so heavily mortgaged that Temperance could barely afford the conversion of School House.'

This was beginning to sound like a dead-end to Bridget. Unless … 'What relationship was Millie to Temperance?'

'Millie's mother was some sort of cousin. Millie was born here, then they left, then came back. Lisa used to take more of an interest than I did.' He looked at the counter. 'I mostly dealt with Feargal when they opened the Miller's Rest together. I used to chat to Millie occasionally, but then Lisa was ill and …'

'Sorry.'

'Well, when I started to take an interest in the world again, they'd split up and Millie had signed the death warrant on the café. It took a long time for it to die, though.'

Perry made the last statement with way too much relish for

Bridget's taste. Did the man enjoy putting his tenants through the wringer or what? She was about to ask why Millie and Feargal had split up when Perry pointed behind her.

'You're wanted,' he said. 'I don't think Kat's quite ready to make Esmeralda's coffee on her own.'

Bridget turned round. Perry was right: Kat was emitting distress signals and a stern white-haired woman in a paint-smeared artist's smock was standing tapping her feet at the counter.

Bridget hot-footed it to help and dispensed coffee without a single word exchanged. All Kat would say was that their third non-paying customer was, 'A mad artist woman. She's replaced Temperance Easterby as the village witch. You should get on well with her.'

The chilled and ambient deliveries arrived in time for Bridget to make her own lunch and to realise that until Kat could be rushed through a food hygiene course, she was going to be very, very busy.

After Kat had satisfied her digital cravings, Bridget set about proper training on the coffee maker. With added interrogation, of course. 'What made you drop out of college?' she asked. 'And where were you?'

'Chester. Doing Criminology and Psychology. I was gonna join the police.'

'Thermometer. It's not for decoration: it's crucial to the perfect cappuccino. What made you drop out?'

Kat shrugged. 'Just didn't like it. What about you?'

Serves me right, thought Bridget, regretting her earlier disclosure. She decided on a tactical lie. 'Bereavement and change of priorities.'

'I know you're a senior manager now, but you didn't start out as one, did you?'

'No. There was a guy who grew up in Garston who became rich and famous, and he needed someone to make ice cream part-time and serve coffee part-time in Southport, so I didn't quite start at the bottom, but I wasn't far above it when Lucy took over the coffee shop. I'd say that the rest is history but it only feels like five minutes ago. The main thing is that I was like you: I decided to earn a living instead of piling up debt like a banana republic.'

'What's a banana republic?'

'Look it up. After you've told me how *you* came to be earning a living here.'

'I started when I was sixteen. Saturday job – clearing up and whatever. Better than being in the village shop with Mum and Dad. I did summers, too, then Millie and Ferg split up and I came full-time.' She smiled brightly. 'So now I can put on my CV that I spent three years making bad coffee. Not that I could tell the difference, anyway.'

'What do you mean?'

'I can't stand coffee.'

'I … I don't know what to say. And the fact that you look happy about it is doing my nut.' Bridget shook her head mournfully. 'What am I gonna do with you, eh?' She paused, and the answer was obvious. 'You actually wanted to be a bizzy, right?'

'*Bizzy*. That's a police officer?'

'It is.'

Instead of answering, Kat nodded her head. There was something there that needed to be winkled out, and Bridget was a proven master of the winkle picker, whatever that might be. However, she had only known the girl two days, and there would be plenty of time for winkle picking later. 'Go on then, apply your detective skills to Millie's murder.'

Kat turned half away and shook her head. 'I can't do that! She was like … like … like I knew her. It's not right.'

'And it's even less right that people are calling Lucy for it. I'm very sorry about Millie. I am. She seemed really nice, and nothing like that should happen anywhere, but it's happened here, and it was someone she knew. There's someone out there who killed her, Kat, and we need to find out who.'

'There's no such thing as amateur detectives,' said Kat with some finality. 'Do you want me to have another go with the latte?'

'Yes please. In a takeout cup this time, then you can give it to whatshername upstairs and have a break.'

When Kat had made a perfectly acceptable latte and disappeared, Bridget wandered over to the windows and stared across the millpond to the chimneys of Byford Lodge, one of which was smoking gently. There was a lot to discover about this village.

Bridget was a born outsider, and the rural scene beyond the windows shouted *and you always will be an outsider* in floral accents. Bridget needed to clear Lucy's name, and she needed a way in to

Byford. A mole. No, not a mole. Too troublesome. She needed a full-time agent, and who would make the better spy, Kat or Perry? Perry was both a loyal professional and possessed of nice buns. Too distracting. It would have to be Kat.

Bridget checked her phone and saw a message from Lucy. *OMG! Commander Ross is coming to the café at 2:30. He has news!!!!!*

'I'd like to be a fly on the wall for that,' she muttered, and shoved her phone away. There was something not right about the layout of tables in here, and she couldn't put her finger on it. Time to make some salad, ready for tomorrow.

'Will you be able to cope?' asked Lucy. She was standing on the customer side of the counter and sort of lifting herself up with her hands. It was quite a high counter by Lucy's standards. Even higher by Mina Desai's.

Lilianna didn't answer her straight away. She peered into the utility area and shouted, 'Latte glasses!' Their new trainee was somewhere in there, probably wondering what he'd let himself in for.

'Okay,' came the reply, with no great conviction.

Lilianna turned to Lucy and planted her hands on the counter. 'I am fine with the little one. Will *you* be fine, boss? Commander Ross is the only man who scares Scarywoman, no? And where is she gone?'

Tom's closest colleague was DC Elaine Fraser. They had been thrown together by circumstances and did a very creditable Good Cop/Bad Cop routine. Tom, of course, was good cop, but that wasn't the only reason for Lucy calling Elaine *Scarywoman*.

'Shh! Don't let people hear that name. I'll get it in the neck, Lili.'

'Too late. All station knows. Where she gone?'

'Barrow-in-Furness for a few days. They're short-handed.'

'Hmmph. Remember that Ross cannot hurt you.'

'He's nice! He made a special point of introducing me to everyone at the leaving do last month. Tom says I must remind him of his daughters.'

Lucy glanced at the clock. She had ten minutes, nothing to change into and no one to get it for her – Tom had left the house before she was awake this morning and gone to Preston for an urgent meeting of the National Crime Agency: strictly no phones allowed, ring this number in emergency only. Maybe she could raid Bridget's wardrobe?

'Why you laughing now?' asked Lilianna.

'I've just realised that it's too easy to get wound up about things. Take five minutes before he comes, Lili.'

Lilianna was a smoker, and she shot off to the side alley before Lucy could open her mouth. Lucy pushed herself up again, leaned right over the counter, pulled herself even further forwards and checked the prep area. 'Stop!' she shouted.

The new lad looked up, his hands poised over a wire rack that had just emerged from the dishwasher. 'Lilianna told me these were latte glasses, boss,' he said. 'Was she winding me up?'

'No, and they are latte glasses. They are also boiling hot. Take the rack from underneath, okay?'

And that was how Commander Ross found her: flat on the counter, legs off the floor and bum in the air.

'Are you alright, lassie? Need a hand?'

She could hear the smile in his voice, and that somehow made it worse. She cringed, squeezed her eyes shut and took a breath. 'No thanks, sir, but if you've got any spare dignity, I could do with some of that.'

While he laughed, she slid back down to earth and tried to bounce up. Now she just looked demented. With the grace of a dancer, Lilianna slid back behind the counter and smiled as if she'd been there all along. 'Good afternoon, Commander Ross. How can I help you?'

Every single eye in the coffee shop was on them. To be accurate, they were on the Commander and his uniform, and at least three regulars were sitting up straighter and trying to look innocent and two more were hiding their faces.

Ross turned to the counter and pulled a piece of paper out of his pocket. 'I believe you know young Barney Rubble … Lilianna?'

'Everyone know Barney. And his handwriting.'

'Then if you could make these up, I'll have a word with Ms

Berardi. Is there somewhere we could go, Lucy?'

If Lucy took Ross up to the flat, Bridget would have a turn. Whatever else had been planned for tonight would be cancelled in favour of disinfecting, cleaning and polishing every room of the flat bar the bedroom (which was padlocked). Lucy would not do that to Bridget unless she had to. 'Erm …' she said to Ross.

'Do you have a coat? It's not shirt-sleeve weather outside.'

Lilianna managed to pour boiling water into a mug and hand Lucy's coat over the counter at the same time, without being asked; not for the first time, Lucy wished she could clone Lili and make all of them branch managers. She took the coat and walked through the door that Ross was holding open for her.

He was right: it *was* a bit nippy. She fell into step with the Commander, and he asked if there had been any word from York.

'No change, sir.'

'Lucy! You don't need to call me *sir*. I'd prefer it if you used my Christian name, which I'm sure you know fine well.'

'I'll try.'

'Good. The café here in Cairndale is already looking better, by the way. Not too corporate. I like that.'

They had passed the library and turned down Bridge Street. This was the old, old Glasgow Road, and once upon a time, all the traffic from the Midlands to Scotland passed through here and over the bridge. Lucy knew this because Tom had told her, and she still wasn't sure that he hadn't been winding her up: the road wasn't much wider than a heavy lorry. Maybe trucks were smaller then, or maybe he'd meant horses and stuff.

Ross carried on asking questions about the Cairndale coffee shop and her plans for it. He even seemed interested in her answers. Politeness or genuine? Hard to tell. Whatever the reason, he stopped abruptly in the middle of the bridge and leaned on the parapet. Then he stood up when he realised that Lucy couldn't do the same.

With a casual hand, he brushed grit off his sleeve and smiled. 'What I'm about to tell you isn't confidential as such: it's just rather privileged. It's nothing that Tom wouldn't tell you himself if he hadn't been in a huddle with the anti-gang boys in Preston. In fact, you telling him will save me a job.'

'It sounds like good news?' she suggested.

'Pretty much. The good Doctor Jepson delivered his findings to me this morning, and they tell a very interesting story.'

Lucy used to think she wasn't good with blood and stuff, and then she'd been on a First Aid course and surprised herself by not fainting at any of the videos. More recently, she'd been in a farmyard after one of Conrad Clarke's *encounters*. Now she knew she really did have a strong stomach. 'I thought the postmortem was yesterday.'

'It was, and yesterday's proceedings didn't tell us anything we didn't already know: that poor lassie died gasping for breath from acute cyanosis. And after Jepson had done his bit, some poor sod had to work overnight on the contents of her small intestine.'

'Oh. Do I want to know why?'

'Your friend Bridget is very perceptive, Lucy. Amygdalin is … Something to do with glucose. Nothing happens in the stomach, but as soon as it hits the small intestine there's this enzyme that whips off the glucose molecule and thinks it's done its job. Unfortunately, it leaves behind active cyanide, and that's what got into Miss Easterby's system.'

Ross paused and raised his eyebrows. 'I can see from your face that you've cottoned on,' he observed.

'Yes. How long before she died was she poisoned?'

'At least an hour and a half. No more than three. And it was consumed in or alongside some sort of gluten-free cereal. I'm not going to insult you by checking your alibi: you were at Ford Mill throughout that period. So, unless you snuck into School House and put amygdalin on Millie's porridge, it wasn't you. As soon as Liz and the team have enjoyed your coffee, they'll be heading back out to Byford.'

'So can I!' exclaimed Lucy. 'Sorry. That came out more enthusiastically than I'd intended.'

Ross gestured towards the hill back to the Market Square. 'Shall we?' They started walking, and he continued, 'If you could hang fire until tomorrow, I'd be grateful.'

'Of course.' A few steps later, she said, 'But someone poisoned her breakfast or whatever. Have you any idea who?'

Ross didn't answer her question straight away. 'You were never a *suspect*, Lucy. Not even a *person of interest*, but you were and are an important witness, which leaves me with two enormous headaches.'

'How come?'

'Thomas is still barred from acting as SIO, and I could really use his detective's brain on this one.' He smiled at her. 'People say I never became a detective because I like the uniform too much. Not true. I never became a detective because I wouldn't have been any good at it. And don't tell Tom that, please. I don't want to spoil the illusion.'

'Your secret's safe with me. What's your other headache.'

'I have to tell Tracey Kenyon that all the work she did in the tent was for nothing.'

Chapter 15

Lucy and Ross returned to Caffè Milano, where the Commander collected the CID coffee order and paid Lilianna with a generous tip. As soon as the ramrod straight back had left the coffee shop, several customers breathed a sigh of relief and Lilianna invaded Lucy's personal space to the point where Lucy's eyes almost unfocused.

'Well?' said the Polish barista. 'You are innocent? Yes?'

Lucy backed off a step. 'I always was innocent!'

Lilianna's mouth turned down. 'You are what the police say you are.'

Lucy opened her mouth. *You are what the police say you are.* That was an aphorism she would *not* be sharing with Tom – it would send him off on one and no mistake. She closed her mouth and decided that what her audience wanted was a simple statement. 'They have evidence which shows Millie was poisoned while I was at Ford Mill. End of story.'

Lili gave a curt nod of satisfaction. 'Good. Now what?'

'Now I call Bridget. Can you wait a bit?'

'Yes. I will show the boy how Bridget likes her disinfectant made. She know the strength by smell, I think.'

Sounds about right, thought Lucy. When she was happy, her body's natural response was to shimmy, as if she were on the dance floor. She hadn't been to a club for *months* until Mina's hen party had delivered them to not one but two clubs on successive nights. She'd enjoyed that (apart from losing her car, but hey – she'd been compensated), and organising a girls' night out was coming close to the top of her to-do list. To the best of her knowledge, Tom had *never* visited a nightclub during opening hours, so if she wanted some dance action she'd have to provide it herself.

She shimmied outside and called Bridget. 'Hey! Guess what!' she began, and then quickly filled her friend in on the evidence which Allister had disclosed, along with a strict warning to keep it under wraps today.

Bridget breathed heavily through her nose, a sort of half snore. 'Luce, I am so made up. This is brilliant.'

'I know. Not that I was ever *really* worried.'

'Neither was I, but it means you have to come up here and do some work.' She paused, but not quite long enough for Lucy to splutter her outrage. 'Because we open tomorrow, and we need you on site for the publicity. And then you're off to see the vicar.'

Lucy was genuinely baffled. 'What on earth for?'

'Because you said it yourself: Ross is no detective.'

'Liz is a good detective. Tom rates her very highly.'

'I'm sure he does and I'm sure she is, but she's not in charge, is she?' Bridget sighed. 'They're already closing ranks, Lucy. No matter what the cops say, if they don't finger someone's collar, you'll always be the girl found with the poison in your handbag.'

'That's what I love about you, Bridget: your glass is not only half empty, it's been spiked.'

The sharp intake of breath was like nails on Lucy's inner blackboard. *Oh dear God, I've done it now.* 'I am so sorry, Bridget. I didn't mean that. I really didn't.'

There was an agonising pause down the line. Lucy's nails bit into her palm as she squeezed her fist and forced herself not to dig a deeper hole. Finally, Bridget exhaled with a *whoosh*. 'I know you didn't mean it. And to prove you didn't mean it, you can grill the vicar tomorrow. It's your penance.'

'Can I not say three Hail Marys?'

'No. Now, what are we gonna do about the car?'

'Tom's back at Cairndale tomorrow, so he can give me a lift. We'll go in together.'

'I doubt there's room for you, me and the cakes.'

'What?'

'I've just had Tabor's Bakery on the phone. They've only just realised that Byford isn't in Cairndale. They won't deliver out there.'

'But it's only ten minutes! Twenty minutes max.'

Lucy prided herself on supporting local businesses, and Tabor's Bakery in Garstang did a superb line in cakes and pastries.

'We're not the only café, you know,' said Bridget. 'Their early driver has a lot of deliveries with a tiny window, apparently.'

Lucy pinched her nose with her fingers. Was it only five minutes ago that she'd been dancing out of the door? She let go of her nose and snapped her fingers. Why hadn't she thought of that before? 'I've got a plan, Bridget. Two plans, actually. What time are you packing up?'

Bridget started to moan about Kat Chester and food hygiene, but Lucy wasn't listening. The main point was that Bridget wouldn't be leaving Byford for another hour at least.'

'Fine. Perfect. See you soon.'

'Wha—?'

'Bye. Got to go.'

Bridget was tired. 'I must be getting old,' she muttered.

'You are old,' said Kat. She paused. 'Maybe not yet, but definitely on the way. You'll soon be as old as Mum.'

Jackie Chester must be in her mid-forties, nearly a decade away. Before Bridget could point this out, her phone rang: Lucy.

'Could you bring the car keys outside?'

'You what? Are you *here*?'

'Flying visit. See you in a sec.'

There was no window from the Spinning Room to the car park, so Bridget had no choice but to grab the keys and head outside. What on earth was going on?

'Surprise!' said Lucy.

Seeing her friend was scarcely a surprise; seeing her leaning against a small white van was another matter. Lucy held out a pair of ignition keys. 'Swap!'

Bridget's hackles went straight up, and she folded her arms to prove the point. 'No.'

Sometimes when Bridget said no Lucy reacted like the proverbial smacked puppy. Not this time. She lowered her hand and said, 'It's on a week's contract. You can get your own car in that time or I'll lease a van for work.' She raised the hand with the keys again. 'It's the only way Byford will work. And I hired their only automatic, just for you.'

Damn. Bridget hated it when other people were right; for a week, at least, she would have to become White Van Woman. If Natalie could see her now …

'Fine.'

They swapped keys, and Bridget peered suspiciously into the front. It looked okay, she supposed, and the seat looked much easier to get in and out of than the one in the Mini. Satisfied, she turned to talk to Lucy about tomorrow, but Lucy was already unlocking her car.

'Gotta dash,' she said. 'See you tomorrow at half past eight. Brad Nicol is coming to take pictures and do interviews at nine. And don't you even think of saying no.'

Bridget rolled her shoulders and headed back inside for the more difficult conversation. 'Kat, I need to pick you up at eight o'clock tomorrow.'

There was no hesitation in the answer. 'No chance.'

'Just this once. We open tomorrow to paying customers, and Lucy's coming in. We need everyone to pull together.'

'Still no.'

Bridget nodded slowly, to give Kat the impression that she was thinking about it. 'What would be worse, d'you reckon? Me seeing your Ma tonight and telling her to get you up, or me seeing her first thing tomorrow?'

'No! That's … that's harassment.'

Bridget loaded her voice with extra Scouse. 'Nah, kid, it's just how we old people do things. D'you wanna lift home or d'you want some extra sulking time?'

The lights were all on inside the village shop the next morning. Bridget knocked on the glass and got a smile and a *come in* wave from Jackie. Bridget entered and raised her eyebrows.

'She's up, she's had an energy bar and she's just getting dressed. Won't be a minute,' said Jackie. She was busy writing names on the top of newspapers. Surely they didn't still have a small boy who pedalled furiously around delivering these things? That would be too twee.

'Do you want to shout upstairs and tell her that the photographer's coming this morning,' suggested Bridget with as much innocence as she could muster.

Jackie's hand froze halfway through writing a name that began with *R*. She thought for a moment, then shook her head. 'I don't mind getting her out of bed, but I don't get paid enough for that kind of trauma. Let it be a surprise. Hang on a sec.'

Jackie kept her left finger firmly on a computerised list and grabbed a piece of paper. She wrote out a phone number and passed it to Bridget. 'My number. If you have a crisis, text me and I can sweep her dressing table into a case and bring it up to the Mill. I was coming along later anyway.'

'Thanks. I've got a few things with me, but that could be a lifesaver.'

'Zombie alert,' said Jackie.

'Eh?'

'Muuuuum, where's my PE kit?'

From some secret passageway, the May Queen of Byford had appeared. The happy, smiling poster girl for village life who had been in the Bake Off tent was gone and had been replaced by a teenager in the uniform of Cairndale Grammar School. It was a weird thing to see, like going to bed with a butterfly resting on your window and waking up to find a caterpillar instead. Reverse evolution.

Jackie picked up her pen and a *Daily Telegraph*. 'Ask your father.'

'I did and he wouldn't tell me!' wailed the girl.

Jackie held the newspaper further away from her eyes and squinted. 'That man is such a wind-up merchant. It's flipping Wednesday, Jazz. PE is tomorrow.'

The zombie shuffled off back to its lair, and its mother put a big tick on her list of newspapers. 'Done! Time to get ready for the hordes.'

'Really?'

'A lot of retired men get up early and come in for their morning paper. Don't ask me why. How's things up at t'Mill?'

'Good, yeah. See for yourself later. Kat's been ace.'

Jackie smiled broadly and dropped the papers into a rack by the door labelled *Reserved*. Bridget had been looking around and noticed something very interesting, high on a shelf. She smiled to herself and said, 'Thanks, Jackie. I'll wait outside and I'll see you later.'

'Great. I'll go and give Kat a shout.'

Bridget went back outside. It was going to be a beautiful spring day. Nice. Some would see it as an omen for the new branch of Caffè Milano, but not Bridget. The worst day of her life had been a beautiful spring day, just like this one: sun shining, warmth in the air but not the stickiness of summer and even down in London there had been the smell of new life, especially in the pub garden where she'd gone for a drink after a day in the university laboratory.

When you feel yourself being sucked back in, focus on an exit, her therapist had told her. *Focus on a doorway and go through it into the future.*

Bridget turned left and took a good look at the driveway that separated the shop from School House. She even walked down it a few yards so she could turn around and go back, through the exit to the main road. The original wall that kept the Victorian children penned in was still very much in place. Perfect.

She turned back and flinched, not with a regression to *that* day, but with a horror very much of the present: it was a full-blown zombie apocalypse, and it was happening here. From left and right, from down Church Lane and from across the bridge, black shapes were converging on the village green, from where presumably the school bus would collect them. Some of them.

Interspersed among the black shapes of children were the grey ghosts of Byford's retired residents. Some walked quickly, outpacing the kids and looking around with interest at what the morning might bring; others were slower. In a way. They were all going as fast as they could.

A couple of cars appeared, paused for a second to eject their teenage occupants, then carried on towards Cairndale or up the valley heading for Hackthwaite and Lunesdale.

Bridget didn't call it an epiphany, but it was definitely a *moment*. Out here in Byford, the exact same scene had been played out yesterday and the day before. If she'd been here a century ago, it would have been quieter, and the teenagers would have been heading to work, not school, but it would have been basically the same. 'I think I'm starting to get it,' she said to herself. 'It's not for me, but I'm starting to get it.'

A few of the kids bustled into the shop in search of sweets and energy drinks, and Jasmine Chester emerged. She was followed a couple of seconds later by her older sister, and it looked like Kat had put on clean jeans, which was good enough. Bridget clicked the locks and smiled. 'Morning.'

'Hi,' said Kat. And that was the last word she spoke until they arrived at the Mill.

Bridget opened the back of the van and grabbed a tray of rolls. 'You can't make me carry that lot,' said Kat.

'Why not? If I can manage, so can you.'

'It's the smell. It's too nice.'

'Then take that one, the one with the jumbo slicing cakes. They don't smell until you cut into them. And you can make me a double espresso while I carry the rest in.'

Bridget waited until they'd started to fill the display cabinet before she broke the news. 'These need to be extra neat for the pictures.'

'What pictures?'

'Press are coming. Well, Bradley Nicol is coming. He's the local reporter for the *Lancashire Mercury*, and he's gonna …'

Bridget looked around and found herself alone. No sign of Kat whatsoever. In the quiet of the Mill, she heard a cubicle door slam from the ladies' toilets. She got out her phone and the scrap of paper which Kat's mother had given her. She added *Jackie the Shop* as a new contact and sent a message: *What has Kat got against Brad Nicol????*

Thirty seconds later she got this reply: *Oh dear.* There were several gasping, open-mouthed monkey emojis, too.

How long since he dumped her? was Bridget's next question.

The second message was even worse. *He two-timed her. It was terrible.*

Bridget sighed and went to her secret cupboard in the kitchen. She took out the packet of malted milk biscuits and started to make her special indulgent hot chocolate. It was going to be a long day.

As Lucy drove through Byford, she resolutely turned her face away from the Old Rectory, because thinking about vicars would spoil her mood, and Lucy was carrying her good mood like a newly lit candle in a draughty house: it wouldn't take much to knock her off course. Hang on. That was a spectacularly mixed metaphor. *It must be true love,* she thought, *if I'm starting to crucify the language like he does.* No one could mix a metaphor quite like Tom.

One night, over grappa, Bridget had told her that it was one of those things that was *endearing* at first but would later become *grounds for divorce,* to which Lucy had responded, 'He would have to propose first.' She shuddered, because thinking about marriage proposals led her mind inexorably to Mina and Conrad's wedding, and she hadn't processed that fully yet. And there was still no word of the happy couple, either. Even Conrad's commanding officer was starting to get worried.

Lucy arrived at Ford Mill and parked her car *enthusiastically* before grabbing her holdall and bouncing into her new premises. She was home now, her metaphorical candle safely behind glass, like she would soon be safely behind the counter. She put her holdall on a table and went round to get herself a coffee, but something was wrong.

Bridget never, ever, left the chocolate jug out like that. *And the top was off the jar of marshmallows.* Something must be wrong. Seriously wrong. And where were they?

A shadow crossed the archway, and Bridget appeared. Lucy's friend had a face like thunder and was holding an extra-large cup at arm's length. Lucy's little candle of good mood flickered and nearly blew out.

'Bradley Nicol is a snake in the grass,' declared Bridget as she passed. 'That man deserves castration as an absolute minimum.' Verdict delivered, Bridget sailed through into the kitchen and Lucy heard the rattle of china on wire rack, followed by running water.

'What's up?' shouted Lucy.

Bridget reappeared, drying her hands on blue roll. 'Do we have to use him for publicity?'

'Yes. Why?'

'Because he's just forced me to serve chocolate in the ladies' toilet and dispense malted milk biscuits. I don't know which was worse. Kat will be out in a minute, and you will tell Brad Nicol that he has to apologise to her. After you've made me a double.'

'Coming up.' Lucy knew better than to push it, so she slipped off her coat and got to work. They were having a soft opening today – no publicity material, no fanfare on social media. That would come in a couple of weeks, when they were up to speed and when they had enough staff to cope. Right now, the curious locals and the passing trade heading to the gallery and workshops would do the trick.

Drinks made, Lucy took them into the kitchen and politely asked for an explanation.

'Nicol two-timed Kat with a kid from ULIST,' declared Bridget. 'One of us has to put him in his place.'

That was Bridget all over: she would fight the battles of every underdog and wounded stray she came across, just like she'd done for Natalie. It probably explained why she was determined to stick her nose into Millie Easterby's death, not that an explanation would save Lucy if Bridget screwed up the police investigation.

'I've already done that,' said Lucy. 'He's under orders to be positive and to make no connection whatsoever between the Bake Off murder and our coffee shop. He'll cover Millie's death in Thursday's paper and feature us in a fortnight.'

Bridget looked suspicious. 'How did you manage that? Do you own shares in the paper or something?'

'No chance. I got our marketing agency to call the editor and told him we'd commit to six months of display ads in colour, and they can't afford to upset their advertisers, can they? I'll tell you what, I'll let you have at him when he gets here. If Kat sees that you're on her side, it should cheer her up no end.' Lucy slurped her espresso and found it perfect. 'Now, what needs doing? We open in less than two hours.'

Bridget thoroughly intimidated the young journalist and managed to wring half an apology from him while Kat hid in the kitchen and Lucy maintained a safe distance. Kat didn't actually want Bridget to act as her avenging angel. Lucy knew that, and Lucy knew exactly how

Kat would feel – doubly mortified. She also knew what was really bothering the young woman: the photographs.

When Nicol got out his camera, Lucy stepped in and shoved Kat behind the high display cabinet, then posed herself in front of the counter and put Bridget behind it. This way, Kat's height and Bridget's hips would be hidden and Lucy could show off her smile.

Pictures taken, Nicol glanced nervously at Bridget. The poor little man was almost walking around with a hand in front of his groin, so vicious had been the verbal assault. 'Do you mind if I do the whole entrepreneur interview some other time, Lucy? I could come to Garstang …?'

Lucy started putting paper napkins on the tables. 'Oh no, Brad. You can come to Cairndale. You'll be using it regularly now, won't you? Our coffee's much better than Rhona's place. You can interview me one day when you pop in.'

'Yeah. Great. Thanks.'

Nicol fled, and the next hour flew by in a blur of last-minute preparation. They paused at ten o'clock, half an hour before the off. Things were well in hand, and Lucy was even worrying that they were *too* good. Naturally, Bridget chose that moment to blow out Lucy's inner candle.

'I've just been on the St Peter's Church website,' Bridget announced. 'Rev Deb is available in the church for parishioners for the next two hours. Look for her in the Children's Corner, whatever that is. Go on then, off you pop.'

'But …'

'It's a nice walk. You'll enjoy it.'

Bridget took the napkins out of Lucy's hand and blocked her path to the counter and the kitchen. *Might as well get it over with,* thought Lucy. 'See you later.'

Bridget was right about the walk. As Lucy breathed in the country air, she calmed down and paid attention to the important thing: the houses. Mentally, she ticked them off as she passed: *too small, too twee, too public … not bad, not bad.* And then she sighed deeply when she saw the Old Rectory peeking over its wall. *Now that's what I call a house.* Shame it was both taken and well beyond her budget.

She crossed the road and went into the churchyard, then followed the winding path through the marble monuments. In this section, the decaying stones were peeking out from uncut grass and flowers, no doubt left to grow for the bees, and there was a much neater and polished section to the west of the church.

She made a mental note to tell Bridget that it deserved four gravestones on *Gothadvisor,* one of the many businesses they'd dreamed up over cocktails in Layla's bar back in the day, with Natalie making sure their glasses were never empty. Lucy's favourite had been *Bluedate,* an app for people who wanted to date police officers. Maybe one day …

She strode into St Peter's and immediately shivered with the change in temperature. Or that's what she told herself. The sudden darkness and sense of what might be lurking had nothing to do with it. Nothing at all.

Chapter 16

If asked to describe St Peter's, Byford, Lucy would have said that it was *Old, dark, plain and pointy*. Which it was.

Tom often struggled with his faith, or lack of it. It didn't keep him awake at night, but sometimes he would check out of the moment and reflect on his place in the universe. When he checked back in, it was always with a smile and an extra hug.

Tom would undoubtedly walk slowly up the nave and admire the church, too. Not Lucy. Instead of pausing to note the fan vaulting, she genuflected and made a beeline for the vicar, who was standing in the far right corner, or *Children's Corner* as it proclaimed itself.

The Italian church where Lucy had made her first communion had a chapel to Our Lady and a couple of shrines to saints. Obvious enough. A casual non-Christian visitor to St Peter's would assume that Children's Corner was part of some weird cult of the child, because the school's achievements and central role in the village were spelled out in exhaustive detail, and there were lots of cushions, children's Bible stories and other things designed for little ones. Thankfully, there were no actual children present at the moment.

Lucy was barely halfway over when the Reverend Deborah Giddings turned to face her. The vicar had swapped her tasteful blue clerical blouse from Saturday for a black one, and the change did not suit her. She waited until Lucy was almost there and spread her arms.

'Lucy! Welcome to St Peter's. How are you?' An embrace didn't seem optional, so Lucy gave the vicar a hug, then found her hands being held on to when she'd rather they weren't. 'Come and sit down,' said Deborah, leading her towards two padded institutional chairs. 'Is everything alright with you? Saturday was such a traumatic day. For everyone.'

It was well known in Caffè Milano that Bridget kept a vial of hand sanitiser in her handbag. She wasn't overly obsessive, but it was there. Lucy preferred a different detergent: soft soap. She used it on the vicar now. 'It was traumatic, Deborah – I can still call you Deborah in here, can't I?'

The vicar patted her hand. 'I'm still Deborah in here, just as I'm still the priest outside the church walls.'

'Of course. I came today because I felt such a … a *spectator* on Saturday. It was horrible for me, but I feel so sorry for Millie's family. How are they, Deborah?'

The vicar composed her face to match her message. 'It sounds so sad to say this, but Millie had no family except the church and the school.'

It was Lucy's turn to put out her hand and grip the vicar's (it was quite rough). 'Then you must all be devastated.' She looked up at the display of school pictures and spotted Millie more than any other teacher, including the Head. Of course, the Head might have been taking the pictures, but Deborah was the more likely candidate for that. 'She seems to have been such a huge part of the village.'

'She was. Since she came back, she's done so much.'

'Oh? Where did she go?'

Deborah sighed. 'It was before my time, of course. I've been here seven years, and Millie moved in with Temperance at School House the same summer. She'd have been twenty-five then, and she was taken to London when she was twelve.' She shrugged. 'Two years after I moved here, Temperance died. I can honestly say that Temperance Easterby's funeral has been the biggest event during my ministry here.' She smiled sadly. 'And now they're gone. No more Easterbys in Byford, though there are some in Canada.'

Deborah looked at Lucy and seemed to realise that there had been a role reversal, and that she didn't have the energy to swap back yet. 'It's normally me trying to explain God's ways to people, but this is one of those times when the best I can do is to say that He has gathered up Millie for His own reasons.'

Lucy was fairly certain that while God might have gathered Millie into His arms, He hadn't had much to do with the woman's death apart from creating amygdalin – a point she did *not* make to the vicar, because Lucy was more interested in someone who had been airbrushed out of the story so far.

'So did you marry Millie and Feargal, Deborah?'

The vicar folded her hands in her lap. 'Oh no. Let's see: they split up three years ago, and they'd been married seven years at that point.' She smiled and tried to regain the initiative. 'She must have met Feargal just after you knew her.'

Lucy was ready for this, and tried to match the vicar's earnest face. 'I never knew her. The police finally got hold of Diego Luiz – the guy in the picture. He's a Uruguayan holding midfielder. A footballer. He told the police that it was Millie's boyfriend who took the picture, and he – Diego – only dragged me in because he was trying to get my dad to be his agent.'

'Your father. Yes. I'm sorry about your brother, Lucy.'

This was another gambit that Lucy was ready for, and countered with, 'Thank you. It's one of the reasons I came to see you: I've seen what something like this can do to a community.'

Deborah opened her mouth and realised that she had nothing to say. Before she could regain her balance, Lucy gave her another nudge. She crossed her legs and tried to look like she was happy to be in the church. 'When it becomes obvious that someone from the village has done this, it could tear Byford apart.'

Lucy's remark didn't just knock the vicar off balance, it nearly floored her. 'Someone from the village?' was all she could say.

Lucy nodded earnestly. 'The police came to see me and tell me that I've been downgraded from being a *key witness* to being just an *irrelevant bystander*.' She smiled. 'I'll try not to take it personally.'

'Are you sure?'

It was a desperate appeal, and Lucy didn't have the heart to rub the vicar's nose in it. She clearly loved Millie and missed her desperately. 'I'm sorry, Deborah, but yes. Commander Ross is looking for the person who put that poison in my handbag, and he knows that it wasn't me.'

The Reverend Deborah Giddings went very pale suddenly, and Lucy realised that the Vicar of Byford had something to hide.

'Are you expecting anyone?' asked Lucy.

'What? No, I'm not, but …'

'But nothing. Let's go for a walk to Ford Mill.'

'I can't leave the church.'

'Yes you can. If ever there was a day for someone to treat you to something, it's today.'

As soon as Lucy had set off for the church, Bridget drifted back to the counter. She had been pushing things this morning, and pushing them to create this moment when she and Kat were alone. They were half an hour ahead of schedule for the opening, and it was time to begin *Operation Eliminate.*

After her *moment* this morning, Bridget had decided that she was going to play the village of Byford at its own game. The problem with village life was that everything was so *close*. You couldn't just message people or hide behind an email because they'd come round and knock on your door (and wasn't *that* a frightening thought). Good job Bridget's front door was in Cairndale.

Now she was here, she'd have to play them at their own game, using their rules and tactics. It was time to put not-so-little Kat on the spot and see if she had the mettle to be Bridget's secret agent. She drifted into the kitchen and casually said to Kat, 'I must have a word with Perry about the CCTV. Have you got the Securi-Fast app on your phone?'

Kat couldn't help herself. As well as the compulsion to pick up her phone (which she did), it was also ingrained in her to be helpful, and with Bridget being right in front of her, to be helpful right away. 'Yeah, I've got it,' she said, 'but it's no use because the Mill uses a different system.'

Bridget closed the gap. 'Never mind. You've got access to the shop CCTV, though, haven't you?'

Kat's antennae started twitching. 'Yeah, but why?'

'When I was waiting for you this morning – and well done for getting up, by the way. Couldn't have managed without you. When I was waiting for you, I saw the Securi-Fast CCTV monitor, and one of the cameras covers the road to Cairndale, including the front of School House. Have the police been on to you for the footage?'

Kat shifted uncomfortably, holding on to her phone and uncertain whether to put it down or hide it in her apron. 'No. They haven't.'

'Hasn't your mum offered it to them?'

'Mmm. Yeah. Well. It's like this: we shouldn't have it pointing that way. Not really. It was Millie who asked us for it, actually. Parents aren't supposed to drop off anywhere near the school entrance, and she wanted evidence. It's less of a problem now that they have the walking bus from the station, but Dad hasn't got round to moving the camera.'

Bridget had no idea what a *walking bus* might be, and it sounded like just the sort of thing the locals did in their spare time. Never mind. She nodded sympathetically and said, 'I see what you mean. Puts your mum in an awkward position, doesn't it?'

'Yeah.'

'Shall we help her out? Let's review the footage and see whether it's relevant.'

'What do you mean?'

Bridget grinned. 'I've had a tip off. From the … from the police. Let's have a look and see. We've got a few minutes.'

Kat gave in to her innate curiosity and opened her phone. In seconds, she had the data for Saturday morning on the screen and said, 'What time are the police interested in?'

'We'll start at half past eight and keep going until Millie leaves for the Bake Off.'

Kat moved the slider to the right moment and set the replay going at 10x normal speed, which was way too fast for Bridget but seemingly normal for Kat. Lots of people flashed in and out, doing all the things you'd expect on a Saturday morning: going to the shop, walking their dogs, jogging … 'Stop!' said Bridget. 'Go back a couple of minutes.' She watched anxiously. 'There, see?'

'But … so what?'

Bridget had come armed with an order pad. She wrote down a name and said, 'Keep going.'

Lucy and the vicar left the church in silence; it was only when they went through the lychgate that Lucy asked her first question. She pointed across the road to School House and said, 'When did they build the new school?'

Low-rise brick buildings were visible at the end of a drive, and children were just coming out for playtime. It could have been any modern primary school in Britain.

'That is a very long story,' Deborah began. She stood, staring at either the new school or the old one, and Lucy couldn't tell which. 'When Tobias Easterby bought the Byford Estate, he also bought the right to choose the vicar, so long as he paid the wages.'

Lucy couldn't see the relevance of this, but it was important that Deborah told the story in her own way. 'Really? When did that stop? Did it stop?'

Deborah smiled and grabbed a handful of her long black skirt. 'Clerical dress can be very cheap. So long as you've got the dog collar on, you can kit yourself out from the charity shop. The Easterbys had to stop subsidising the parish a long time ago. That's why I work two days a week at the school.'

'Oh. I didn't know.'

'I was a teaching assistant before I became a priest, and it was carry on being a TA or take charge of three parishes. Even without paying my stipend, Temperance was a rock for St Peter's – pun intended.'

What would Tom do with *that* metaphor, she wondered. *Temperance was the rock who let the vicar spread her wings?* Probably worse than that.

Deborah took Lucy's smile to mean that she'd got the joke about St Peter and continued. 'The Byford Estate became the Easterby Estate, and the family also paid for the original school. When the old building was well past being fit for purpose, Temperance donated the land for the new school and squeezed the last few drops out of her inheritance.

Building the school nearly bankrupted the estate. It was why she had to sell up.' Deborah turned to face Lucy. 'There's more: I don't understand all the legal ins and outs of it, but the school has to pay ground rent to the owner of School House.' She glanced down the road and saw someone. 'If you're going to treat me to coffee, let's get going before we're interrupted.'

They passed the village green, where a police car still stood guard. 'Now I understand the message I got last night,' observed Deborah. 'The police are releasing the marquee at lunchtime. Lots to do.'

The vicar was obviously quite used to striding around her parish, and Lucy had to put her legs into overdrive to keep up. 'Before we get to the Mill, tell me about Feargal.'

'Not my place,' said Deborah firmly. 'I saw you genuflect when you came into the church, so presumably you were brought up a Catholic in Italy?' Lucy nodded. 'The Anglican Church doesn't have the Sacrament of Absolution, but it does acknowledge the sanctity of confession. You didn't waste any time, did you?'

'Sorry?'

Lucy had been about to tell Deborah that her theology was a little out of date, and that the Sacrament was called Penance or Reconciliation these days, so she missed what the vicar was talking about.

Deborah completed her explanation with a gesture towards the new sign at the entrance to Ford Mill, and said, 'Miller's Rest is gone. Long live Caffè Milano.' The sign makers had done their usual fast and efficient job, and it looked good. It was by far the brightest of the signboards. 'Let's hope your coffee is better than Feargal's,' she added with a grimace. 'After Millie left, it went downhill fast.'

Deborah swept along the drive to the Mill and barely broke stride as she waited for the automatic doors to open. Inside the foyer, the A-Board in the entrance to the café now read *Open for Business!* in a much neater hand than Bridget's – and Bridge would never have added the exclamation mark.

Part of Lucy expected the new business to be busy with eager customers. Wrong. It was completely empty.

'Good morning, Reverend,' said Bridget. 'Welcome to Caffè Milano. What can I get you?'

'It's Deborah, please, and I'll have a strong black coffee.'

'I'll bring it over.'

Lucy guided Deborah to the quiet corner where the administrators of Miller's Rest had despaired of the old sofas and given them to Lucy for nothing rather than pay to have them removed.

The vicar looked around her. 'It's so strange. The place is familiar yet … so different. Not that I've come in much since Millie left. Only when in company.'

It was clear that Deborah really didn't like Feargal. When they had met Millie's ex-husband on Saturday, Lucy hadn't been charmed by him – she'd gone out with way too many dreamers to be taken in. Unlike Bridget.

'You're not from Byford?' said Lucy. 'It's hard to know who is and who isn't a native.'

'Fewer than you'd think. Very few in fact. No, I grew up in Cheshire. Not a million miles from Sevenbridge, as it happens.' She tilted her head. 'Do you see that place as *home*? I can't imagine what it must have been like growing up there.'

Lucy had spent her teenage years in an exclusive gated community, full of rich people. Anyone who discovered what her father had done quickly discovered that Lucy had once rubbed shoulders with some *very* famous names. It was not her favourite topic of conversation, so she turned it right round. 'Do you still have family there?'

Deborah shook her head. 'My children both moved to London after university, and when I split up with their father, I took whatever chances God gave me, and they led me here. Perhaps when I'm a grandmother, I might look for a parish closer to them.'

Lucy was trying to digest that when Kat came over with a tray. And ground to a halt, because she was too tall, the table was too low, and table service had clearly not been part of her training. 'Let me,' said Lucy, half rolling off the couch to get upright. She placed Deborah's coffee and her own water on the table, then raised an eyebrow at the Danish.

'Compliments of the chef,' said Kat.

Deborah looked at it. 'Does Bridget bake?' she asked, and Lucy couldn't tell whether she was being funny or naive.

'One day soon, you'll get to taste Bridget's ice cream. Believe me, it's well worth the calories,' said Lucy. She lifted the Danish off the tray and put it in front of the vicar. 'As are these pastries. Freshly made in Lancashire.'

Kat leaned down to Lucy's height and whispered so loudly that Louis probably heard it upstairs. 'Bridget's found something! Can she have a word?'

Lucy cringed, and Deborah waggled her eyebrows theatrically before biting into the pastry. 'I think you need to see your partner and let me enjoy this in peace. It's way too good.'

Lucy dashed through the depressingly empty café to where Bridget was guarding the counter, and Kat kept pace with her. 'What's going on?' Lucy hissed, conscious of the acoustics.

'Show her,' said Bridget to Kat.

Their young assistant whipped out her phone and quickly brought up a view of School House. Lucy frowned. What was this, and where on earth had they got it?

'CCTV,' said Bridget. 'From the morning of Millie's death. Look who popped in for breakfast.'

Kat pressed Play and a car accelerated across the screen. When it had gone, a figure crossed the road and went straight through the gate to School House. As the figure had crossed the road, it had carried on looking for cars, and when it turned to face the village shop, you could clearly see the clerical collar.

Chapter 17

Lucy finished looking at the evidence from the CCTV and announced, 'That's a relief.'

Kat looked alarmed at Lucy's remark, but didn't say anything, turning to glance at Bridget instead, to see what she thought of it all, and Bridget suddenly felt like a dog who'd wandered past a nest of duck eggs while they hatched, and the oldest duckling had imprinted itself on the first thing it saw. 'Why is it a relief?' she asked Lucy.

'Because now the police have some clear evidence to pursue.'

'They will do. When we tell them. Until then, we have a chance to ask—'

'What! Don't they know? You have to tell them now. This minute.'

Bridget turned to Kat. She had already discovered that Kat had passed her driving test ('Because, like, *everyone* learns to drive in the village. You can't survive without it.'), and she handed her the keys to the van. 'Go and fetch your mum. And while you do it, you can tell her that you've shown the CCTV to DCI Morton's girlfriend, and she says that the police won't care where she points her cameras.'

Kat looked at Lucy. 'Thanks, boss. That's a weight off my mind.'

'But …' began Lucy.

Bridget gently pushed her duckling in the back. 'Off you go. We need some more bodies through the door, even if we have to go and collect them ourselves.'

Kat headed off, and Lucy was about to have Strong Words with Bridget, but Bridget got in first. 'What's the vicar's story, then? What did you get out of her? And yeah, I was always gonna tell the bizzies. Cough it up, Luce.'

Lucy cast a furtive glance at the vicar, who was blithely finishing her pastry and sipping her coffee, blissfully unaware that she was now a suspect in Millie Easterby's murder.

Lucy dropped her voice. 'She's divorced, she misses her kids and she works two days a week as a teaching assistant in the school because she's as poor as one of her own church mice. She has a shrine to childhood in a corner of the church and she loved Millie Easterby as a surrogate daughter.'

Bridget nodded slowly. 'And most murders are committed by family members. Looks like we have our first paying customers, so you serve those old dears who've just walked in, and I'll see to the vicar.'

'You can't! It could ruin …'

But Lucy was talking to Bridget's back, and Bridget had her sights firmly fixed on the comfy corner. She grabbed a standard chair and took it over, because she wasn't going to sit on one of those sofas. Lucy thought they were a bargain, but Bridget knew better: she had seen Feargal's attitude to dirt, and it was very much from the *out of sight, out of mind* school of cleaning. New sofas were definitely going on the list.

She sat down as Rev Deb was wiping her hands on a napkin. 'That was delicious, thank you, Bridget. And the coffee is superb. For that alone, I am very grateful, and I wish you all the luck for the future.'

'It's alright, Reverend,' said Bridget. 'You can bless the coffee shop if you want. I won't mind. We sacrificed a goat yesterday, so that's all good.'

'I look forward to trying the stew. You're not going to waste it, are you?' The vicar lifted her cup, and her eyes smiled over the rim. 'Not much shocks me, Bridget. Saddens, yes, but shocks, no.'

Bridget shifted on the chair. She'd put on a newish pair of jeans this morning, and that might have been a mistake. The vicar was clearly a cool customer; *let's see if we can heat things up a bit.* 'Lucy told you that the police are working on some new evidence, didn't she?' Rev Deb gave a cautious nod. 'Part of that evidence means that they'll be looking at who had access to School House on the day of the Bake Off. You ran off to get something, didn't you?'

'Yes. Millie had forgotten the certified gluten-free oatmeal, and it was quicker for me to get it than send Chris Chester back to the shop.'

'But you could also have been getting something, couldn't you? Like the bottle that was found in Lucy's handbag. The bottle of poison. The bottle you left behind when you popped in for breakfast.'

The unshockable reverend was gone, and Bridget wasn't sure what had replaced her. 'That's a terrible thing to say, Bridget. I hope you didn't make the same suggestion to Katarina.'

'Don't need to: she'll work it out for herself sooner or later. And as for it being a terrible thing, so was circulating the picture of Lucy with Diego Luiz. Not that I'm suggesting you had anything to do with that.'

'I wouldn't know how.' The flick of the vicar's eyes to the left told Bridget everything she needed to know: Rev Giddings may not have shared the image, but she was covering for whoever did.

Bridget could be remorseless when she wanted to, and with the vicar trapped on the squashy sofa, she wouldn't get a better chance. 'So why *did* you go round so early?'

'Millie was a much-loved member of the congregation. I relied on her for a lot, and she relied on me. I was her TA. There's a lot of pressure on all the teachers at St Peter's.'

It was a smoothly delivered explanation, and Bridget was having none of it.

'Every teacher I've ever met likes to leave the job in their bulging briefcase. I doubt she'd have enjoyed being reminded of it on a Saturday morning.' That got another flicker. 'This isn't the first serious crime I've been next to, and every single copper from Cairndale nick is a valued customer. I've even had dinner with Tom Morton a couple of times. I know what they're like. They find out everything. They may never find enough evidence, but they soon know what people have got to hide.'

'Millie had nothing to hide,' said the vicar resolutely. 'She wore her heart on her sleeve.' Rev Deb looked down at Bridget's arms. 'A bit like you and your tattoos. What story do they tell, Bridget?'

That was good. Smoothly delivered and sharp as a knife; Bridget knew she was getting closer now that the vicar had gone on the attack. 'Millie had steel, Vicar. I got that from two minutes watching her despatch that Neapolitan traybake. It's you I'm worried about. Compared to Liz Swindlehurst, I'm a pussy cat, and she has no love for the Church, or so I've heard. If you don't talk to me and get your story straight now, who else will you talk to?'

Rev Deb's eyes were going all over the room now, desperately seeking a friendly face. Bridget resisted the urge to turn round and relied on village politeness: if they saw the vicar huddled with a new parishioner, they wouldn't interrupt.

Finally, the vicar's eyes settled on her empty cup. She pushed it aside and said, 'Millie was in trouble financially. She inherited the house mortgage-free and in her own right. She made three mistakes when she married Feargal, and marrying him at all was the first. The second mistake was making him joint owner of School House so that they could borrow the start-up money for Miller's Rest.'

That was unexpected. Bridget hadn't seen money as a potential motive: it just didn't feel right, somehow, but the iron was hot …

'So does Feargal get to keep the house?' asked Bridget.

'No. Absolutely not. Millie's third mistake was not telling the police about what he did three years ago.'

'Go on. You've started …'

'It's going to come out to the police, whom you seem to know rather well.' When Bridget didn't respond to that, the vicar sighed. 'He took out another loan and forged her signature. It's why they split up, and he signed over his interest in the house to her as part of the divorce. What he couldn't do was take over the loan: the bank was adamant that it was secured on the property.'

'That's fraud,' said Bridget indignantly.

'Millie could have got out of it if she'd reported him to the police, but she wouldn't, so she's been trying to repay the money on her own. It hasn't been easy. In fact, she's in arrears. I went over to see her on Saturday because she left me a message that she'd had the place valued by the estate agents. She was going to sell up, and I went over to see if I could talk her out of it in the short term.'

Bridget sat back and shuffled her bum again. These jeans were definitely a mistake, and Feargal Hulme was definitely a total shitehawk, as her dad would say. 'How could he do that to her, Deborah? Was he playing away, too? You don't do that to someone you love.'

'Love is a mysterious thing, Bridget, and by the way, thank you for calling me *Deborah* at last.' She gave a wry smile. 'Not sure if the price was worth paying, though. I think Feargal Hulme is a terrible person, but he never stopped saying he loved Millie, and he hasn't been seen with another woman since she kicked him out. For the first year, he even paid money towards the mortgage, but that only made things worse in a way.'

'How come?'

'It meant that he could keep talking to her, for one thing. And for another, it only hastened the death of Miller's Rest. Feargal Hulme may not have been an adulterer, but unlike Lucy, he's not a natural entrepreneur.'

Deborah had glanced at her phone a couple of times, and now it started vibrating. The vicar picked it up and sighed deeply when she saw who was calling. 'That's the police. If you'll excuse me ...'

Bridget stood up and whisked the chair away, allowing Deborah to make a swift exit through the side door.

When Bridget turned to put the chair back where it belonged, she was pleasantly surprised: they had customers. Real people paying real money. She scanned the dozen punters and they split into two neat groups. Three quarters were retired couples or friends, and the others were young and not-so-young mothers with buggies. Bridget grinned to herself. *Point to Gorrigan,* she thought proudly. It had been her idea to put up a large notice saying that bottles and baby food could be warmed in the microwave.

Kat was back now, and Lucy was leaving her to do most of the serving and drink-making. It was how Lucy operated – she let the local staff get to know the customers while she cleaned tables and kept an eye on things. Lucy was also in charge of staffing; Bridget had made that very clear.

At some point in the near future, they would need at least two more part-timers, and according to Kat, both the other girls who'd helped out in the past had gone to college and weren't interested in having their old jobs back.

Bridget picked up Deborah's empties and Lucy came over with the microfibre and spray bottle. 'She's left her bag,' said Lucy. 'I'll pick it up.' She gave the table a thorough polish and they adjourned to the kitchen.

'Well?' said Lucy. 'Are we on the vicar's hit list?'

'No, but I'm not on her Christmas card list, either. Unlike you. She likes you, or at least she respects you, which is better.'

Lucy always looked bewildered when people liked her; it made Bridget wonder just how bad her gilded childhood had been. 'Why?

What did she say?'

'She called you a *natural entrepreneur*. Unlike Feargal Hulme. What did you find out in the church that made you drag her back here? Which was a smart move, by the way.'

They exchanged news with repeated glances outside to see if Kat was coping. When they'd finished, Bridget asked where Kat's mother was.

'Having a free and frank exchange of views with her husband about CCTV. She's coming over for lunch. Look, here comes Deborah looking for her handbag.'

'I'll take it.'

Bridget went back out and intercepted the vicar. Something Lucy had said niggled at her, and when she'd handed over the bag, she asked, 'If you're the chair of governors at the school, who interviewed you for the TA job?'

'What an odd question. It was Temperance who interviewed me, because she was chair at the time. I took over when she died.'

'Oh. Right. Sorry. Good luck with Liz Swindlehurst.'

Deborah made a face and left.

Something still didn't sit right, and she indulged in a little Google. The results made her grunt with satisfaction for a hunch played out. She now had a very difficult question to ask *Deboraaaaah* the next time she could corner her.

Chapter 18

Offering to warm baby food might drag in more mothers, but they had to offer changing facilities as well, and Bridget left the accessible toilet carrying a metaphorical bone to pick with Perry Lockwood when he turned up. There was another issue, too, and it was written on Bridget's order pad: *Talk to Perry.* Perry Lockwood had been Millie's second visitor on the day she died. And talking of the Devil…

'Here,' said Kat, offering Bridget a cappuccino when she re-entered the Spinning Room. 'I told Perry you'd take it over to him. He's over there, by the wall.'

'I know that,' snapped Bridget. She examined the cappuccino. 'Your chocolate sprinkles are a work of art, kid. Like your calligraphy.'

'Thanks.'

'So why do I have to do table service for our landlord?'

'Because he likes you,' said Bridget's duckling with a smirk. 'He asked where you were, and it wasn't business because the boss said hello to him and he only made polite conversation with *her*. It's you he's interested in.'

'Me? Are you daft?' said Bridget brusquely. She could feel the heat rising under her industrial grade foundation, and she wasn't happy. She snatched up the hot drink, and had to swerve to stop the perfectly foamed milk from slipping over the sides. Oops.

She took the coffee to Perry, and he lifted his bum off the seat a fraction, as if he were going to stand up but had thought better of it. She placed the drink down with a professional smile. 'Was there something you wanted, Perry?'

His smile was more uncertain. 'I was just going to ask how it was going, that's all. I can see you're busy, so thanks for bringing this over. I'll let you get back.'

And now it was Bridget's turn to be uncertain. He was trying to be nice, that's all. Nothing to get wound up over. She decided to deal with the hygiene issue first, because if he clammed up after being accused of murder, Bridget might end up doing the cleaning herself.

'We're coping fine right now,' she said brightly. 'And thanks for asking. It means I can talk to you about something I'd rather not have discussed at the counter. I'm afraid the toilets, especially the ladies and the accessible one, are a bit of an issue.'

'Aah. Oh dear. Feargal wasn't that bothered about them. It's just that the management contract specifies only once a day for cleaning.'

'It does, but that only applies to the staff toilets upstairs, the ones used by the workshops and gallery. I have no idea why the arts centre is a tenant of its own building, but there you go, and we have to offer service to all patrons of the arts centre while it's open. I double checked, and technically the arts centre is allowing us to use the foyer as an entrance, presumably so you can close it when you want to, so everyone who comes through the front door is entitled to clean loos, whatever the time of day.'

Perry sat back and smiled, which was an odd thing to do. 'That's one interpretation of the agreement. We could argue about that for some time.'

'Or I could get Lucy's Uncle Paul on the case, and he works for nothing. You'd need to get your solicitor to respond, and he doesn't work for nothing, so you'd end up losing a packet even if you won. So how about you employ a full-time caretaker instead of relying on evening contractors and Louis's good will?'

He frowned and blinked at her. Then he shook his head. 'No one gets round you, do they?'

Having sorted the toilet issue, she decided to give him five minutes before dealing with his visit to School House. 'I'll leave you to enjoy your coffee and have some quality thinking time.'

She went back to the counter, where Kat was taking off her apron. 'Break time, Bridget. If I don't take it now, Mum will be here.' She folded her apron and cast a furtive glance behind Bridget. 'I told you he was interested. You two get on like a house on fire.'

'We were talking about toilets, actually,' said Bridget. It had been a long time since she felt she needed to justify her behaviour to anyone, let alone to a kid like Katarina.

'That's what they all say. Back in half an hour.'

Things were ticking over in the café. It was nowhere near the business they'd need to do long-term, but for the first day of a soft opening, it was quite good. Bridget's gangly duckling was still on her break, and Lucy had swapped to be on the counter when Mike the Milk strode through the arch.

'Morning, Mike, and welcome to Caffè Milano. What can I get you?' asked Lucy.

'Oh. Right. Yeah.'

The cheek of it! From the look on his face, he clearly hadn't been planning to spend any money. Bridget would have frowned at him, but Lucy just stood there with a tray in her hands and a smile on her face. At least Bridget was spared trying to interrogate him: Mike Mason had not been one of Millie Easterby's visitors.

'I'll take a latte to go, thanks,' said Mike, and Lucy got to work. He continued, 'Got to get to the green, because it's all hands on deck. The cops have released the marquee, and there's a hell of a lot of clearing up to do. I just stuck my head in to ask if either of you had left anything inside?'

'No,' said Lucy. 'How about you, Bridget?'

'No. Nothing. Sounds like a big job.'

Mike made a face. 'Tell me about it. Not a good day – the sunshine has brought out the jam and preserve makers, and I can't afford to be too long. Amos is great with cows, not so much with fruit. It's helped your trade, though.'

'You've lost me,' said Lucy, placing the cup on the counter.

He glanced around. 'That table, and that table, and that one over there. They all came to buy from me first. I've got ten acres of pick-your-own fruit on the sheltered side of the hill, including the Easterby cherries.'

The girls exchanged glances: how had they missed this bit of market research?

'Good to know,' said Lucy, keeping her hand on the drink. 'Isn't it a bit early for strawberries up here?'

'And what are the Easterby cherries when they're at home?' added Bridget, because she'd just joined some dots in her head.

'You're right: strawbs next month. No, the Easterby cherries are an acre of early fruiting sweets. Tempe's dad bred them from some US variety, and they're doing great right now. Can I have my drink?'

'Of course. Three pounds, thanks.'

'Oh. Are you sure? Of course you are. Put it on the Meadow Farm tab. Got to go. Thanks, and good luck.'

The nerve of the man! Bridget could see that Mike had expected it to be free, and tabs were not something that Caffè Milano operated, a point she made to Lucy.

'True,' said Lucy with a reflective inflection. 'Maybe we should start. For people who we know are good for it. Might encourage them to spend more if they don't have to worry about the five-pound minimum spend on debit card transactions. One thing's for certain, though: I am not Feargal Hulme, and that coffee is the last one that goes on anyone's tab without a signature on an agreement. I'll download one from the internet tonight and see about setting it up on the point of sale.'

The lunchtime offering at Caffè Milano varied from branch to branch. At Cairndale they did a lot of takeout sandwiches for people on the go, while at Southport they catered mostly for people wanting to eat in, and it was going to be the same here. It also led to their first complaint.

The guy Bridget had seen on her first trip to Cairndale appeared – Allan it turned out his name was. He was about seventy, a retired engineer and, so he loudly declared, the chair of the Byford Artists Society. 'Feargal gave us a discount for being Friends of the Mill,' he announced. 'And senior discount on top of that. And where's the sausage sandwiches? I can't see them on the menu.'

There was no way Kat was going to stand up to that. Yet. Lucy was nearest, and she gave the spiel.

'We have senior discounts before eleven, so you've missed them, I'm afraid. They're on every day from Monday to Thursday, just so you know, and I'm sorry about the sausage sandwiches. Try the chorizo salad, it's freshly made. And I haven't heard of the Friends of the Mill. Is it a heritage society?'

Allan didn't look happy, and was trying to decide whether or not he should carry on moaning. 'No. Friends of the Mill is what Feargal called us. The regular customers. He knew the importance of repeat business.'

'I couldn't agree more,' said Lucy. 'Which is why we're determined to put the café on a sustainable, long-term footing. And I think a loyalty subscription might be an excellent idea. What do you reckon, Bridget? We could roll it out to all the branches.'

'A good idea. You could look into it along with sorting the tabs.'

Allan hadn't noticed Bridget, and he gave a good look up and down when she spoke. 'You're different. Weren't you one of those vampire girls last time I saw you?'

'We all wear the uniform, Allan. Even the boss.'

His eyes went back to her bare arms. 'That's good work, that. The detailing on the thorns is superb, as is the shadow on the rose petals. I'll have a pot of tea and a scone.'

'I can't tempt you with the salad?' asked Lucy.

'I don't like spicy food.'

That was the first time Bridget had heard chorizo referred to as *spicy*. And the first time that anyone other than a fellow Goth had commented on the artistic merit of her ink rather than its symbolism. When he'd gone, Bridget said, 'I wonder what he'll complain about tomorrow.'

'Hopefully the weather,' said Lucy. 'And no, I am not going to introduce a subscription scheme. Way too much hassle. Here comes a big group.'

Chapter 19

Bridget didn't get a chance to go back to her list of names until after lunch. The midday service had gone well, though she was surprised not to have seen Jackie Chester, and there hadn't been any more complaints about the food or pricing.

Bridget needed a moment when the café was quiet and she could get Kat on her own. She braced herself and said, 'I know that Perry's PA works part-time. You've been here a while, do you know which days she's here?'

Kat burst into a radiant smile. 'You gonna go and see him? I told you he was interested in you!'

'I don't believe I'm having this conversation. You saw the CCTV. You know he was at School House, and if that wasn't enough, I've had to check the toilets three times today, which is three times too often. And for the record, just because I'm single, it does not mean I'm in the market, okay? Now, what about his PA?'

'Is it Wednesday afternoon? Right. No, she's not in, and he has to cover the phones.'

'Won't be long.'

'Hang on! You've got to take him a drink.'

'Why do I?'

Kat was already filling the portafilter and pouring milk into the jug. 'Catch him unawares. I'll have something for you when you get back as well.'

Bridget wasn't going to let a cappuccino go to waste, and it wouldn't hurt to turn up with a peace offering. She collected the takeout cup and made her way across the car park to the estate office and up the stairs. Perry was at his desk and staring at his computer.

'Hi there,' he said, pushing his chair back. 'You found me then.'

'Regular bloodhound, me. Have you got a minute?'

He got up and pointed to the chairs round the table. Bridget had forgotten about that. 'Shouldn't this be in the café?'

'It was. I took it in part-payment one month when Feargal was struggling with the rent.'

The feeling Bridget had had yesterday made sense now: there was a table missing from the coffee shop, and that's why the balance was off. This table was coming home somehow. It was on her list.

But not for today. She held out the coffee. 'Here. Thought you might like something to get you through the afternoon.'

'That's very kind, Bridget. Cheers.'

They sat down, and he took the lid off his drink. After the space and acoustics of the Spinning Room, it was almost womb-like in here, despite the office furniture and lighting. Nice carpet, too. Even so, Bridget had a purpose. 'I noticed you snuck out before I could talk to you about a caretaker. Have you given it any thought?'

'I did not sneak out! You were busy, and besides, I wanted to have another look at that service agreement.'

'And?'

'And you're right: patrons of the gallery and the theatre, even patrons of the theatre foyer, they all have the right to access clean toilets. However, your patrons don't. As such. It would be up to Louis to complain about the situation, not you.'

Bridget's mouth was open to object, and she was bracing herself on the table to get up and walk out when Perry held up a hand. 'Hold on, hold on. I'm just taking it one step at a time.' Infuriatingly, he took a sip of coffee before continuing. 'I do not want Louis to be subjected to a concerted campaign of psychological battering from you over this.'

Bridget relaxed again. Perry had put his finger right on it: she had been going to head straight for Louis, so naturally she denied it. 'As if I would. Go on.'

'I need to run this past Edwin and Fliss, because another extra cost is going to be hard to swallow. And there may have to be a quid pro quo.'

It was a sign. A tiny sign that Perry respected the Scouse Goth who ran the café, because he didn't try to mansplain the concept of *quid pro quo*. 'You're into hypotheticals here, Perry, and the dirt is not hypothetical. That accessible toilet needs an upgrade, too, if it's going to get five stars as a baby-changing room.'

'No, the dirt isn't hypothetical, and yes, we've got plans to refurb the facilities. I'll action it as soon as you've gone. Even if Edwin agreed to a caretaker tomorrow, we'd have to recruit, so we need something in the interim. Have you met Josie yet?'

'Not that I know of.'

'She does a couple of hours a day for me. I couldn't survive without her, and she could come over before lunch. If you offer her cash in hand and free coffee, I'm sure you could work something out.'

This was wrong on several levels: it should be the estate paying, not Caffè Milano, and Lucy had a strict *no cash in hand* policy for staff. It was the price for having Tom in her life that she was a stickler for anything that might generate bad publicity if it came out: "DCI's partner in tax scam" was not a headline that anyone wanted. On the other hand, it was how business round here was done, and if anyone could hide a few quid in cash, it was Mina Desai.

'Thanks, Perry. Send her over sharpish, eh?'

'I will.' He stayed seated, relaxed even, and he said, 'Was there something else?'

Bridget felt embarrassed again. This man was not easily wrong-footed, and that was normally her role. 'Should there be?'

He sipped coffee. 'I thought you might have come about the CCTV. Jackie dropped in before, and she's notified everyone who was caught on camera. She also told me that the vicar was lucky to escape from your interrogation without handcuffs. Now that I would have paid good money to see.'

'It's not a sport, Perry.'

'I agree, but what's it to you?'

'Millie had no one except Deborah, and Deborah has to support the whole village, so look on me as Millie's avenging angel.'

He gave a hollow laugh. 'You're right, but for the wrong reasons.' He leaned forwards. 'Lucy and you are innocent, right? The police are sure of that?'

'Yeah, but …'

'But nothing. If our vicar can't pin it on one of you two, she'll pin it on whoever visited Millie from the Dark Side.'

Bridget didn't know whether to be afraid or bemused. She'd joked to herself about pagan practices in Byford, but was he telling her that there was something to it? 'Sorry, Perry, you'll have to explain that.'

He stood up suddenly and crossed the office space without a word before rummaging behind one of the desks and pulling up a picture frame. He came back and placed it carefully on the table for Bridget to see.

"Stop This Dark Satanic Mill" screamed the headline on an old copy of the *Lancashire Mercury*, dated from just before Edwin Duke had bought the Easterby Estate. The headline and picture took up so much room that there was only space to report a growing local opposition to the sale of Ford Mill and that the reader should turn to page two.

'The Dark Side,' said Perry, 'is everyone who supported and continues to support Team Duke over Team Calvert. We call them the Angels. It's a joke now, but it wasn't then. Not that I was involved.'

'What on earth did Dom Calvert want with the Mill? And I thought that Anya was friends with Fliss. Wasn't she taking Anya's kid to baby ballet or something equally horrific?'

'We only put this up when we want to annoy people,' he said, lifting the framed article and returning it to the corner. When he'd sat down again, he looked serious. 'I try not to get involved, Bridget. Whether or not Anya and Fliss are friends, I can tell you that Dom and Edwin still haven't forgiven each other. I couldn't say how much of the rest of it is a "bit of fun", but we have to make a living, don't we?'

'Fine. You don't have to gossip, Perry, but what *did* Dom want with the Mill?'

'He wanted to turn Ford Mill into a high-tech hub and link it to his businesses and the university, but he wanted it on the cheap and he didn't want the rest of the estate, not the land or the properties and definitely not the farms. Couldn't afford it. Edwin could afford it, and Fliss wanted her arts centre. Once it was clear that the Mill wasn't going to become housing, the village calmed down and got on with it.'

'There's more. You're holding a lot back.'

Perry finished his coffee and put the lid back on. 'You should know that Fliss calls herself a *neo-Pagan Spiritualist*, whatever that might be, and the Duke children are going to private schools when they're old enough.'

'So?'

'Anya is a bishop's daughter and very much a practising Anglican. She is a big ally of the vicar and supporter of the school, which is a state school. Right. Do you want to know what I was doing at School House or not? I'm sure you're busy over there.'

'Did your Lisa and Millie have anything to do with each other?'

He frowned at that. 'No more than anyone else in the village who has two kids at St Peter's. Both boys did well, as it happens. Millie was a good teacher. Lisa's best friend was Jackie, which is why Jackie came to see me first. She wouldn't tell me who else was on the CCTV.'

'Cherries. Talk to me about cherries. You put last year's jam into the Bake Off. Have you made any this year?'

He looked really uncomfortable at this point. Not guilty, but very uncomfortable. 'I wasn't planning to, no. What on earth are you asking that for?'

Perry Lockwood was a master of playing his cards close to his chest. He was also a man, and had a male reserve to him. Lisa's death was still very close in the Lockwood rear-view mirror. What Perry could not do was act, and his bemusement regarding the cherries wasn't faked.

'You'll find out about the cherries soon enough.' Bridget got up from the table and smiled. 'Just one more thing. Who told you that School House was coming onto the market?'

He lifted an imaginary hat from his sandy hair and said, 'Respect, Bridget. There aren't many who know yet, and no, my lips are sealed on that one.'

Bridget took the empty cup: Lucy had insisted on a supplier who offered a genuine recycling service. 'Thank you, Perry. Don't forget to message Josie, yeah?'

'On it. Feel free to bring me free coffee any time. I'll come out with you.' He grabbed his coat and followed her down the stairs.

At the door, Bridget risked another question. 'Jackie Chester. Angel or Dark Side?'

'Divided loyalties. Katarina works at the Mill, and Jackie was really good to Lisa, which puts her on the Dark Side. On the other hand, Jasmine is in the choir and Chris is a Churchwarden, so … I'll see you later.'

Chapter 20

'Where've you been?' hissed Lucy when Bridget got back to the café. 'It's got very busy all of a sudden, and Kat said you were on a date!'

Bridget wrapped the apron round herself. 'I'll murder that girl and cook her with orange sauce one day. I was on *Operation Eliminate*. Perry is in the clear, Lucy.'

Lucy gave her a bug-eyed grimace. 'Whatever. Accident in the accessible toilet. Apparently.'

Bridget sighed and went to get the cleaning kit. Making ice cream in Southport had been *so* much easier.

The next time she got a minute to breathe, Kat produced a piece of paper but held it out of reach. 'Is Perry a suspect?'

'No.'

'Good. I told you so. I can't say the same for the others on your list of suspects, though, and talking of lists, I've made a special one just for you. Here.'

The paper had seven names on it. 'What's this? A new line-up for that quiz team that Perry was banging on about the other day?'

'Quiz team? You what?'

Bridget took a proper look at the list and recognised Perry Lockwood, Mike Mason, Nathan Frost, Brad Nicol and Feargal Hulme. 'If they're not a quiz team in the making,' she said, 'then are they new suspects or something?' She looked again. 'Anyway, who's Gerrard Scott, and why is Feargal's name in brackets? And why does this Joseph Hayton have an asterisk next to his name?'

'These are all the single men in Byford who own or rent their own home. All the other single men live with their parents, and believe me, they are *not* worth it. Gerrard Scott is the landlord of the White Hart, and Feargal's name's in brackets 'cos he's sort of still in love with Millie. Oh, and Joseph Hayton is Coffin Joe's real name. I put an asterisk because, well, he's Coffin Joe. Technically single, though.'

Twin reactions of disbelief warred inside Bridget: disbelief at Katarina's bloody nerve and disbelief at he shortness of the list. Two years ago, the first would have won, but she found herself saying, 'Is dat it? Seven men in the whole village?'

'You know Carter's, yeah? Opposite side of the Market Square.'

'The estate agents and lawyers? I've seen them. Don't know them by name yet.'

'Have a look in the window when you get home. It explains a lot about the village, because only couples with big deposits or large salaries can live here, and if they get divorced, they usually leave.'

Bridget put the list in her order pad without thinking about it. 'Good job I'm not planning on moving in, then, isn't it?'

She had no intention of ever living in this village, or any village come to that, but she would definitely be paying a visit to Carter's Estates tomorrow morning.

Lucy didn't get home until late on the first day of trading at the new Caffè Milano. She and Bridget had a lot to go through, given that on Saturday it had still been operating as Miller's Rest. After a long discussion, they had put staffing at the top of the list, both recruiting new people and putting Katarina Chester through a food hygiene course as an urgent priority. When Lucy finally opened the door of their rental in Garstang, she was shocked to see Tom carrying a suitcase downstairs.

Lucy had been betrayed by her last serious boyfriend. Badly betrayed, and her heart lurched when she saw the man she loved walking out. Then she took a closer look and saw his face.

'Is it Granddad Alex?'

Tom nodded sadly.

'Why didn't you call me? What's happened?'

'He's had a stroke. It doesn't look good.' Tom sighed. 'We knew it might happen, and I'm not his only grandchild, am I? You had enough on your plate today. I'm so proud of what you've done, Lucy.'

Her heart swelled, and she had to grab him into a hug. 'Oh, Tom, Tom, Tom. It's only a coffee shop for goodness' sake. Let me run and pack.'

He pushed her slowly away and shook his head. His face was sad, yes, but he was right: Alex Morton had a wife, two sons, two daughters-in-law, six grown-up grandchildren and umpteen great-grandchildren, not to mention a mysterious clutch of wealthy cousins over the moors. In fact, Lucy would only be taking up space.

Tom brushed the hair off his forehead and squeezed round her to get at his car keys. 'Besides,' he said, 'you have a village to interrogate. Apparently.'

Lucy's knees shuddered together and a chill ran down her back. 'Are you in trouble?'

He looked amused. 'Me? Why should I be in trouble? The Commander doesn't hold me accountable for what my women get up to. Except Elaine. And Liz. I am accountable for both of them.'

She punched his arm, making sure it was the right one, not the left one with the scars. 'They are not your women. I am your only *woman*, so there. What did Allister say?'

'*Allister*, is it? He has said nothing because he knows nothing. Liz, on the other hand, was most pleased. She said that you and Bridget had tag-teamed the vicar and softened her up nicely, as well as Bridget uncovering that CCTV evidence. How was the day job, love?'

'Fine. Better than fine, actually. It went brilliantly, all things considered.'

He bent down to kiss her. Properly kiss her. 'That's because you're a genius and you have a great team. I'll call you from Skipton way. You should have finished in the shower by then.'

'Shower?'

'It's a measure of how much I love you that I am still in the same hallway as your smell of *Eau de Café*.'

Before Bridget could investigate the Byford property market the next morning, there was the small matter of a day's work to get through, starting with the early morning delivery of aromatic oven-fresh goods from Tabor's. Even earlier today, because Thursday was market day in Cairndale and the council would soon be along to fence off the northern half of the open space for the traders.

She parked the van in the square, ready for a quick getaway, and glanced into the café. Lights from the back told her that Lilianna was throwing herself into her new role as branch manager with an equally early start. So early, in fact, that her little boy was sitting in the window, suited and booted for school and staring at a reading book, moving his lips soundlessly behind the glass as he practised his English.

The sun peeked over the mishmash of buildings which formed the square, and Bridget leaned on the van to enjoy a moment's warmth and peace. It lasted all of ten seconds before a voice from the Clyde interrupted her morning mindfulness. Not that Bridget had any time for *mindfulness*.

'Are ye open or what?' demanded a young woman.

Bridget blinked and saw a sweaty, red-faced student staring at her. The kid had been running, and now one dangling earbud thumped bass into the air. *Are you open or what*. How rude was *that*?

'You'll damage your hearing with that racket,' said Bridget, pushing herself off the van.

'Who're yoo? Ma gran?' asked the woman. On second glance, the runner wasn't one of the ULIST sports science students, though she might be a teacher. Nah. The running gear was too new and too designer for lecturer's wages.

'I'm Bridget,' she said. 'And I'm off to Byford in a minute. If you ask *very* nicely inside, Lili might make you a skinny latte.'

The woman laughed. 'Sod that. I need a triple-shot. Off to Byford, you say?' Gears had been turning behind the woman's eyes and something had clearly clicked.

'I sure am,' responded Bridget.

The woman swapped her phone around. *Please don't let her want to shake hands. Not with all that … sweat.*

No such luck.

Hand extended, the runner modulated her Glasgow accent and identified herself. 'I'm Abigail Tennant, from McEwan and Co.' She shook hands, then pointed to a horrible 1970s building with a ladieswear shop on the ground floor. *That* shop wasn't called McEwan's, so where had Bridget heard the name before? Ah, yes.

'The solicitors,' Bridget said. She stepped closer. 'And why haven't you been in Caffè Milano before?'

Abigail stepped back. 'Rhona's is nearer the courts. And I've heard the polis own this place.'

'Lucy owns this place, and everyone is welcome. Including some of your clients, I'm guessing.'

'Another reason to avoid it.'

Bridget stepped aside and pointed to the door. The little student looked up from his book and turned to smile at his mother, who deposited a fully loaded hot chocolate and gave him her phone to play with. 'Tell Lilianna I said to give your first coffee on the house. You'll never go to Rhona's again after that.'

Abigail looked from Bridget to the door, just as the Tabor's Bakery van roared into Market Square. 'You're Bridget and Lucy's the owner. Bridget Gorrigan and Lucia Berardi. Of course. You're the witnesses in the Bake Off murder.' She gave a wicked grin. 'I bet your ears were burning last night.'

'What's that supposed to mean?'

The van rocked as the driver threw it into reverse and backed up to the café.

'Thanks for the coffee,' said the lawyer, stepping lightly away on air-soled shoes. 'See you around, no doubt.'

She was gone inside, and the delivery driver hopped out of his cab. Bridget got her bag and reached for the sanitiser with her left hand, having carefully avoided touching *anything* since Abigail's sweaty palm had gripped her. Eurgh.

Chapter 21

On the drive up to Byford, Bridget went through the obvious reasons for Abigail Tennant to have been talking about her and Lucy. With a client? With the police? She didn't work for the CPS, so almost certainly a client. If so, had she been at the station, and who was her client?

Bridget first noticed that something was wrong when she saw the crowd outside the village shop. She was planning to pull in there, but all the spaces were taken, and a good half a dozen Byfordians were standing talking and looking at newspapers. She had to turn on to the green and walk back, and as she approached the group, all heads swivelled to train their eyes on her. At least they didn't have pitchforks. She vaguely recognised a couple from yesterday (who'd said they liked the new coffee shop), and there was no mistaking Allan.

He turned and lifted his folded newspaper to her. 'Did you lot write this, or just give the journalist free coffee for life?'

'Or something else,' muttered a tall man from the back. Bridget chose to ignore that.

'And a good morning to you, too, Allan. What's going on then?'

'Have you not seen this?'

'Give over. It's all well and good for you, but some of us have to work for a living, you know. I was taking a delivery at seven o'clock and today's pastries are in the back of me van.'

'And I shall be up later.' He turned to the rest of the chorus and said, 'Did you know you only get senior discount before eleven under the new regime? That only gives you an hour and a half, so you'd best be sharp about it.' He turned back to Bridget. 'At least we know it's safe to eat at the Mill now.'

Without a goodbye, he strolled off and the tall man shuffled forwards. This guy was another retiree, perhaps in his early sixties, and he had a big grey beard, neatly trimmed but still making his face and head seem huge. 'Let me read you this. It's Bridget, isn't it?'

He was holding the paper up, blocking her way and waiting for an answer.

'Yeah, that's right. Bridget Gorrigan. Why? Do I get a mention?'

'No, but your boss does. Listen, "Police discovered vital evidence early in the enquiry, but they now believe that an attempt was made to divert their attention by implicating blameless café owner Lucia White, twenty-eight. Commander Ross of Cairndale Division is keen to speak to everyone in the village who had access to Ms Easterby's home at School House." Is that right? Is she only twenty-eight, and did she interfere with the enquiry?'

Bridget didn't know whether to get upset, be thankful or be annoyed. She decided to just be angry for now. 'It's *Lucy Berardi*, actually. We want to help the police as much as you do. I hope. We're both shocked that something like this could happen in Byford. Thanks for telling me, by the way. Hope to see you later.'

She sidestepped the tall man and nearly barged into the resident zombie. She couldn't resist it. 'Morning, Jasmine. Got your PE kit? Scuse me.'

She left the youngest Chester to have her existential crisis on the threshold and slipped into the shop. 'Have I missed the sandwich guy?' she asked Jackie.

'Nope. He's down the bottom checking the sell-by dates.'

A man only slightly younger than the chorus outside was holding a bread tray against the chiller cabinet with his hip and rooting through the sandwiches.

'Sales have been good,' he shouted down the shop. 'Nothing like being the centre of attention to shift sandwiches.'

'Hiya, Rodrigo,' said Bridget. 'Did Jackie tell you about us?'

'Rodrigo! We haven't met and you're already calling me *Rodrigo*. Only long-standing customers get to call me that.' Then he actually winked at her. 'Here. Free sample.' He chucked a sandwich at her; good job that Bridget was awake. She caught it, and he grinned. 'That makes you a long-standing customer. If you like it, call the office before two o'clock and I'll see you tomorrow morning. Mine's a regular coffee with two sugars.' He slipped a business card out of his overall pocket, placed it theatrically on the shelf, then moved to take the tray in both hands. 'Nice to meet you.'

He pivoted and went the long way round the shop, dropping off a delivery note by the till and timing his exit perfectly so that someone opened the door for him. Suddenly, Bridget was alone in the shop with Jackie. She picked up Rodrigo's business card and walked over to the counter.

'He's a bit of a whirlwind, isn't he?' she said.

'You could say that. What did you say to Jazz? She went white, then pulled her tongue out at you and stomped off.'

'Nothing. Honest. Maybe she doesn't like to be spoken to before ten. Like her sister, in fact. Do you think you'll make it up to the Mill today?'

'Big delivery later. I'll see what I can do. Kat said it went well. Not that she said much about herself. Was she okay?'

'She was great. Honestly. Couldn't have done it without her. Right. Can I have a copy of the *Mercury*?'

'On the house. You can swap it for a coffee.'

Bridget glanced at the masthead. 'Sorry, Jackie, can't do that: it's a lot cheaper than a coffee, but I'll comp you one for getting Kat out of bed yesterday. In fact you can have several for that. Cheers.'

If they staggered their breaks sensibly, there was no need for three staff at Ford Mill most of the time, and Bridget knew that now the first day was done, there would be slack periods after they'd coped with setting up. Kat was exactly on time (as promised), but Lucy was uncharacteristically late.

'Sorry. I didn't get to sleep for ages. It's Tom. He had to go to York last night. His granddad's had a stroke, and it was late when he left.' She sighed. 'Tom says it's a matter of time now.'

They started service, and it was much busier than the first day with a big influx of local seniors. When the initial rush had died down, Bridget got her chance to escape after she asked Lucy if the extra latte glasses were in the back of her car.

'Oh no! I forgot to pick them up! Have they got any spare in Cairndale? I'll go and get them.'

'I'll go. No problem. You can read this while I'm away.' She handed over the paper. 'I don't want to pile on your misery, but they've called you *Lucia White*.'

'Shit. Oh, sod it. I'm past caring. Every man and his dog knows what my dad did. Even the bloody cows probably know by now.'

Bridget quite liked her new van. She doubted that Lucy would buy one exactly the same, but it was nice to drive it while she had the chance. It turned out that (so long as you were careful), driving was almost as easy to remember as riding a bike, and hadn't vehicles become a lot *nicer* since she last drove one?

She had to go the long way round to the back of the Cairndale coffee shop, under the railway arches and then reverse down an alley which she had vowed *never* to walk along, day or night. And the reason for today's diversion? No parking in the square on market days.

Glasses loaded in the back of the van, she messaged that she was going to take her break here and grabbed herself a coffee. She took a few minutes and indulged in her first walk through the market – on every previous Thursday, she'd been behind the counter racking up the extra sales. She marvelled at just how cheap the meat was when bought from the farmer's stall. Those sausages looked delicious. Maybe she should bring back Allan's favourite butties.

On the other side of the square from the coffee shop were the two buildings which made up Carter's. One was tall, thin and very old; the other was low, squat and brutally modern. In the old building, the firm of Carter, Webb and Carter practised law, while in the new addition, the abbreviated Carter's Estates sold and rented houses. Mindful of Kat's words about the cost of houses in Byford, she spent a few seconds looking at the properties in the window.

They'd been helpfully organised into districts, and she zoomed in on Byford. 'Bloody hell,' she exclaimed. 'They're having a laugh, aren't they? *Four hundred thousand* for a three-bed semi? Give over.'

'Byford *is* much sought after,' said a woman close behind her. Rather too close.

'Jesus! You gave me a fright.'

'I'm sorry, Miss Gorrigan. I'm Andrea, the senior negotiator.'

'Oh! You work here?'

The middle-aged woman in the corporate suit was a regular in Caffè Milano. She was carrying one now and she even gave tips, but she'd never said where she worked. Maybe she was embarrassed.

'That's right. Are you just window shopping or are you interested? That flat over the shop is pretty ropey, isn't it?'

'How do you know that?'

'Let's go inside so I can drink my Milano fix.'

There were two more negotiators and an admin assistant in the open plan office, all of whom had taken their turns as Milano customers, and none of whom had worn their ID badges to do so. They had them on now, so what was the story there? Andrea led them to the desk at the back and offered Bridget a very comfy customer chair.

Bridget looked suspiciously at the woman when she put her own lanyard round her neck, but she didn't comment. Instead, she said, 'I wasn't involved in buying the place over the road, but I know it wasn't sold by your firm.'

Andrea sighed. 'Alas no. They went with that mob from Lancaster, unfortunately, but I had a good look round before Lucy came along. I'm surprised you've stuck it out up there as long as you have: that flat would give me the creeps.'

Bridget bristled. 'It's great, actually. Yeah, it needs work, but it's way bigger than anything else on the square.' Point made, she realised she needed to be nice if she was going to get her information. 'Thanks for all your business, by the way. It's much appreciated.'

'Pleasure. I'll have to say hello now, I suppose. I should have done it weeks ago.'

'Why didn't you?'

'I was half hoping that you'd make a mess of the business and I could be on hand to make you an offer. On the whole I'm glad you've succeeded, because your coffee is miles better than the old lot.'

'Thanks. I think.' She finished her own brew while Andrea got started on hers, and while she did, Bridget saw the paper to one side. It was the perfect opportunity. 'You've read the main story in the *Mercury*?'

'I have. All publicity is good publicity, I suppose. Terrible way to get it, though,' she added, shaking her head.

Bridget tried to look unthreatening. 'I only met Millie once, but she was really nice, wasn't she?'

'She was …' It was out before Andrea realised the slip.

'So it *was* you who did the valuation on School House. I thought it would be.'

Andrea didn't even go red. Totally unflustered. 'It's no secret, although she did ask me to park in the school car park in the evening and use the rear entrance.'

That was news. 'Rear entrance?'

'The old playground is the back garden. Temperance put a gate in the wall and even had a remote electronic lock fitted. Very forward thinking.'

Damn. Bridget hadn't noticed that, and it meant that anyone could have sneaked in to School House – if Millie had unlocked the gate for them. 'What happens now?' she asked Andrea.

Andrea smiled. 'You first.'

'Sorry?'

'You tell me the gossip first. Your place is practically the police station canteen, and we all know that Lucy is the future Lady Throckton.'

This woman would get in where a draught wouldn't, thought Bridget. Almost no one in Cairndale Division knew that the ailing Alex Morton was also the third Baron Throckton and that, in time, Tom would become the fifth.

Bridget glanced at her phone: no emergency texts, and it was still early; plenty of time to enjoy the comfy chair. 'It was definitely someone who knew her …' she began. Bridget didn't give away any direct evidence, but she sailed as close to the wind as she could, and Andrea lapped it up.

'Thank you,' the estate agent said when Bridget had finished. While she'd been telling her tale, Bridget had studied the woman. Her hair was immaculate, but it didn't move like hair should. It couldn't be a wig, could it? Either that or Andrea had shares in a hairspray company.

When she'd thought for a moment, Andrea shuffled in her seat and adjusted her skirt. 'Well I can tell you one thing, Bridget: the vicar would be a very happy woman if she weren't in mourning.' She pressed her lips together and leaned forwards. 'This is the only house I've ever seen which comes with an attached school. St Peter's Primary is part of School House, or vice versa. It's on a thousand-year lease, but even so. The whole lot will now go into a trust for the benefit of the school, and I'm telling you this because the governors will have had a letter from Mr Patrick this morning.'

Andrea sat back and smiled.

'Who's Mr Patrick when he's at home?'

'Mr Carter's son, of course. He runs the estate agency and handles residential property law.'

That muddied the waters no end, and Bridget didn't know what to make of the news. It wasn't even what she'd come in for, but it gave her an opening. 'And presumably one of the Carters is executor.' Andrea nodded. 'And you'll want it sorted quickly, won't you? That's you personally, not the firm, because you won't get sales commission otherwise. You have nothing to gain from a court case delaying things because at least three of the suspects are school governors, and there could be a challenge to the will.'

'Where are you going with this?'

Bridget raised the stakes by sliding over a small black skull with plastic gemstone eyes, a gift from Natalie. Totally kitsch, but totally lovable. Just like Natalie. She prised off the bottom to reveal the USB connector. 'It's a flash drive. Drop the pictures of the kitchen and any larder cupboards on it.'

Andrea rested her hands on the desk, about six inches away from the skull. 'That would be deeply unprofessional.'

Bridget put a stack of vouchers next to the skull. 'Free coffees. The office will think you're Mother Christmas.'

Andrea snorted. 'No chance of that. I'll take the vouchers, but that's not going to sweeten the pot.' She leaned even further forwards, and Bridget did the same. 'What I want is for you to become Lady Felicia's best friend. She could do with one.'

'I'll take your word for it. I cannot see how on earth that's gonna happen, but if it did, what do you want from *her*?'

'Her husband's residential lettings business. Don't ask why we don't already have it, because it's a long story.'

'Isn't that up to Perry Lockwood?'

She raised her eyebrows. 'That would be even better, but I wouldn't force him on anyone.' She grimaced at something and continued, 'I'm not asking for a guarantee, just your best shot.'

Bridget hesitated. She had already agreed to pay Josie cash in hand and recruited Kat to be her unwitting secret agent, and now here was Andrea asking her to join in the country maypole dance and work her non-existent charms on Perry Lockwood. She shook her head. 'I can't do that. It's not that I *won't*, I just can't. If I thought I had that sort of power over men, I'd use it to promote world peace, but you're barking up the wrong tree there.'

'You're a woman. Of course you have power over men.'

The pain was a reflexive stab. *Don't go there,* warned her inner therapist. She smiled at Andrea. 'How about I just owe you a favour, eh? It's no skin off your nose.'

'Deal.'

The vouchers disappeared into a drawer, and seconds later the red eyes of the skull were flashing brightly as the drive was accessed, written to, and ejected. 'Nice to meet you properly,' said Andrea when she slid it back.

'And you. Thanks for that.'

Chapter 22

Lucy had learnt from bitter experience in Southport that you have to be careful when dealing with senior customers who identify as senior customers. A lot don't, and wouldn't dream of turning up early for a special offer, but for the ones who did …

At eleven o'clock, there was a small queue of grey-haired patrons at the counter, and Lucy picked up the weighted sign which said *Senior Special Over*. She carried it to the end of the line and placed it beyond the last customer. She wasn't sure which provoked more complaints: denying discounts to those already here or offering them to those who arrived late.

She was starting to clear the empties when Bridget bustled back in with a laptop under her arm. 'Got it!' she declared.

'Got what? And did you get the glasses?'

'Safely in the van. They can wait. Let's see what the crime scene looks like.'

'Eh?'

Lucy trailed Bridget into the kitchen and gave a shrug to Katarina on the way past. She stopped to load her tray into the dishwasher, and by the time she'd finished, Bridget had the computer up and running. Lucy wiped her hands and found Bridget staring at a country kitchen with oak doors and black granite worktops. 'What on earth is this, and where did you get it?'

'It's the kitchen at School House, and don't ask how I got it.'

Lucy's mouth dropped open. 'Please tell me these are not from HOLMES2.'

Some of Tom's jargon had rubbed off on Lucy, including the computer system used for Large Major Enquiries, a wonderful bit of applied tautology to get the acronym *HOLMES2*.

'Give over,' said Bridget. She sighed. 'If you must know, they're from Carter's Estates. There's loads, but they're all pretty similar, just different angles.'

'What is this going to tell you? It's been tidied and staged. On the day of the Bake Off, it would be covered in jars and ingredients.'

'I know that. Don't forget, someone put *liquid* amygdalin into her food. It wasn't put into dry ingredients, was it? I needed to see what sort of kitchen it was – social or catering. And there's the answer: look at the size of the place. It must take up half of the house.'

Bridget was right. The kitchen was spacious, accommodated a classic farmhouse kitchen table, and ran through to a south-facing conservatory. Whoever had visited Millie on the day of the Bake Off would have spent their time in here. They could easily have come with a distraction prepared – *Could I borrow that book? Here's the paperwork you wanted …* Anything to get Millie out of the room. Not even that: anything to get her back turned for long enough to pour the poison into … what? What would disguise the flavour. Did it have a flavour?

'Does amygdalin have a flavour?'

'No. The molecules are too big to have flavour on their own, but there's always some degradation to benzaldehyde, and that's what smells of bitter almonds.'

Lucy scanned around the kitchen. 'Those units would have to go. They'd need a completely new kitchen for the sort of money they'd be asking. Sink's in the wrong place, too.'

'What are you like! We're murderer-hunting, not house-hunting. Focus, girl.'

Focus. Right. Slight bitter flavour. 'Zoom in on the coffee machine.'

Bridget did so. It was a top-of-the-range domestic model and worth more than any other appliance – even more than the Artisan KitchenAid in off-white. Lucy would only consider having a red one in *her* kitchen. Iconic doesn't come into it. Having a shiny new KitchenAid might even tempt her to learn how to bake …

'You're right,' said Bridget, maintaining the focus that Lucy was struggling with. 'That coffee machine is clean, but look how discoloured it is round the drip tray. That's seen a lot of use.'

'Mmm.' And then she saw it. 'Those mugs,' said Lucy. 'Look at them!'

'*Changing Lives One Class at a Time,*' said Bridget, reading the message on one of the mugs. 'End of year present. Must have loads tucked away.'

'Yes, but what about the one just behind it.'

The *Changing Lives* mug was half hiding another, and Bridget tried to read it. 'Teachers have more … in their … I don't get it.'

'*Teachers have more lead in their pencils,*' supplied Lucy.

'That's gross. And tasteless. Left over from when she was married to Feargal, d'you think?'

'No. It's too new, way too new. It's not something a parent would give either. Not in a primary school, anyway, and certainly not to a woman.'

'You should have tried my school.'

'I think that Millie bought it for a boyfriend, and a recent one at that: she left it out because that's the one in use.'

'Who on earth buys something like *that*?' asked Bridget aghast.

'Someone in a new relationship,' said Lucy with some indignation. 'Just after Tom and I hooked up, I was tempted to buy him a *Feel My Truncheon* T-shirt.'

There was an ominous pause. Lucy had forgotten herself again, and now she would pay for it. Bridget turned slowly and stared at her. From the look on her face, Bridget was channelling a great aunt of some vintage. 'I am so glad you didn't, Lucy. I might never have spoken to you again.' She paused. 'You're right, though, and I discovered something else this morning: there's a back way in from the school grounds. I think we need to add Nathan Frost to the list, don't you?'

Lucy was dubious, but she could see Bridget's point. The St Peter's headteacher, Nathan Frost, was the only male member of staff. Unless Millie had been dating someone from outside the village, of course. But why hide it? No one had mentioned a boyfriend or lover, and there would be a strong imperative to keep an in-house relationship quiet.

Bridget interrupted her thoughts by asking a sensible question. 'Liz and the team will have been all over Millie's phone records. If she's having a relationship, there will be evidence. Do you think they know who? It could be crucial. This is the second day since they changed their focus from what happened in the tent, and they're bound to have made some progress.' She slapped her hand on the stainless steel counter. 'We need to know what they're thinking.'

'Not gonna happen. They won't tell, and I won't ask.'

'Oi! You two! I could do with a hand out here,' said Kat from the doorway.

Bridget looked unhappy and frustrated. She made fists of her hands, then slammed down the lid of her laptop. 'Sorry, Kat. On our way.' She stood up and pushed the stool away. 'I don't want access to HOLMES2, Luce. I just want a chat. Is there nothing you can do?'

Lucy sighed. She'd been dreading this moment, dreading being forced to choose between her loyalty to Bridget and her loyalty to Tom. It was a harsh decision at the best of times, but with Tom away in York and about to lose his grandfather …

Over the next hour, Bridget slowly updated Lucy with the other news about School House and what Millie Easterby had done in her will.

'But who benefits from that?' asked Lucy during a shared moment at the coffee machine.

'Everyone from the school, I reckon. If Millie had gone ahead and sold the house on the open market, it would have opened up a can of worms for the school, and everyone from the school would know about the situation, even if Rev Deb played dumb with you about it. I think this clears Perry one hundred per cent. The Dark Side would rather Millie alive and desperate for cash, than dead and handing everything over to the Angels.' She gave a savage twist to the steamer valve, and Lucy winced. Engineer callouts to these machines were astronomically expensive, and heavy-handed abuse was not covered under warranty.

Having shown the steamer who was boss, Bridget continued, 'Feargal was on the CCTV, too. He doesn't benefit financially, but revenge and bitterness are definitely motives for him. He is not ruled out, and we've left it too long. We need to see him. Well, you do.'

'Why me?'

'Did you not see the way he was eyeing you up at the Bake Off?'

'He only had eyes for Millie!'

Bridget smiled innocently. Or tried to. Bridget didn't really do *innocent* very well. 'Maybe you remind him of her.'

Lucy put her hands on hips. 'I am not going alone to visit a potential murderer who thinks I look like his ex-wife, which I don't by the way.'

Bridget was unmoved. 'Treat him like one of the fairies: just don't eat or drink anything. Midland Terrace is up from the church. Good luck.'

Lucy flinched back at the mention of *fairies*. She did not want to go there, metaphorically speaking, nor did she want to go to Midland Terrace in real life. On the other hand … talking of the *Fae*, to use their preferred name, reminded her of something.

She picked up a toasted teacake and got ready to deliver it. 'You can go see Feargal. I'm going to summon Barney Rubble and get him to spill the beans.'

'How the flip are you gonna do that?'

'Judicious application of blackmail. Show you in a minute.'

She delivered the teacake and shuffled through her phone on the way back to the counter, earning herself a dark look from Kat in the process. She found what she wanted and showed it to Bridget.

'Oh my good God. Who is he dancing with, and has his girlfriend seen this?'

It was a scene from The Wedding. Detective Constable Barney Smith was dressed in an Indian outfit and was getting rather close to a curvy young woman with auburn hair in an emerald green tunic and trousers. Barney's blonde girlfriend was nowhere to be seen.

'She's one of the beauty team,' said Lucy, forgetting that this was supposed to be a secret.

'Team? There was a *team* of beauticians?'

'Mostly hairdressing,' said Lucy dismissively. 'This is Alicia, and she danced with everyone, I think. Can't remember who she ended up with. What happened after the happy couple disappeared is all a bit vague.' She frowned. 'Did I see her with two blokes at the same time? Whatever. It's just that Barney was more enthusiastic about dancing with her than the others. Watch this bit.'

'Ouch. His girlfriend – what's her name? Erin? She won't like that one bit. The way she's nibbling his ear …'

'It brought him to his senses, I think. I'll send him a link to it and offer free coffee this afternoon. If he's around.'

Feargal Hulme was every inch the divorced, bereaved, unemployed man when he answered the door. From his unshaven face to his stained dressing gown (at half past two in the afternoon), from his bird's-nest hair to his hungover breath, there was no part of Feargal Hulme that was not a wreck. Even his smile had deserted him. Bridget suddenly wished that she'd hated Millie Easterby, then she could walk away and leave this man to grieve in peace.

'Bridget,' he said, spurting out the word like a burp of memory. 'Don't you look different? Very on brand, if I may say so.' He frowned. 'Is everything okay?'

'With me, yes. I'm sorry to disturb you, Feargal, but I didn't think we should ignore you or pretend you don't exist.'

'I feel like I don't exist. You're right about that much.'

'I'm really sorry about Millie. Totally.'

He stepped closer to the door, perhaps to get a better look, then the afternoon sun hit his eyes. 'Oh God, I can't cope with that. If you promise to make me coffee, will you come in?'

'I've got one in the van for you, made not two minutes ago. If that isn't sleeping with the enemy.'

'Ouch. I can see you're sorry about Mills, but you're not sorry about the Mill. If you see what I mean.' The smile sputtered into life, then died, like Bridget's first car used to. 'Ach, come on in why don't you?' He disappeared, leaving the door open, and Bridget dodged back to the van to retrieve the strong Americano.

Midland Terrace was a run of five narrow redbrick homes, the clue to their name being given by a stone inset above the door of number three – *Midland Railway Company 1867*. When Bridget got inside, she discovered that very little had been done to number four during the hundred-plus years since its construction beyond rewiring and the erection of a rear extension for a galley kitchen. A much-abused galley kitchen in Bridget's eyes.

She gave thanks that she didn't have to rescue Feargal from what had happened here. Her skin tingled at some of the things lurking in bowls on the worktop. Whatever else he'd been doing since Saturday, cleaning up after the Bake Off hadn't been one of them. Even the food he must have retrieved from the tent yesterday had just been left to fester.

'Here you go,' she said, handing over the coffee.

He popped the lid and sniffed. 'You have no idea how good that smells.' He sniffed again. 'You probably do, don't you? I hope your supplier is more generous with credit than mine was.' He sipped the coffee to check the temperature, then slurped a good third of it.

'We can buy in bulk,' said Bridget apologetically. 'Makes it easier. There's lots of savings when you're buying for multiple premises.'

'And when you're backed by someone with deep pockets.' He took another slurp, and a little life returned to his eyes. 'There's me being bitter, and this coffee is anything but. Unlike mine, as several people a week told me, and repeated it on Tripadvisor.'

He took a deep breath, deep enough to loosen the cord on his dressing gown. *Please let him be wearing something underneath,* prayed Bridget. He caught the garment and pulled it tight with one hand. 'I'd say I'll get dressed, but that really needs a shower first, and you've not come for that long.' He paused. 'Have you?'

'I came to say hello and offer my condolences.'

He tied the dressing gown cord with a proper bow and lifted a tea towel from a baking tray. He sniffed the contents and grunted. 'Still good.' He pulled out a lump of flapjack and stuffed it in his mouth. From round the sticky mess, he muttered, 'So how's it going, Bridget? How's Kat getting on?'

'Fine so far. Kat's been brilliant. You trained her well, and we couldn't have got off to such a start without her.'

He washed down the flapjack with the last of the coffee and put down the cup. 'Flatterer. Ach, she's a good kid and no mistake. I really do wish you well, you know, and if the coffee is this good, I'll be up to scrounge some. Obviously I can't afford to actually *buy* any at the moment.'

Bridget was running out of things to say, so she opted for a platitude. 'I'm sure you'll be back on your feet soon.'

'I always have before, but it doesn't get any easier, you know. Losing the business *and* Millie in one week is a whole heap of shit, that's for sure.' He shook his head. 'Right. Enough self-pity for one day. Thanks for coming, Bridget. As soon as you've gone, I'll get my arse into gear. For one thing, it's about time I found a lawyer.'

'Oh? What for?'

'Because I spent a long time last night making a "witness statement" to the girls in blue, and they were not impressed that I'd failed to mention my visit to School House during my first interview with them.' His brain was waking up now. 'You wouldn't happen to know anything about that, would you? Is that why you're here? They showed me the shop CCTV, and what they've seen, Kat will have seen, and for all I love her, that girl won't have hesitated to show you as well.'

Bridget wasn't going to admit to being the one who'd uncovered the evidence, but she couldn't deny knowing something. 'Yes, as it happens. I've seen the whole thing.'

She looked round the kitchen again, and this time he watched her face as she did so. 'Tell me, Feargal, do you have any friends in Byford? Real friends?' she asked.

'I suppose it is a bit obvious, isn't it? Clever you: now that I'm not one of the Angels, friends are hard to come by. Edwin and Perry have been good to me, but I burnt a lot of bridges when I got kicked out of School House, and ever since then, I've been working so fecking *hard* that I've not had time to go to the quiz, to join a five-a-side team or do any of the other things that men are supposed to do to find friends and look after their mental health.'

Bridget pointed to a jar that was hidden behind a dirty mixer bowl. Shudder. 'Are they preserved cherries?'

He looked startled. 'Are you actually *working* for the cops, Bridget? They took half a dozen samples yesterday, and I'm beginning to kick myself that I didn't ask for a warrant first. Then they dragged me down to the nick and asked me about fecking *cherries*. Are you? Working for the cops?'

'Absolutely not, and if you weren't a suspect, I'd ask you to wash your mouth out for suggesting it. Look, Feargal, I'm with you on this one. I'm from the Dark Side, but I'm batting for Millie. And for you. All of Rev Deb's lot will point the finger firmly in your direction, so help me out here, eh? What happened when you went to Millie's on Saturday morning?'

'If you seriously want me to answer that question, you'll have to wait until I've had a shower.'

'Have you got any rubber gloves? If you have, I'll wait.'

Chapter 23

Detective Constable Barnabas Smith, known to all as *Barney Rubble,* stared morosely into his cup of tea. 'Nothing happened, you know,' he said.

Lucy patted his hand comfortingly. 'I know, Barney, and I wouldn't *dream* of telling Erin about it. Honestly.'

Barney used to play rugby. He still had the shoulders for it, and how no one had managed to tie him down before now was a mystery to Lucy. Whatever the reason, he'd been well and truly hooked by Erin, and also *on the hook* for this video. 'I just thought it was a bit of fun, that's all,' she said calmingly. 'I only got sent it the other day, and I know you've been busy.'

Panic flared in his eyes. 'Who sent it? Who else knows?'

'Don't worry. It came from one of Tara Doyle's people, and Tara doesn't know you from Adam. She only got to see it recently, and she knew that I'd find it ... amusing. She won't pass it on to anyone else.'

He tried to muster some defiance. 'I've heard the stories, Lucy. The next time you all get drunk, it'll be on WhatsApp before you know it.'

Unfortunately there was more than a grain of truth in that: it was how the pictures of Mina and the stripper had got into circulation. 'If I had something to take my mind off it, Barney, the video might get lost.'

He looked suspicious – cornered, yes, but definitely suspicious. 'Such as what?'

'Well, look at this way. The Sheriff's going to be out of town for a while, I'm afraid.'

The whole station called Tom the *Sheriff,* even though none but Elaine had known him when he got the nickname. He even had a mug with a star on it to prove he didn't mind. Of course he did really mind, but the alternatives were much, much worse.

'How is he?' asked Barney. 'It's his granddad, isn't it?'

'Yeah,' she sighed. 'Not good, I'm afraid. Not unexpected, but not good either.'

'Pass on my regards if you get a chance.'

'Of course.' She smiled at him. 'If Tom were here, he wouldn't *dream* of interfering in the case, would he?'

Barney knew the answer, and he knew the answer was no. He was still suspicious, though. He had the look of a bull about to be led by the nose. Maybe this was what it was like all the time with Erin. 'No,' he said eventually.

'But he might pop into the Commander's office and say *How's the case going?* mightn't he?'

This time the answer was yes. 'Yes.'

'So imagine that I'm Tom and you're Allister. How's the case going?'

This was a different kettle of fish altogether. Barney knew that Tom wouldn't *ask* how the case was going, and Barney knew that he didn't have the authority to answer on Ross's behalf. Lucy was banking on him choosing the least worst option, and that's what he did.

'Well, I think that the Commander *might* tell the Sheriff that we've discovered that Millie Easterby was in a relationship with her boss, Nathan Frost the headteacher. A relationship that he is most anxious *not* to become public knowledge. We've also analysed all the gluten-free cereals in the house, which turned out to be a waste of time.' He paused and fixed her with a knowing look. 'At this point, the Sheriff would have questions but he wouldn't ask them, would he?'

Touché, thought Lucy. Barney was right: unless her name came up in the enquiry, Tom would ask nothing and say nothing.

'If it were me,' continued Barney, 'I'd desperately want to know if we tested the crockery, too. We would have done, but the dishwasher had been filled and set to run before Millie left the house.'

Lucy unlocked her phone and passed it to Barney. With clumsy but determined swipes, he consigned the video of himself and the hairdresser to the digital crematorium.

'Thanks for the tea,' he said as he returned the phone. 'Liz has been mithering to come in here since you opened. I guess it's safe enough.'

'Thanks, Barney, and don't worry: this conversation never happened.'

Bridget confined herself to emptying, tidying and putting things to soak rather than doing any actual cleaning or washing up. For one thing, Feargal only had disposable gloves to hand, and they conduct heat way too effectively for serious cleaning. When it comes to having a good scrub, you can't beat yellow Marigolds.

Nevertheless, the kitchen looked a lot better when he returned, and Bridget even had two mugs of tea brewing. He entered the kitchen still towelling his hair, and there were damp patches already soaking through the hastily thrown on T-shirt. She tried not to think of the damp jeans and the possibility of chafing.

'You are amazing,' he said. 'Thank you. I woulda got it done today, honest. Talking to the Guards was a real wake-up call, I'm telling you.'

His eyes were alive, but still bloodshot. 'Were you drinking on your own last night, Feargal?' she asked.

He looked at his bare feet. 'Not so much drinking, more *topping up* after the police let me go. I carried on till I finished the bottle, and I'm not going back to the shop to buy any more until I've cleaned up properly and found meself a lawyer. Obviously, all the decent ones are taken by the powers that be in the village.'

'Oh? I met someone this morning who might be your perfect match: Abigail Tennant of McEwan and Co on the market square.'

He grunted. 'They must be new. Weren't around when I got divorced. You reckon she could go ten rounds with DS Swindlehurst?'

Bridget tried desperately to keep the image at bay. And failed. Totally inappropriately she was assaulted with a vision of Abigail's sharp-elbowed silhouette and Liz's formidable bulk entering the boxing ring. She shook her head to clear it. 'It would be a points decision, I'm sure. Unless Liz got her cornered, then the seconds would need a big sponge.'

He leaned back. 'You've taken that metaphor a lot further than I would have. Good to know her name, though, and I'll certainly need someone *in my corner*. As it were.' He gave a wry smile. 'I've been here for years. As long as your man Perry or his lordship the Duke. I'm still the outsider, though.'

'I thought about elocution lessons once, you know,' said Bridget.

'You're joking!'

'Course I'm bleeding joking. Who wants to fit in when you can be yourself? Right. Tell me about Saturday morning.'

He removed the tea bags and fired them into the bin with a practised flick of the wrist, then went to the fridge and took out a bottle of milk.

'Stop!' said Bridget. 'You are not putting that in my tea.'

'What? I've only had it since Monday.'

'It's *unpasteurised*!'

'And all the better for it. Go on. Live a little, eh?'

'That stuff is *alive*. It's a white soup of bovine bacteria. Tell me you didn't used to serve it at Miller's Rest.'

'We did, for a bit. Then we had to start stocking all the non-dairy crap and there wasn't room in the fridge. We always used it at home, though, and we both still do.' He paused. 'Did.'

'If you've got no proper stuff, I'll take it black.'

'Suit yourself.'

He poured his own milk and slid Bridget's mug along the counter. The one thing she had cleaned was a section of the worktop so that she could lean on it, which she now did.

'You know that Millie only stepped in to the Bake Off at the last minute, right?' he began.

'Someone did say, but no, I don't know the story.'

'It was supposed to be Fliss herself until the weekend before, not that I've ever heard of her cooking anything except the books at Ford Mill. That woman went straight from living on takeout pizza as an "actress" to employing a cook-housekeeper when she married Edwin.'

'And what's wrong with that?' said Bridget, blowing on her tea. 'Why should she have to do the cooking?'

'Fair point. Anyway, Fliss dropped out the week before when she found out that she was going to be visited by Jorie Lutworth and Little

Gidding, and that she had to prove she'd made everything herself. No way would Lady Felicia open herself to scrutiny like that.'

'Who's *Little Gidding*? Do you mean the vicar?'

'Sorry. English poetry in-joke. TS Eliot wrote a poem called "Little Gidding", and it's big on the Anglican Church.' A twinkle came into his eyes. 'Scrutiny by the vicar wasn't the only reason Fliss dropped out: she discovered that you'd be one of the judges.'

What was that about? 'I only met her once! What's she got against me?'

'She decided that you were too much of a free spirit to be bought off. According to Perry.'

Bridget was used to strange looks and people pointing at her. Came with the territory. What she found disconcerting was that a whole chunk of the village might be talking about her, and she redoubled her determination to appoint a branch manager for Ford Mill and get out of Dodge asap.

'That is very disturbing,' she said.

'You get used to it. Millie had a week to get her shit together and enter the competition, and of course she put her back properly into it, and when she needed a helping hand …' He trailed off, lost in memory. His face twisted into a grimace, and he continued with a snort. 'When she needed a helping hand, she called the one sap who couldn't say no and who wouldn't report her to the vicar. That would be me.'

Bridget couldn't believe it. Millie cheating? Feargal helping her? 'But you were a competitor, too!'

'Ah, Bridget, I've bad news for you: the world doesn't always play by the rules.'

Anger fought with embarrassment. Or maybe it was anger trying to defy the guilt that snatched at her insides. 'You don't need to tell me that. Then again, a man who'd forge his wife's signature wouldn't think twice about cheating at a village baking competition.'

He flinched, then slowly put his tea down. 'So they've got to you already, have they? Blame the Irishman. Doesn't ever change.'

She pushed off from the worktop and jabbed a finger at him. 'Are you deaf, soft lad? Did you not hear my last name? *Gorrigan* is about as Irish as you can get, and my grandfather lived up to every Irish cliché in the book, including drinking himself to death. Cut the crap and tell me what you did and when you did it.'

Feargal didn't answer the question she thought she'd asked him. She thought she'd asked him to talk about baking, but that wasn't what he'd heard. Guilt is a very powerful thing.

'I did it for our dream, Bridget! We had no chance without that extra loan. She couldn't see that building a business for our future and our children's future was more important than her Auntie's obsession with a fecking school! Isn't that exactly what Lucy's doing? Building a business for the future?' He ran out of steam. 'And look at me now, eh?'

Was there a grain of truth in Feargal's oyster of self-deception? Could he have been fighting against the dead hand of Temperance Easterby's vision for Millie's future? And if he was, did it make the slightest difference?

Bridget was wearing a comfier pair of jeans today, with plenty of room in the back pockets for her order pad and pen. She took them out and said, 'Take it from Friday night? What did you do and when did you do it?'

'Did you throw any papers away when you tidied up?'

'No. I put them all together under the bread bin.'

He fished out a miscellaneous selection of leaflets, printed recipes and A4 lined paper from where Bridget had tidied it and quickly sorted out a couple of hand-written sheets. 'Have a look.'

Bridget looked, and she realised that you could frame these documents as a testament to Feargal and Millie's characters. One was neat, ordered and legible; the other belonged to Feargal. 'How did you get to be a teacher?' asked Bridget. 'I've seen doctors with neater writing. If the kids you taught learned to write like you, the nation's doomed.'

He laughed. 'Thankfully I was not called on to do that. I was a high school English teacher, for my sins, so they could write before they got to me. In theory. I taught at Lancaster until we set up the Miller's Rest.'

Bridget grunted. 'What am I looking for?'

'I co-ordinated our menus so that I could leave stuff to cool and nip down to help her out. And yes, some of it I did for her. See there? There's Madeira cake on both menus, and I baked it. She iced hers, or she was going to, and I used mine as part of a cake smorgasbord.'

She gave him a blank look.

'Never mind. The point is that I baked on Friday afternoon, and I had my scrutiny visit from Debs during school hours. As soon as the bell went, I nipped down to School House and mucked in with Millie.' He drifted off and looked down the hall towards the front door. 'At least we had one happy moment together.'

She gave him a second to come back from his reverie, then asked, 'Did you know that she was going to put School House on the market?'

He snorted. 'I know you won't believe me, but I didn't. First I heard of it was when the big scary detective put it to me. Things went downhill from there, I'm telling you.'

Bridget had a tick list of questions and wrote *Ignorant????* next to *Sale of S.House*. While she wrote, she said, 'Barney Smith's not really scary. He's a teddy bear at heart.'

'It wasn't him. Saw him in the tent on Saturday. No, it was that ogre DS Swindlehurst. I would not like to meet her on a dark night.'

'Liz isn't *that* big,' said Bridget. Feargal's eyebrows went up, but he didn't say anything. *No. Not the image of Liz in the boxing ring again. And definitely not with me wearing silk shorts ...* To take his mind off any thoughts about the relative size of Liz vs herself, she added, 'But yeah, she can totally do scary.'

And then the flashback. *And on a dark night, she'd still be a woman and you'd be a man. There would be no contest.*

She blinked her eyes closed while he slurped his tea and she took a cleansing breath. 'What else did Liz ask you?' she said when she'd stabilised herself.

'Like I said, it all went downhill. I was still trying to deny knowing about Mills putting the house up for sale when your pal Liz hit me with a secret boyfriend.' He studied her face. 'You're not surprised! You knew!' He squared his shoulders. 'Did they tell you? Did anyone else tell you?'

'No,' said Bridget hastily. 'We worked it out for ourselves. Did you really know nothing? Didn't anyone say anything in the café? They do like to gossip.'

'Tell me about it. What you might not know yet is that they have ways of turning the knife into you. If anyone knew about this "secret boyfriend" they wouldn't discuss it directly. What they'd have done is say things like *Millie looks so much happier recently* or *Millie has a glow in her cheeks these days*.' He gave a hollow laugh. 'Now I look back, the sale of the house and the alleged boyfriend explains an awful lot, but I was too drunk for it to sink in last night.'

The faraway look returned to his eyes. 'What do you mean?' prompted Bridget.

'Sorry. I was thinking about Millie and how nice she was on Friday. For an hour, it was like the old times: me and her against the world, fighting our corner in the Bake Off. You know, Bridey, I think she wanted to say goodbye, like she knew it would never be the same again.'

Bridget did *not* like being called *Bridey*. She let him off this time.

'And I did ask about the mortgage,' he continued. 'Right at the end we shared a glass of wine and she asked how I felt about leaving Miller's Rest. I told her it was water under the bridge for me and asked how she was doing. She told me she was going to sort it. I thought she meant she was going to consolidate her debts in a new mortgage.' He shrugged. 'That was it.'

'And on Saturday?'

'I only nipped in for a minute. Ten minutes tops. I just wanted to drop off some sausage rolls, make sure that she was okay and that she'd finished most of the prep, and she had. If Mills had any faults, one of them would be a tendency to perfectionism. There were a couple of corners cut, but she was all ready to start baking.'

'Did you eat or drink anything together?'

'Nope. Nothing. I did take a full flask of Mike's Magic Milk, but that's it. She put it in the fridge, but didn't touch it.'

'Thanks, Feargal. I'm sorry to intrude, really I am.'

'No, Bridget, thank you. Dragging me out of my pit did me a favour, and going through it all again helps me fix it in my head for when I have to testify in my own defence.'

'It won't come to that. Not if I can help it.'

'I love your confidence. Wish I felt the same. Perhaps this Tennant girl can protect me with her mighty shield of justice.'

'Pop in to Caffè Milano when you're ready, Feargal. It might help you exorcise a few ghosts.'

'A few? I'll ask the Archbishop to join me, shall I? It'll take more than a free coffee to exorcise my ghosts or banish my demons.' He paused. 'I do get at least one free coffee, right?'

'And a muffin if you've had a shower first. I'll see myself out and let you get started on the washing up.'

Chapter 24

Katarina cracked when Lucy got a message from Bridget saying that she was on her way back from Feargal's.

'How is it that you two get to use your phones all the time but Bridget makes me put mine in the kitchen!'

Lucy looked up from typing her reply. 'Nothing to do with me.'

'But you're the boss!'

'I know,' she said, putting all the weight of the world into her sigh. She sent the reply and gave the young barista a mischievous grin. 'Just be thankful that I used my omnipotent powers to stop Bridget designing the staff uniforms.'

Katarina glared at her for a second, then stropped into the kitchen, where she no doubt sent a *woe is me* message to someone. Lucy glanced at the foyer: no one was on the radar, so she picked up a large tray and headed out to clean up.

She was on her way back with the first load when Bridget appeared. Lucy continued into the kitchen, and Bridget followed. Yup, Kat was on her phone. Lucy coughed loudly, and Kat left them alone (after tucking her phone into her apron).

'Well?' said Lucy.

'I don't know,' said Bridget after she'd gone through the headlines of her meeting with the rather tasty Feargal Hulme. 'He's a mess alright, but he's got charm coming out of him like sweat in a sauna.'

'Euw.'

'I know. It's nice to experience, but when you step back a bit … He could easily be channelling his grief into denial. I've seen it before. In other contexts, obviously.'

'Hmm.' Lucy had been waiting patiently to share her *yes* moment. 'Well I was right: Barney confirmed that Nathan Frost was Millie's boyfriend-slash-lover,' she announced with triumph.

Bridget offered a fist bump. 'You go girl. Well done, Miss Junior Detective.'

Lucy bumped back and sighed. They still knew very little, really. 'The only thing he let slip that we didn't suspect was that Nathan is desperate for their involvement to stay a secret. Did Feargal really not know?'

'Like I said: he could be lying. If I had to put money on it, I'd say he really didn't know *who* the other guy was, and I certainly didn't tell him. Whether he's accepted that there *was* another man is another question, and whether he goes looking for him is another matter. I'm sure he's got his own version of Kat's list. Oops …'

Bridget looked alarmed. And guilty. 'What?' insisted Lucy. 'Tell me.'

Bridge pulled a piece of paper from the fold of her order pad. 'Kat gave me a list of all the single homeowners or renters in the village. Here.'

Lucy glanced at the list. 'I don't know which is the most disturbing thing here: the fact that the list is so short, the fact that she gave it to you, or the fact that she's put a ring round Perry's name.' She stared at Bridget. 'It was Kat who did that, wasn't it?'

'Might have been. Look, Luce, how do we get to see Nathan Frost? He's got to be next.'

Lucy put her finger to her lips, then jumped sideways and turned towards the doorway. Her ballet teacher would have been proud. Hypercritical, but proud. As expected, Kat was standing by the opening, listening to their every word, and like a naughty child, she scuttled out of sight.

'Kat! Any sign of the after-school rush?'

Katarina shuffled back. 'Not yet.'

'Have you got Nathan Frost's number?'

'Why would I have the headteacher's number? That's gross.'

'Who do you know who would have it and would also give it over with no questions asked?'

'Umm … Dad. Well, he'd give me the number, then ask questions when I got home. I can deal with Dad, no problem.'

Lucy turned back to Bridget. 'Come on. Let's give Kat a break. She can text me the number.'

'She can. How are you gonna get to him? Won't they be having an emergency governors' meeting after that solicitor's letter? They've just been told that they've inherited a house, for goodness' sake.'

Lucy thought for a moment. 'You know I said we should consider starting a mobile coffee van?'

'Yeah, and I told you that it was one of Mina Desai's less sensible ideas. Let's try to make the bricks and mortar outlets work first.'

'I'm going to call Nathan and tell him that I'll drop a full order round in an hour. On the house. As a pilot for our delivery service.'

'You're mad. If you start doing delivered takeout, people round here will expect hot chocolate at bedtime and complain if they can't get it.'

'It's a pilot! A trial.'

'Whatever. You do know that schools have staff rooms with kettles and fridges with milk. They don't need a delivery, and he won't let you near the place.'

'Oh he will. Especially when I tell him that I could get his mug back from School House. And it's the perfect time for you to visit the Old Rectory.'

'Why?'

'Because Anya Calvert is the governor, so Dom will be at home with the kids.'

'How's that gonna help? And you should see him, not me.'

'Can't,' said Lucy with some finality. 'I'd have too much house envy. You have no idea what it's like living out of a suitcase for months.'

'You are bonkers, d'you know that?'

'Yes, and you love me for it, Bridget.' Lucy's phone pinged, and she stabbed the screen to add Nathan Frost as a contact, then pressed Call before Bridget could talk her out of it.

It took rather more persuasion than Lucy had anticipated to get herself admission to St Peter's School. Nathan Frost had simply pulled a curtain over the conversation at first, and Lucy had been forced to come *very* close to issuing a direct threat, and that was not her style at all. In the end, she thought he'd agreed to see her more to get her off the phone than anything else, a point he made when he let her into the reception area soon afterwards.

'You weren't going to say no, were you? The other governors will be here shortly, so make it quick.'

When Lucy had met Nathan at the Bake Off, she'd got the impression of a man with a strong sense of his own position in the village. Deborah Giddings had smarmed all over him, and he'd handed out the refreshments like he was doing them a favour, not providing a service. He wasn't physically imposing, but he carried himself with confidence, and he made the rough cotton patch-pocket jacket look *almost* fashionable.

'Here,' she said. 'On the house. Extra fuel for you.'

Nathan had declined the coffee delivery for the governors outright, but Lucy simply couldn't turn up with nothing. It was against her principles. She offered him the large takeout cup and said, 'Strong black. I'm sure you've got milk here if you need it.'

He accepted the cup and said, 'This way.'

The staff room at St Peter's was tiny, as you'd expect, though it did have the sink and kettle that Bridget had predicted, along with half a dozen mugs and a tin of biscuits set out ready for the governors. Nathan opened the fridge and took out some milk, adding a generous splash to his coffee. Lucy shuddered: how could the man taste it like that?

He carried on into an equally tiny office, and immediately apologised. 'Sorry for the tight squeeze. The architect wasn't going to include a head's office at all until someone pointed out that there had to be somewhere secure to keep records and have confidential interviews. You won't find it as hard to sit down as some of our larger parents.'

She paused a second. 'Well at least you didn't offer me one of the kids' chairs. I'm not *that* short, you know.'

'Of course not. Sorry. And thanks for the coffee, by the way. I shall definitely stroll up to Ford Mill in the near future.' He smiled when he said it, then turned the smile off. 'What you hinted on the phone is a serious matter, Lucy. Another reason to ask for this discussion to take place in private. What went on between Millie and me was just that – between us. She didn't tell anyone, and neither did I, so how did you know about it? We've all heard who your boyfriend is.'

'You may have heard of him, but you haven't met him. Tom would never disclose information like that, nor would his team. I was half joking about your "Lead in the pencil" mug, Nathan, but that's how we found out. It couldn't be anyone else.'

He looked annoyed. Annoyed and upset. He drank more coffee and put his arms on the desk. 'Well spotted. So what? Why is it any of your business? We're oversubscribed here, you know. I've had parents try to bribe the school, and one even tried to dig up some dirt on me at my last school. They failed, by the way, because there was no dirt and because the school told me what they were doing. You don't have children, so you're not blackmailing me into admitting them.' He nodded to himself. 'Then why are you here?'

It was the most direct challenge yet, and Lucy had no intention of telling the truth. Anything but. This was Bridget's crusade, so she had no hesitation in dropping her friend right in it and laying it on with a trowel, if that wasn't too much of a mixed metaphor. 'It's for Bridget. She fancies you, and I insisted that you were effectively widowed.'

He jerked back. 'I beg your pardon?'

'You're clearly a private man, Nathan. Not much on social media, never been married. Bridget liked the way you mucked in and helped out on Saturday, as well as the obvious attraction. She didn't believe me when I spotted the mug. I came down to say that I know, Nathan, and that I'm sorry. I really am.' She looked down and twisted her fingers. 'I had to keep my relationship with Tom strictly platonic at first, because of his job, so I know what it's like, and I'm very sorry.'

'Of course. It must have been hard, given what was going on in your family.'

Lucy didn't rise to the bait. 'Was the sale of School House Millie's way of bringing your relationship into the open? Was she thinking of leaving St Peter's?'

'Who knows,' said Nathan curtly. 'Millie was a private person, too.' He waited until he had eye contact before continuing. 'She was selling the house because of what Feargal Hulme did to her. How that man is still walking around, I don't know.' He laughed mirthlessly. 'Well, I do know. It's because Millie was too good for him. Deborah thinks she was too weak, but she was too good. Didn't have it in herself to send him to prison. Couldn't stop him sniffing round, either.

That was the clean break she wanted.'

'I can't imagine being betrayed like that.'

'Be thankful.' He turned his palms face up in a gesture of openness. 'You're right about one thing, though: if we were going to go public, one of us would have had to move on. The governors would not be happy with forty per cent of the teaching staff being married to each other. If anything, it would have been Millie who moved on, because she *should* be a head somewhere. Should have been.'

Lucy left it a moment before she spoke again. 'I never got to say goodbye to my big brother.' She paused. 'Gianni and I weren't getting on when he was murdered. Did you at least get to tell her you loved her when you went round on Saturday?'

'How … Yes, I did. I only popped in for two minutes with some of that disgusting unpasteurised milk she drinks. I didn't offer to help, because as I told you, my baking isn't up to much.'

'Couldn't she have walked next door to the shop? They stock Mike's Magic Milk.'

'Millie liked to have it ultra-fresh. She kept it in special vacuum flasks, and I took the one she'd left at my house, filled it and dropped it off. I wished her luck and asked if there was anything else she needed. There wasn't. Don't forget, I was going to be in the tent near her all day.'

Lucy barely listened to the last part. 'She went to your house? Enough to keep *milk* there?'

Nathan wasn't so open any more. 'And a toothbrush. And other things. Do you know the Glebe?'

She shook her head. The Glebe had been mentioned a couple of times by customers. It was a development of 1980s houses on the way into the village, and had as many residents as all of the old village houses, cottages and mansions put together.

'If you go through the churchyard, there's a back gate. The new Vicarage is just on the other side, so anyone who saw her would think she was going to Deborah's. My house is next door but one to the Vicarage.'

The conversation with Barney was still in her mind. 'You didn't help clear up or anything?'

'No point. At that stage, she was still in full flow, and she'd already had Deborah and Dom Calvert round. The last thing I wanted was to get in the way. She was on top of things and Millie was one of the tidiest people I know.'

There was a buzzer sound from outside his office, and he stood up. 'That's the front door. The other governors are here. Thank you for the coffee, Lucy, and for your sympathy.' He blinked. 'And understanding. It's good to know that someone else knows how I feel, and how I'd like to keep my grief like my love: private.'

Lucy stood, too, and said, 'Of course. You've got a lot to discuss.'

He led them at a quick march to the front door, where Deborah was waiting to get in. He held the door open, and that meant Lucy didn't have the chance to do more than say hello to the vicar before she was outside and the door shut behind her.

As she drove out of the grounds, she saw Anya Calvert walking in with one of the buggy brigade – the crew of mothers who came to Caffè Milano every day, just before playgroup in the village hall. She grinned to herself and wondered if Dom Calvert was looking after the kids. That would make Bridget's visit an interesting one, and talking of Bridget …

Her phone was ringing and Bridget's grumpy face was flashing. Lucy stopped the car and took the call. 'Hi. How did it go?' asked Bridget.

Lucy looked around before answering. 'I don't know whether he loved Millie, but he certainly loves himself. Says he only popped in to drop off a vacuum flask of that raw milk and was there for two minutes just after Dom Calvert left.'

There was a pause. 'Change of plan,' continued Bridget. 'You get home, 'cos I'm seeing Dom tonight.'

'How? Where?'

'At the am dram. I'm thinking of joining.'

Lucy's mind immediately rejected this idea. 'Right. Of course you are. Whatever. Are you sure? I was late in this morning, so it should be me who stays on.'

'You can owe me. You get home, and I'll call you later.'

'Ah, thanks, Bridget. I feel a long soak in a hot bath coming on. Talk later.'

She checked her rear mirror before pulling out of the entrance, and saw the women waiting outside the locked doors of the school. A thought struck her: Deborah Giddings was chair of governors and a teaching assistant. Why didn't she have her own keys to the school?

Chapter 25

When Lucy had left to see Nathan Frost, Bridget had grabbed the cleaning kit and gone to check on the accessible toilet: Josie had started work today, and Bridget was going to make sure it was up to her own standards. She donned a disposable apron, heavy duty gloves and pinned her hair even further back. Naturally, when she exited the facilities, that was the exact moment she had her second encounter with Lady Felicia Duke.

Her landlord's wife was leading a couple through the glass tunnel and practically *wafted* in front of them like a pixie (if pixies can waft), her long rainbow skirts swishing around her ankles. She was talking over her shoulder and said, 'I never use the lift, so we might as well go up the stairs. Gives you an honest idea of where the studio is.'

Studio? What studio?

The couple were mismatched in the extreme, and none of their body language said that they actually *were* a couple in the romantic sense. The woman was one step ahead of the man, and had dressed for some sort of public appearance, everything neat, clean and possessed of strong lines, including her hair and the contouring on her cheeks.

The man was her complete opposite, and if he'd bought new jeans in the last ten years, there was no evidence of it. Ditto for the faded T-shirt with a giant talking strawberry. As it often does, Bridget's mouth went off on its own like a jack-in-the-box.

'Space Fruit!' she blurted.

The man immediately looked at her with a big grin, his partner frowned and Fliss stopped in her tracks. 'Who? Oh! Bridget! I didn't recognise you in your … your uniform.'

'Well that's a relief,' she managed. 'Wouldn't want my cover blown.'

The woman looked impatient. The man was staring at her tattoos. Bridget's first-hand knowledge of real aristocrats was precisely zero, and she wondered what Fliss would do now.

'Bridget, I'm just heading upstairs to show off our studio space to Hayley and Anthony. We'll be down later.' She pointed to Bridget. 'Bridget runs the coffee shop and is our resident sleuth, apparently.'

Bridget waved her rubber gloves. 'I won't offer to shake hands. I didn't know there was a studio space. What sort of studio?'

'It's whatever you want it to be,' said Fliss blithely. 'In this case, it's going to be an online channel studio and warehouse.' She arched her eyebrows at Hayley. 'Maybe?'

'Hmm,' said Hayley.

'I look forward to trying your coffee,' said Anthony with a nod of his head. 'Triple-shot Americano with plenty of air,' he added, then both of them moved to catch up with Fliss.

'That industrial unit has *no* stairs,' hissed Hayley.

'And no atmosphere,' countered Anthony. 'Still less does it have a coffee shop on the ground floor ...'

They disappeared round the bend, and Bridget shrugged. So what if Hayley Glossylips thought she was the cleaner? No skin off Bridget's nose. And Fliss had looked proud when she introduced her to them. Maybe she'd practised on the servants at boarding school when she was a kid.

Bridget packed away, washed her hands thoroughly and got ready to organise her next mission: a visit to Dominic Calvert. To achieve *that* objective, she would need Kat to do some overtime. She left the kitchen and found her duckling rearranging the cakes without being asked. Excellent.

There was no reason that Kat shouldn't work an hour's overtime. None at all. She had nothing on. She was going nowhere. There was no task waiting for her at home. That didn't stop her complaining, though.

'This is my free time!' she said. 'You've got no right to ask me to stay on.'

Bridget considered the best way to train her duckling and decided that a direct order wouldn't cut it. She thought of Anthony's T-shirt with a grin, and asked, 'Do you like strawberries, Kat?'

'Hate them.' Totally unfazed by Bridget's question, she carried on.

'When I went to the Grammar School, Mum made me go up to Magic Mike's PYO fields when the customers had gone. I had to scavenge and pick what they'd left and we got them at a special rate. She sold them in the shop next day.'

Bridget hadn't been expecting a story like that, but it played perfectly into her hands. 'Okay. Look on the next two hours as being perfectly ripe strawberries. Can you do that?'

'Of course I can! I don't see why, but yeah: the next two hours are actually *strawberries*. Got it.'

'Not just any strawberries. Perfectly ripe strawberries sitting on the counter in the shop. You've got two choices: you can sell them or eat them, because they'll soon go off.'

'Not if I put them in the chiller for Dad's tea.'

'And if I had a chiller that would preserve time, I'd be Doctor Who, but I'm not. You can work for me and get paid, or you can go home and eat your strawberries in whatever way you want.'

'But that means my life is like … a commodity! It's not!'

Was she really this naive? It seemed that she was. 'Bad news, I'm afraid. That's *exactly* what your life is. At least you get a choice about who you sell it to, unlike some. Why don't you agree to do some overtime, then you can think about it while I go and talk to Dom Calvert?'

'Fine. Doesn't look like we're going to be busy, so I can cope on my own.'

Bridget was tempted. Sorely tempted. A part of her wanted to swipe Kat's phone and take it with her to the Old Rectory. Nah. You don't slap a duckling.

While Kat went into the kitchen to text her mother, Bridget checked the fridges and got two portafilters ready in case Lady Felicia hadn't been putting on an act and really did bring the odd couple back. Two minutes later, Bridget heard the clear tones of Fliss from round the corner, telling the others that she'd get the drinks, then they appeared, and Fliss urged them to take an empty table by the window.

'I'll give you a moment to talk things over,' she told them, then she wafted up to the counter and turned on a smile. 'Hello again!'

'Hi. One triple-shot Americano for Anthony. And the others?'

Fliss flicked back her hair. 'Perry told Edwin how professional you are, so I shouldn't be surprised that you remembered Tony's order.

Hayley wants a decaff skinny latte, and I'll try the tea, please.'

Bridget nodded and set the machine running. 'Did Perry also say that I was an amateur sleuth, or is that just the whole village?'

Fliss tilted her head. 'Not the *whole* village. I'm sure most people don't know who you are. Yet. Do you want my alibi?'

Bridget gripped the second portafilter and reminded herself that the pixie with the purple streaks had power here. A simple *This isn't a game, Felicia* would only make an enemy for no reason. There was plenty of time to make an enemy out of Fliss later, so she ignored the question and asked one of her own. 'What sort of online channel are those two planning?'

Fliss blinked. 'No idea. Hayley used to work for some ghastly telly shopping outfit and keeps changing the subject when I ask about it. Part of me hopes they plan to shoot pornos and sell adult novelty toys. That would get a rise out of the village.'

'That's one way of doing it. We could put Viagra in the cakes, too.'

'Don't! You'll be overrun … a bit like this tray is overloaded.'

Three drinks do not overload a tray. That didn't stop Fliss projecting her voice across the Mill and asking Anthony to give her a hand, then simply leaving it there.

Anthony ambled over and stopped to take out his phone. 'Smile.'

Bridget frowned. Surely he wasn't going to take a pic— too late. 'That's rude,' she told him. 'You should ask.'

'I know. But you just looked so *right* standing there. I promise not to share it without your permission.'

'In that case: never.'

He didn't look put out at all and came to the counter. Totally unabashed, he peered at her arms. 'Wow, that's some ink, Bridget. I wish I had your pain threshold.' Before she could answer, he pointed to the strawberry on his T-shirt. 'You're a bit old to be a fan yourself. Kids?'

'No kids or plans for any. But I was a post-grad student …'

'… And students love kids' TV. Yeah.'

He picked up the tray, and she checked his arms for aborted tattoos, then looked at his hands, and suddenly she knew what the books were on about when they described men as having fingers like concert pianists. Despite his paunch, despite his messy, thinning hair, and despite his less than perfect teeth, Anthony's long and elegant fingers, the most beautiful she'd ever seen, made her bitterly regret the rubber gloves from earlier, because she really wanted to shake that hand before it disappeared. *Now that's a fetish I never saw coming,* she thought. *Must be me age.*

He turned away, then turned back. 'Has Felicia paid?'

'No chance. I'll send the bill to Perry. I've got to go now, so I'll drop it off. Don't want to disturb your negotiations.'

'Thanks, Bridget. Might be seeing you soon.'

'Maybe. Good luck.'

Bridget put the bill on hold and printed a summary. She shouted goodbye to Kat and checked her phone. Damn, she'd have to drop the account off some other time. She was out of the foyer and heading for her van when the man himself shouted for her in an *I want a word* voice. For the first time since they'd met, Perry looked a little flustered.

'Hiya,' she shouted across the yard. 'I've got to rush, so I can't stop long.'

'Thanks. I've just had Close on the phone.'

He jogged over, and Bridget said, 'Who?'

'C-L-O-S – Cairndale Light Opera Society. Not to be confused with the North Lancs Players.' He shook his head. 'They wanted to know if Ferg had passed on their rehearsal schedule to you. I told them that you hadn't dealt with Mr Hulme personally.'

'CLOS. They're doing *Kiss Me Kate,* aren't they? It's on the noticeboard at the entrance. Why on earth would I want their rehearsal schedule?'

'They're starting to rehearse in the Cowan Theatre from tonight. I don't know how to put this, but Ferg used to keep the Miller's Rest open for them, and they expect the same.'

Bridget burst out laughing. 'That's priceless that is! I hope you told them that it *wasn't in the lease,* 'cos that seems to be your favourite saying.'

'I would have done, if I'd had the chance, but like you, I don't care a damn about them, except where it impacts my life, and if they don't get their refreshments, they'll complain to Fliss. I don't think either of us want that.'

Bridget was so tempted to ask him if she looked bothered, but he was right. No sense in looking for trouble. On the other hand …

'You're right, Perry, there's no point in upsetting Fliss. She's in there now with those porno directors. At least I hope they're the directors, not the stars.'

Perry grimaced. 'You mean Anthony Carson and Hayley Horst?'

'I do. Here's the bill that Fliss didn't pay. We take cash or card.'

Perry glanced at the bill and dug out a ten pound note. 'Give me the change later. Now, about CLOS ...'

'How many of them are there?'

'About forty, all told, but that's not the issue.' He tried to keep his face straight before he went on, but Bridget could see his eyebrows go up and a smile twitch at the corner of his mouth. Made him look a lot younger. Under forty, even. 'Apparently they used to give Feargal twenty quid for the drinks and eat whatever cakes were about to be chucked away.'

'Now I know you're joking. They can whistle for that.' She reflected for a second. 'Is there anyone in the group I know?'

Perry thought for a moment. 'They're mostly from Cairndale, but I do know that Dom Calvert acts as a sort of tech guru, so he'll be here. He used to do a lot more before they had the kids. Why do you ask?'

She ignored the question. 'What time do they want?'

'Seven until eight tonight; later for dress rehearsals.'

'Leave it with me. Kat's already agreed to stay until six, so getting her to stop until later won't be a problem.'

He looked alarmed. 'Don't let her near them!'

Bridget groaned. 'Let me guess: the leading man dumped her.'

'I couldn't possibly comment. Good luck.'

She started walking rapidly away, towards the Mill, then half turned and risked walking backwards. 'No problem. Oh, and Perry, thanks for sending Josie round to do some cleaning. Her work is first rate and she's a star. I'll deduct her wages from the next rent cheque, shall I?' She spun round and pretended not to hear his reply.

Chapter 26

Bridget decided to go home and get changed before CLOS came out to play, and not just because she was getting a bit sweaty and had spilt milk down her polo shirt. She needed to put them off balance in any way she could, and if she turned up in black with the purple lipstick, they'd either think that she was a couple of sandwiches short of a picnic or they'd be scared. Either would work. And she'd feel a lot more comfortable, which was even better.

She got back to Ford Mill at half past six and asked Kat if she'd reflected on her status as a unit of production in the capitalist economy.

'Yeah. And it sucks.'

'Welcome to adulthood. I can see your brain needs a rest, so you can clear off early. Don't worry, you'll get paid for the next half an hour.'

'Oh. I was gonna clear out the fridge.'

'I've got plans for that, but …'

Bridget had lost her audience because Kat was staring at the man standing in the archway. In her shoes, Bridget would have stared, too, but probably for different reasons. In Bridget's humble opinion, any man who turned up in a bow tie and a herringbone jacket should be stared at until he fled screaming. However, she suspected that Katarina knew exactly who this man was and why he was here.

'Hang on one sec!' said Bridget to Mr Bow Tie, holding up a hand to keep him at bay. She leaned in to Kat's space and whispered, 'Off you go, girl. Sharpish.'

'Right. See you tomorrow.'

Bridget strode forwards to create maximum dynamic impact and to give Kat a chance to slip away. 'Hi. I'm Bridget Gorrigan, operations manager of Caffè Milano. I understand you're interested in contracting for us to stay open.' Having spoken, she offered the man a hand. It should be safe enough, given his fastidious (if awful) dress sense.

He returned the handshake. 'Oh, hello, I'm Derek Fisher, secretary to CLOS. Nice to meet you. I came in early to have a word, and I wouldn't put it so formally as *contracting*. We had a very good relationship with Feargal. He was most supportive.'

'I'm afraid that Miller's Rest went into administration. Sorry 'bout that. We're very keen to support local groups, too, which is why I've come back specially. The only problem is that I have to pay for someone to open up late, see? I can't ask people to volunteer for this. Well, I could, but that would put them in a very awkward position, and you wouldn't want that, would you?'

Mr Fisher didn't wilt in the face of a Gorrigan onslaught. He frowned slightly, then smiled. 'I see your problem, Bridget was it? Yes. I see your problem. Our problem is that we paid extra to rent the theatre with access to refreshments.'

'Then it's not my problem or your problem, is it? It's Perry Lockwood's problem. Look, I know you're going to have thirsty thespians on your hands soon, and I've got nothing else on. Why don't I offer the senior discount to all your members? And yeah, you can have what's left of the cakes. Just for tonight.'

Fisher looked at the price list. He blinked. He adjusted his bow tie. 'How about this: I give you forty pounds, and you make as many pots of tea as are needed? You can charge what you want for coffee and soft drinks.'

That was a better offer than Bridget had been expecting. 'Sounds good to me. Just for tonight, though. You'll have to talk to Perry about the next time.'

'Quite. And one more thing: this is between you and me, okay? I don't want the cast arguing about refreshments when they need to get their fingers out, so the money's coming out of my own pocket.'

'Of course, Derek. No problem.'

Two twenty-pound notes changed hands, and Bridget tried to be casual when she asked, 'Who does the audience refreshments on performance nights? I see there's no bar in the foyer.'

'Gerrard Scott from the White Hart does it, and there's a small bar upstairs in the gallery. Extortionate doesn't come into it. We barely make any money at all from contracting him to run the bar.'

'Don't the Dukes run the bar? Or Louis on their behalf?'

Derek shrugged. 'No idea. Something to do with licensing and Louis's job description.'

'Interesting. Could you do us a favour, Derek? Could you tell Dom

Calvert I want a word with him when he comes in.'

'Of course. He's usually early, too.'

'Right. I'll get some teapots ready.'

Bridget got stuck in, spreading crockery on tables and putting out cake under clingfilm. She saw a couple of people arrive and go straight into the theatre, then one of them came back out and headed towards the café. She straightened up and got ready to meet the richest (if not the most powerful) of the Angels.

'Is it a rule or something?' asked Bridget. 'Do male members of Cairndale Light Opera have to wear bow ties, 'cos it does nothing for the image, I'm telling you.'

With him being a Village VIP, Bridget had made sure to memorise Dominic Calvert's face when she'd seen him (briefly) in the tent. He was clearly older than Anya, and his hair was going grey in all sorts of places. He looked healthy in a sort of weedy runner way, and although he wasn't tall, his arms seemed too long for his body. Maybe his mother had made him hang from parallel bars as a child. And the printed check shirt looked way too casual for the bow tie. That was definitely a mistake. Not that Dom seemed bothered by her remark.

'Nice to meet you, too, Ms Gorrigan,' he said. They shook hands, and he continued, 'I found that black didn't suit me, and purple lipstick isn't my colour either. You stick to your outfit, and I'll stick to mine.'

'Pot of tea? Coffee?' She dropped her voice. 'I'll do you a free cappuccino if you don't tell anyone. Call it a bribe.'

He looked round theatrically – well, he was a *thespian,* wasn't he? 'Where's the Cheshire Cat, because I feel like I've dropped back fifteen years into our production of *Alice in Wonderland*.'

'You should revive it. Better than bleeding *Kiss Me Kate*. This is the twenty-first century, Dom. Do you want that coffee?'

'I'll pass on the coffee, thanks, though I take your point about the committee's choice of production. Derek said you wanted a word, and it's not about light opera, is it? I've heard that you and your sidekick have been poking a stick into the village wasps' nest.'

'Other way round. I'm her sidekick. Can we cut the crap, Mr Calvert?'

He looked suspicious. She'd just gone from calling him *Dom* to *Mr Calvert,* and the switch hadn't gone unnoticed. Dominic Calvert was a *third-generation* software designer (whatever that meant), and he'd created a product that took advantage of the early stages of the World Wide Web. He'd sold his baby, LancsPay, to one of the big payment companies and married his assistant compliance manager. After she'd left her husband.

Since then, he'd stopped creating programs himself and become a start-up venture capitalist and one of the Angels of Byford. Bridget took a good look at him and mentally shrugged: she didn't have to live with him.

'I'm all in favour of minimising bullshit,' he said, 'and I don't care that you're not with the police. They've interviewed everyone who went near School House, apparently, and they haven't made an arrest yet, which tells me there's no conclusive forensic evidence. Just tell me one thing: why do *you* care about Millie Easterby?'

Somehow, the challenge from Dom Calvert struck her harder than objections from the other people she'd spoken to, like he was the physical manifestation of the *pillar of the community*, and he wasn't going to be shaken by a mild tremor. Why *did* she care? She suddenly felt very uncomfortable, like she needed to adjust her skirt or tuck in her blouse or retie her bootlaces or something, anything but think about his question. But what would he take as an answer?

It went right to the heart of what she'd felt since Lucy had turned right and headed into Byford four weeks ago. Bridget didn't belong here. She was meant to lurk in the urban shadows, not be standing in the spotlight taking a sledgehammer to pillars of the community.

Dom was waiting for an answer. In Bridget's shoes, Lucy would come straight out with it. Bridget couldn't do that, so she opted for a convincing lie. 'It's because I'm naturally nosy,' she suggested. 'Can't see a situation and not want to stick my hooter in, and once I'd started, I couldn't stop. Same for Lucy.'

His face said that he wasn't buying it when he replied. 'If you say so. What do you want to know?'

'To start with, what did you think of her, Dom?'

'Why me? Haven't you spoken to everyone else?'

'We have, but you don't have any skin in the game. Not really. St Peter's will still be a good school without her, and you didn't have designs on her house.'

They had to step aside for a moment as the first of the cast arrived and went to collect their pots of tea. One of them, an older lady, took two pieces of cake, surreptitiously folding one into a napkin.

When it came, Dom's reply was unexpected. 'If you want my honest answer, I think Millie Easterby spent her whole life wishing she was someone else.'

'Sorry?'

'She was a great teacher but a poor Easterby, according to those who've lived here a lot longer than me. She wasn't much good at being Feargal's wife, either.'

Bridget was instantly outraged. 'You what? That's a terrible thing to say after what he did to her.'

Dom had his answer for that ready and waiting. 'I think Liz Swindlehurst would have made a good Mrs Hulme. Both feet firmly on the ground to stop Feargal floating away on a cloud of his own making.'

This was too much. Pillar of the community? Pillar of the patriarchy, more like. 'Oh yeah? And why should a woman have to do that? Why shouldn't Feargal take responsibility for his own life?'

He didn't answer her. He kept eye contact long enough to know that he'd heard and understood what Bridget was saying, then he looked at his bejewelled, distinctly non-digital watch. 'Got to go in a second. If they try to power up the lighting rig without me, it'll take all night to fix it.'

Bridget shook her head and moved on. 'What happened on Saturday morning?'

'You've seen the CCTV?' She nodded. 'Then you'll know I wasn't there long. I'd heard about Carter's doing the valuation, and I wanted to make her an offer. I told her that if she was serious about selling, I'd buy the house without going through an agent. It could save her five thousand.' He spread his arms open. 'That's it.'

'What did she say to that?'

'She seemed quite open to it, especially when I told her she'd be mad not to get the high-end agents down from Kendal. They have a much richer client list than Carter's. I told her to get School House valued at least twice. She thanked me and I left.'

'What was she doing at the time?'

'Trying to make choux pastry. Not entirely successfully, I might add. I said I'd get out of her way as quickly as I could. After all, I wouldn't want to be accused of trying to distract the opposition on Anya's behalf, would I?'

'She didn't have a cup of coffee on the go, did she?'

'Not that I saw. She was a bit busy for that.' He paused. 'Though her last act was to tip the pastry in the bin, so that might have been a prelude to taking a break.'

'Thank you.'

'You're welcome. Do you need to bother Anya by talking about any of this?'

What an odd question. Anya didn't look like she needed protecting, and she was nowhere on Bridget's radar. 'I doubt it very much.'

'Then I'll ask on her behalf, because it's been bothering her ever since you said it. What on earth were you on about in the tent? I take your point about the fire extinguisher – someone should have thought of that – but what was that about the ice cream?'

'That? When you add alcohol it lowers the freezing point quite a lot, way below what you can achieve with domestic machines. Rookie mistake.'

He had the grace to smile. 'I shall tell her. It won't happen again, not that she's inclined to use the machine for a while: when it was locked in the tent, the contents mutated into a new life form.'

From the foyer, a voice shouted (quite plaintively), 'Has anyone seen Dom Calvert? The board says it wants to update itself.'

'Oh shit,' said Dom. He left the café at a fast walk, saying, 'Call me first the next time you want a word.'

Bridget was loading the dishwasher and wondering just how long Lucy would need in the bath before she called her when Bridget got a message: *Granddad Morton has passed away. Can you cope on your own tomorrow?*

To which she replied: *Course I can. You get over there. But go TOMORROW.*

?????

You had a drink before your bath. I know you.

HaHaHaHa. Oops. Yeah.

Give my condolences to Tom. Call later if you want.

You get to see Dom?

Yes. It was a CLOS encounter.

????

Tell you later.

She put her phone away and went to see whether there was any spare cake left. No chance. Time to clear up and go home.

'Hello,' said Perry. 'Glad I caught you.'

He was leaning on the brick arch with his arms folded, and looked like he didn't know whether to be annoyed or amused. 'I've had a phone call from Derek Fisher,' he continued. 'Derek was *ever so polite* about it, but he did point out that since they moved here for performances, the late train back from Byford Halt has been withdrawn from service, which makes it very difficult for some of their audience. In other words, he was threatening to put on their performances somewhere else. That would not go down well at the Lodge.'

Bridget ignored the subtext of what Perry was saying completely: she never negotiated on a passive-aggressive basis. 'So why *did* they move here? Is there no space in Cairndale?'

'The Civic Hall may be cheap, but it doesn't have a stage as such.' He levered himself off the wall and came into the café. 'Do you want a hand?'

'How much?' she said, a little too sharply. She *was* tired, though.

He looked offended, and Bridget had her second Moment of Insight (no way was she going to call it an *epiphany*. No chance). Out here, you had to somehow balance the transactional with the personal. It was something she'd never had to do before, because every other commercial relationship she'd had was either with strangers or with people so close they could be family (a completely different can of epiphanic uncertainty).

Here was a man who had been both nice *and* professional, and she had no experience of dealing with that combination. The same could be said of Kat, Jackie and even Fliss. If the business were going to succeed here, she'd have to find a way through the maze, and until then, she could only deal with one encounter at a time, and right now, Perry deserved more than sarcasm.

'I'm sorry, Perry. That didn't come out the way I meant it. I'd love a hand. If you could take all the plates into the kitchen and bin the clingfilm, I'll get cleaning.'

'No problem.'

They started work, and she asked who was babysitting.

'Homework's done. They're *chillin'* for a bit. I reckon I've got a year before the older one starts wanting to hang out in the evening with totally unsuitable people.' He paused. 'You know the sort.'

It was like being wound up by a ghost: so gentle you might not notice it was happening. It even made her shiver. Or maybe that was the cold breeze from the windows. Better change the subject.

'How come you're telling Fliss that I'm the village sleuth?'

'Because you clearly are.'

'And if I am, what is it to her?'

'Dealing with Fliss is a bit of an art. And if she doesn't hear it from me, she'll hear it from someone else and then bend my ear for not telling her.'

Bridget reflected for a moment. 'So basically, all the downsides of being married to her and none of the perks?'

Perry had his hands full, but that didn't stop him wagging his finger. 'Just don't go there. Have you spoken to anyone else?'

'I went to see Feargal this afternoon,' she told him.

'Oh?'

'Yeah. I woke him up. If you could pop round in a day or so and see how he's doing, I think he'd be really grateful. Not that he'd show it, of course.'

Perry put down an over-filled tray with a non-committal grunt, then barely stopped a platter sliding onto the floor. Bridget didn't say anything about his skills as a waiter because she doubted that he'd be doing this again in a hurry. Instead, she asked about his visit to Millie on the day of the Bake Off.

'You were quite early, weren't you?' she began.

He stepped back to put some distance between them. 'Yes. I left some bread to prove, then I nipped out. Look, Bridget, you've been totally straight with me. If I tell you something, will you promise to keep it to yourself? Not even Lucy.'

Bridget went back to the Spinning Room and started wiping tables. 'Can't give you a total promise, but if it has nothing to do with poison, then I'm the soul of discretion.'

'I was sent to offer Millie ten per cent above the best offer she got for School House.'

That stopped her in mid-swipe. 'Who? Fliss? Edwin? Both of

them?'

He drew a zip across his lips and picked up the last two plates.

'What did she say?' asked Bridget to his disappearing back.

He deposited the crockery and returned, brushing his hands. 'She looked a bit like a frightened rabbit, Bridget. I don't know what our sainted vicar said to her before I arrived on Saturday, or what Dom Calvert said after I left, but when Millie and I bumped into each other in the tent, she whispered, "I'm going to pretend to drop the idea. Who's your lawyer? I'm using McEwan & Co for this. Get your lawyer to make mine an offer well over half a million and we can do it without anyone knowing."' He held up a hand. 'No, I didn't get the chance to ask why she wasn't using James Carter.'

Bridget was stunned, and she didn't know what stunned her more: that Millie was going to Abigail Tennant's smaller firm or that she wanted *well over half a million* for School House. Money won out when she said, 'It's never worth that much!'

'I couldn't say. Anything else you want to know?'

'No. That's great, thanks. Yeah. Hang on, what are you gonna do about the am dram brigade?'

'I'm not going to give them what they want, that's for certain. Could you help me out a bit? Could you leave them a kettle, crockery, tea bags, that sort of thing? We'll cover your costs.'

'I can do, but it'll have to be left out there. We're not insured if we allow people over the threshold when we're closed. It was hard enough to get insurance for a café with no door, never mind unsupervised use.'

He grinned. 'Something Feargal may have neglected to tell his insurers. Thanks, Bridget. I'll email you their schedule. Goodnight.'

Bridget thought about what their costs would be, and mentally added half an hour of her time to clean up the morning after.

Chapter 27

Several things were waiting for Bridget on her phone when she woke up on Friday morning, including the obvious one that today was Friday the 13th. Not that Bridget was superstitious or anything. Not really. Not like her Auntie Susan.

She unlocked her phone and opened the apps to see what else was new. The first thing she checked was a message from Lucy saying that she was setting off for York, ETA ten o'clock. 'I hope she laid off the grappa after her bath,' muttered Bridget. The second thing was a voicemail from Rev Deb.

'Of course I'll talk to you, Bridget. I lead prayers in St Peter's at eight o'clock, and you're more than welcome to join in. We normally finish around eight thirty if you want to meet me at the vicarage.'

Bridget stared at her phone. 'No bleedin' chance of me turning up for prayers. At least she didn't tell me to wait until Sunday.'

The third thing was the first Tripadvisor reviews of Caffè Milano at Ford Mill. She couldn't help herself.

***** *Great new coffee place. Amazing service. Real atmosphere. Glad we stopped by.*

* *Outrageous prices. How can corporate chains be allowed to drive out local businesses like this? The Miller's Rest was so much better.*

*** *Some of the stuff is a bit weird, but we loved Dave Hughes' expedition about paintings with no sky. Real atmosphere. Go see it while you can and B4 there all sold!!!!*

**** *Ladies who lunch, beware!!!! They have great coffee at the new place, and a good selection of cakes but not much on offer for lunches. They said they're going to expand the menu. Hold your fire until then.*

None of the users seemed familiar, though the person who gave the 1* review used an avatar, so they could be anyone. It wasn't a bad start, even if the review of the Dukes Gallery was the sort of random thing that really got on her nerves.

She pulled on a clean polo shirt and peered out of the window;

Tabor's Bakery were a bit early. Good. That would give her time to make Rev Deb a coffee after she'd dropped off the delivery at Ford Mill. An extra sprinkling of chocolate might sweeten the question she was going to ask.

'Abandon hope all ye who enter here,' muttered Bridget to herself as she drove on to the Glebe Estate. She was willing to admit that the Glebe residents would argue otherwise – that she was prejudiced and biased – but in Bridget's head, there was at least one circle of Hell laid out just like this.

At some point in the 1980s, a portion of land on the edge of the village had been sold off and developed into a mix of three and four bed houses, all marketed as *Executive Homes* because they were detached and had tiny en suite bathrooms. The whole thing was an optical illusion, because although the houses had generous drives at the front, the back gardens were mean and boxed-in; on a summer's evening, you could hear your neighbours' TV.

Since their construction, a huge amount of renovation and expansion had gone on, in attics, over garages, behind kitchens, and basically anywhere you could shoehorn an extension. The result today was like going to a very small gym full of very large bodybuilders. One of the few exceptions to all this was the Vicarage.

Not only was Deborah Giddings' home a good twenty years older than the others, it had a proper garden. On the downside, the house hadn't been touched since the builders left. Bridget parked outside and carried the takeout coffee carefully up to the front, right on eight thirty.

The door opened before she could lift her finger to the bell, and she jerked back when one of the zombies dashed out and ran past her. It was a girl, around fourteen, who looked very unhappy. Bridget turned to watch the kid head into St Peter's churchyard with hunched shoulders.

'Good morning, Bridget,' said the vicar.

Bridget watched the girl's head disappear among the graves and said, 'Hasn't she missed the bus?'

'Yes, she has. One of the things I did to upset her was texting her mother to make sure she gets a lift to Cairndale Grammar.'

'*One* of the things you did to upset her?'

'Another was refusing to sign a sick note to get her off for the day.

Come in, and please tell me that coffee is a gift, because if it is, one of my prayers this morning has been answered.'

'That's a first,' said Bridget. 'No one has ever accused me of being an agent of the Lord. The Dark Lord many times, but not Him upstairs. Here. I'll just take my Docs off.'

'No need. Visitors to the Study are usually too busy or too distressed, so I don't bother.'

It went against every fibre of Bridget's being to walk the *Outside* into someone's home. Then again, those laces were a swine for casual use. She followed Deborah into a large hall with an open tread staircase (very 1960s) and several closed doors – the only open one was to the right. Bridget pointed to a far door which had slippers next to it. 'I take it that room *does* need shoes off.'

Deborah did that *surprised vicar* thing where she raised her eyebrows a millimetre. 'Very observant. Most people call that the lounge, but I call it the Sanctuary because it's where the Host lives, and no, that's not an anti-Catholic dig.'

Bridget gave her the eye. 'If that's the standard of joke, your dinner parties must be an absolute riot, Deborah.'

'What dinner parties? Let's sit down.'

Deborah Giddings was in her fifties, average height, average build and just about average in all respects. This conclusion had only come to Bridget now because the vicar had clearly been up early and made an effort. She had put on even more make-up than she had at the Bake Off, and the brushed-back hair was neat and clean. She was still wearing the black shirt, but the trousers suited her better than the skirt.

The study had clearly always been intended for that purpose. The window was big, and gave a clear view of the front path and the church beyond it, just in case the incumbent forgot where their loyalties lay. No wonder the back room was Deborah's *sanctuary*. The left-hand wall was covered with bookcases and had plenty of room for an antique desk which must have come from the Old Rectory. Did Dom Calvert know it was here, and if so, did he covet it? *You shall not covet your neighbour's house, nor his wife, nor his manservant nor his maid* … The Tenth Commandment was strangely quiet on *your neighbour's authentic Victorian desk.*

'Excuse the fireplace,' said Deborah. 'I hate it.'

'Don't blame you.'

The chimney breast was made of the cheapest faux-granite and the generous open hearth was filled with an antique gas fire that could also have been recycled from the Old Rectory. Where Deborah had had the chance to stamp her mark, she had done her best. Six assorted armchairs had been covered in modern fabric and adorned with craft cushions. The vicar stood by one and offered Bridget another.

'Excuse me a second,' said Deborah, removing the lid from her coffee and taking a big hit. 'Thank you for that. Now, what can I do to help?'

'Are you not at school today?'

'Not until eleven. Everyone needs a hand on Fridays.'

'Even the Angels, eh?'

This was the closest that Deborah had come to being angry since Bridget had met her. 'Who span you that line? Fliss? Louis? I thought better of you, Bridget. If there is a divide in the village, it is *not* of my making. I am the last person to describe myself as an Angel, and Millie hated it.'

Bridget wasn't offended, and her curiosity was well and truly piqued. 'It was Perry Lockwood, actually. And it wasn't Fliss who came up with the *Dark Satanic Mill* line. That was Dom or Anya.'

'Actually, it was Feargal.' Deborah tried and failed to restrain a smile. 'That was before he went over to the Dark Side and launched Miller's Rest.' She sighed. 'I thought it was all over. I thought the village could come together and mourn Millie as one. She would have hated her death to bring more division.'

Bridget waited a moment. 'But it wasn't an accident, was it, Deborah? Someone did this to her. When bad things happen, there's bound to be a witch hunt. I'm just glad I wasn't invited round to her house, or it would be me on the ducking stool instead of the Irishman. And tell me I'm wrong. Tell me it isn't Feargal who everyone's pointing the finger at.'

Deborah didn't look away. She forced herself to keep eye contact with Bridget. 'I wish I could. And the worst thing for me is that I can't say anything about it without sounding like a total doormat.'

'What do you mean?'

'If I say *It wasn't Feargal*, then everyone just says *Then who is it?* Because that's the truth: we just don't know. It had to be one of us. One of my parishioners told me this morning that Gerrard Scott is offering to run a book on who did it and told the whole bar that his money was on the vicar. If I preached a sermon saying *Let the police do their job* it sounds like I don't care, when I care very much.'

Bridget hadn't expected to be feeling sorry for the vicar quite so quickly, and she hadn't even asked her questions yet. 'I know you care, Deborah. Going back to the Dark Side thing, I can see why Fliss might cultivate it, but why Louis?'

'Because he very publicly asked me if I would marry him in St Peter's, and when I told him the truth, that I would if I could, he equally publicly said that I should take down the notice saying that all were welcome in God's House.' She shook her head. 'The next time we were both in the village shop, he told me it wasn't personal.'

'I bet it felt *very* personal.'

'If I can't turn the other cheek then who can?' said Deborah, quite reasonably. She finished her cappuccino and put her hands on her knees. 'Thank you for listening to me, Bridget: that doesn't often happen in here. I'm guessing we haven't got to the real reason for your visit, though. Have we?'

'No, but first, could you clarify something? According to the rules, a school employee can't be chair of governors. You had the inspectors in last year, so either they were rubbish at their job or there's something else going on.'

Deborah crossed her legs. 'Believe me, they were anything but rubbish. One of the most stressful weeks of my life. And you're right, if I were an employee, I would not be Chair. I'm not an employee, I'm a volunteer. My two days' salary are paid for by the Calvert Foundation. Simple as that.'

That was not what Bridget had been expecting. Did it change anything? It certainly made a conspiracy between the Angels a more likely prospect, except that Bridget couldn't see Deborah Giddings agreeing in advance to anything that would hurt Millie Easterby That didn't mean she couldn't be pressurised afterwards, though …

'When Lucy saw you last night, you were waiting for the headteacher to let you in. Don't you have your own keys?'

The vicar shuffled in her chair. 'I did, but they … disappeared. Why is that important?'

'Bear with me. Were they lost or stolen?'

'I honestly don't know. At the last governors meeting, I said I'd close up, but they'd disappeared. I had to call Nathan to come back and lock up. I'd had them the night before and put them in my bag, but had not used them. I retraced my steps, but nothing.'

'Where had you been?'

'Morning prayers, then I stayed in the church until eleven o'clock. I went to the school, Millie's house, the Miller's Rest and then back to school for the governors meeting. Do you think it's important?'

'Did they change the locks?'

'I don't have a full set, just the front door, the counselling room and the field gate. There are a lot of those keys around, but they did change the alarm codes.' She looked even more guilty. 'I'm afraid that the code was written on a tag. I think the site manager is punishing me by taking his time getting a new set cut.'

'Site manager?'

'Caretaker in old money. Unlike school caretakers in the past, he lives in Cairndale and commutes. One reason for having so many key holders in the village.'

'I see. Well, I must say it's very generous of the Calverts to pay for your days at the school. Thanks for your time, Deborah. Just one more question: what did Millie say when you tried to talk her out of selling School House?'

When Deborah started blinking back tears, Bridget realised that (with mascara), the vicar's eyelashes might be her most attractive feature. 'You won't tell anyone, will you?' said the vicar.

'I'm your barista. You can tell me.'

'She said that she didn't want to spend the next ten years living like a pauper in a house worth hundreds of thousands. She actually said the words "Not like you". She apologised later, but it still hurt.'

'Ouch.'

Suddenly, Bridget had her motive for Deborah: it was one thing for the vicar's children to make their own lives in London, but if her surrogate daughter had rejected her, that *must* hurt. 'When did she apologise?'

'While you and Lucy were talking to Edwin in the tent. She called me over and said, "I'm really sorry about earlier. You were right. I'm going to take some time to think." And then she asked me to get the reserve flapjack mix.'

Bridget was so busy thinking about what Millie had allegedly also said to Perry during the competition that she nearly missed it. 'Flapjack? You said gluten-free oatmeal last time we spoke.'

'All the competitors cheated a little bit. Millie had some of the gluten-free mixture at home. It wasn't baked. While the Neapolitan traybake was in the oven, she took a good look at the flapjack she'd prepared earlier and wasn't satisfied. That's all.'

It was *plausible*. Like every other account of Saturday morning, it was consistent and fitted with the facts, so who the hell was lying?

'Thanks, Deborah. I'll take your empty: we have a special recycling deal.'

They both stood up, and the vicar passed the takeout cup. 'Do you? You should make more of that.'

'It was hard enough to get the minimum signage space that we needed. Apparently Lucy and Edwin nearly came to blows over sign on the outside of the arch saying *no dogs*.'

Deborah started walking towards the front door. 'That could make you unpopular in some quarters.'

'We're working on an agreement for outside tables. I wonder why Feargal never bothered.'

'Who knows. Thanks again for listening, Bridget, and whether you like it or not I am going to pray for you.' Before Bridget could say that it was no skin off her nose, Deborah caught her off guard and swept her into an embrace. Yeuch. 'I am going to pray that you bring justice for Millie.' She stood back. 'My door is always open – here or across the way.'

'I'll bear that in mind, Deborah. If we had a door at Ford Mill, I'd open it for you, too. See you later.'

Bridget looked at the gate, and was tempted to wander in and explore the churchyard, to see if it deserved the four gravestones on Gothadvisor which Lucy had suggested. Bridget loved cemeteries, old ones anyway, and there was no better place to sit and think about what she'd learned.

She checked her phone: no time for wandering. She leaned on the wall instead, and from there, she could see through the trees to School House. She mentally ran through her suspect list again:

Perry Lockwood
Deborah Giddings
Feargal Hulme

Nathan Frost

Dominic Calvert

And of all them, the only one she had unequivocally ruled out was Perry.

Not only did he have no motive, he had no idea that amygdalin came from cherry pits, and anyone who knew about the poison at all would also know its main source.

Following Millie's death, Deborah was clearly very cut up, but that could be guilt. Feargal had been cast out and was having his male ego royally spanked by Millie. Nathan had just secured a big payday for his school, and Dom Calvert had kept School House out of the hands of the Dark Side.

Was any of this enough motivation for someone to kill a harmless girl like Millie?

Hah. Of course it was.

She tossed the van keys in her hand. When she'd lived in Southport, she'd been aware of *some* of the goings on over the road in Layla's Piano Bar. She'd once tried asking about them, and she'd been blanked. Nothing. And yet there was Perry going around telling everyone she was a *sleuth* for God's sake.

She was definitely going to play them at their own game: round here, people *had* to answer your questions. Even if they were the murderer, they had to talk if they wanted to stay part of the village.

Chapter 28

On the way to the Mill, Bridget got a call. 'Hiya, Lucy. How's things?' she asked straight away.

'Sad, but a relief. Tom's grandmother is doing the stoical thing at the moment. You know, "I wouldn't have wanted him to go on like that." We're going up to Rooksnest Farm soon, so I wondered how you got on with the vicar?'

'Every time I think I've learnt something, I learn something else instead.'

'Right. That makes so much sense, Bridge. What did she say?'

The journey was so short that Bridget was already parking at Ford Mill. Lucy would have enough on her plate today without worrying about Byford. 'I'm getting mixed messages about the sale of School House, that's for certain. I'd better get inside or we'll have customers wondering where we are. Take care and I'm not expecting you back until Monday, okay? We've got this covered.'

'We'll see. Thanks, Bridget.'

Before she went into the Mill, Bridget paused to look at the site it sat on. Outside tables were going to be a must, and not just for the dog owners. There was an ashtray outside their back door, and Bridget had been forced to add an extra stop on empties patrol to reclaim crockery abandoned by the smokers who dropped in – no doubt including Conrad Bloody Clarke when Mina came to inspect the new premises.

She weighed it up, and the only problem was that the car park was ugly, as was that whole side of the Mill. The best place would be on the other side of the mill race, but that would mean a bridge. She shrugged. Another time.

While she worked at getting ready, she also worked at the problem of School House. Had Millie still been planning to sell? *Probably.* Would she have sold to the Dukes and snubbed the Calverts? *Perhaps.* If she'd had a huge written offer from Edwin and Fliss, would she have used it to lever more money out of Dominic and Anya? *Maybe.*

Would she have left the village if she sold up? *Almost certainly.*

All of this was irrelevant, though, because unless she could work out how the hell Millie had been poisoned, there was no point in focusing on motive. She had her theories about that, but she needed more evidence. When Kat rolled in, she sent a message and hoped it would bear fruit, like bread cast upon the waters.

'I'm cracking up,' she told Kat.

'I know. What's your evidence? *Specifically?*'

'I am not only mixing me metaphors, I'm quoting the Bible. That'll teach me to spend time with the vicar.' She put the glass dome down on top of a stacked cake stand and thought for a second. 'Then again, Tom Morton does both of those things. Perhaps it's a sign.'

'It's a sign you're cracking up.'

'I already said that. Have you booked that food hygiene course yet?'

'Oh yeah! I started it last night.'

'Last *night*? Where at?'

'Online. It's cheaper, easier and I can do it at home.'

Bridget shook her head. Kat would pass the course, but until Bridget had shown her how to do things properly, there was no way she was being let loose in the kitchen. On the other hand, that Tripadvisor review had a point: their lunchtime offer was a bit rubbish, given the resources at their disposal.

'Great. Well done, girl. How's your cooking?'

Kat pretended to ignore her. 'Are you sure you can't get any more croissants? We'll sell this amount in half an hour at the weekend. They do love to pretend they're on holiday.'

Bridget was about to push the point about catering when she got an answer to her message: it seemed like she'd hooked her fish, and he walked into Caffè Milano looking a lot better than he'd done the last time she'd seen him. Feargal Hulme stood in the archway of the Spinning Room and turned slowly around.

'Holy Mary,' he announced. 'Would you look at the size of *that*? Do you really need four heads on your coffee machine?'

'Morning, Ferg,' said Kat breezily. 'You should try it: *so* much faster.'

'Maybe I'll apply for a job. You'll be needing more hands, won't you, Bridget?'

Was it bravado or did Feargal really have the resilience to bounce back like this? That was a thought for another day. Right now, Bridget needed to pick his brains. 'What would you like, Feargal?' she asked. 'Take a seat and I'll bring it over.'

'A large cappuccino, two extra shots and one of those pain au raisin, if you're buying.'

'Coming up.'

As Feargal made his way slowly through his old domain, Kat hissed into Bridget's ear, 'Don't you spend too long with him. It's getting busy.'

It was, and Bridget was torn between pressing on with her mission and ruffling the feathers of her duckling. She sent Kat over with Feargal's drink and worked the machine herself for ten minutes until the queue had gone and there was a lull in sight. Then she grabbed a tray and dashed over to Feargal's table.

'I don't miss it at all,' he said. 'Six years of my life gone, and I don't miss it one bit. I only wish I'd had the sort of capital your Lucy does, then it might have been different.'

'Maybe. Look, I haven't got long. Are you planning on staying in Byford?'

'No. When I got your message, I was already gonna drop in. A bit of masochism to add to the sadism that's going to be inflicted on me shortly.'

'Who by?'

'By Perry Lockwood, on behalf of Edwin Duke. He called me last night and said he'd take me out to lunch. He also had the decency to say why: he needs to present the lease on Four Midland Terrace. The one with the rent in it. I'm going to eat his lunch, drink his beer and ask for another month rent-free before I move out. I simply can't afford it. Can't afford anything. I'm *that* close to personal bankruptcy, and I'm *that* close to being arrested. At least I've got meself a brief now. Not that she likes being called a *brief*.'

'Abigail Tennant?'

'The same. She'd been retained by Perry, but when the police told her they had no further interest in her client, Perry told her to give me a ring even before you recommended her. Another decent thing he's done me.'

And that explained why Abigail Tennant had said that Bridget's ears would be burning: she'd been talking to Perry the night before.

'Wait there,' she told Feargal. 'I'll bring you an espresso in a minute.'

'I ...'

But she was gone, filling her tray and making sure that the queue never got big enough for Kat to have a strop. When she'd caught up, she took him his drink and said, 'Try that and tell me you're not in heaven.'

He slurped, and his eyes widened. 'Now that is good. Fair play to you. If you keep plying me with free coffee, I'll move in and sleep on the old sofa. I did that more than a few nights, you know. When Millie chucked me out.'

And there was another reason to get them replaced. The thought of Feargal's bodily fluids was just ... No. Move on. 'I don't know about your finances, Feargal, but I do know that if you leave, you'll forever be the man who killed St Millie and got away with it. You'll be the Byford Scapegoat.'

'So? I know I'm innocent, and Abigail says they've got nothing on me.'

'Help me out here, okay? Just tell me all about this raw milk racket and the flasks.'

'I think Katarina is waving at you, and I need to get over the river. How about I see you later, eh?'

'Half past four. It'll be getting quiet then, and Kat stays until five.'

'Looking forward to it. If you drive, there's something I can show you.'

She headed back to the counter and it was only when he'd gone that she wondered whether it was wise to be heading off alone with a murder suspect.

Before it became the first branch of Caffè Milano, the little coffee shop in Southport had been known as *Giuseppi's Gelateria*, and Bridget had gone there to make ice cream. Because of where she was in her life at that time, she'd kept a baseball bat handy. Later, it had gone into her locker. In the end, having access to a baseball bat had turned out very badly for her best friend, and Bridget quickly decided against going armed when Feargal showed up at Ford Mill.

He didn't look drunk, though she could definitely smell Guinness on his breath. She told Kat very loudly where she was going and picked up the van keys.

'Yeah, yeah, yeah. You've only told me three times. What do you think he's gonna do to you?' Kat waggled her eyebrows. 'You'll make Perry jealous.'

'You can go off people,' said Bridget.

When they got in the van, Feargal belched. 'Sorry. Really sorry. Shouldn't have had the crumble for pudding. Right, when you get to the end of the drive, turn left. Might as well go to the source, eh?'

They followed a small car that crawled along the lane. A short distance later, Bridget saw the sign: *Meadow Farm, Home of Mike's Milk*. There were other signs, too, but they weren't trying to attract visitors, and Bridget couldn't read them without her glasses.

The small car in front turned into the farmyard, and Bridget gave it plenty of room. You could never tell with these older drivers. She drove along a concrete access road and pulled in out of the way. 'Wow. What an operation.'

It was much bigger than she'd expected, with the original stone farmhouse and outbuildings dwarfed by metal sheds. Suddenly, Bridget felt she was being watched and turned round to find that she was indeed being watched – by dozens of large, brown eyes peering out from the familiar ginger of a herd of Jerseys.

One of the sheds had open sides, and the cows waiting patiently for their turn in the milking parlour were having a good look at the new arrivals. The small car stopped by a little installation. A Perspex canopy sheltered a big blue vending machine, and an old man got out of the car with a vacuum jug. Surely he wasn't going to … Yep. He was. The man put his jug under the dispenser and tapped a code into the machine.

While the microbe-filled live soup of infection poured out of the spout, Feargal said, 'And there you have it: Mike's Magic Milk, taken from the udders of those girls only this morning and flash-chilled. If you can get over the ick factor, it's just really creamy, tasty full-fat milk. I love it.' They watched the milk pour slowly into the flask, and Feargal ruminated on the subject. 'Supposed to be full of extra probiotic goodness if you believe all of that stuff. Poor Lisa Lockwood tried it when she was first diagnosed. They come from miles around for it.'

'I don't think I'll ever truly understand country people,' said

Bridget. 'I take it Millie had her own code?'

'She did. You have to pay monthly by direct debit. It should still work if you want me to get you some …?'

'No. Just plain no, okay? Talk me through the vacuum flasks.'

'*Insulated* rather than *vacuum*, but the name stuck. You can put those fellas through the dishwasher no problem.'

Bridget's hands were still on the steering wheel, and she gripped it reflexively, glad that what Feargal had just said hadn't triggered a reaction in her face. So *that's* how it had been done. All she needed now was something, *anything* that would prove it to the police.

'Are you okay?' said Feargal.

'Yeah. Fine. Be honest with me, Feargal. How close was Perry Lockwood to Millie? After Lisa died, I mean.'

'I don't know that he was, and I don't know that he wasn't. If you believe the gossip, he's been linked with every sympathetic woman in the village since he's been on his own. You don't think …'

'Lisa was friends with Jackie, and the village shop is next to School House. Going to one would be a good cover for going to the other.'

'Are you seriously telling me that Perry Lockwood, who couldn't even evict me without getting me drunk first … are you telling me that Perry Lockwood was having a secret affair with my ex-wife and killed her when she decided to move away?'

She turned to face her passenger. 'You believe it now, do you? That she was leaving?'

'Abigail Tenant showed me the valuation from Carter's and her letter of instruction from Millie. I had no idea the place was worth that much.' Feargal was more drunk than she'd thought because he quickly forgot about Perry Lockwood and focused on a drunk's favourite topic: himself. 'I just didn't realise how much she'd moved on from me. Just because I was still in love with her, it really didn't mean that she still loved me back. She'd moved on, and I hadn't. It's time I did. Do you need to know any more about this fecking milk, or can we go.'

'I'll run you home.'

She drove to Midland Terrace, and Feargal lapsed into silence. He twisted in his seat to stare at School House when they turned up Church Lane, but didn't say anything until she'd turned the van round outside the station.

'There's no point in asking you in for a coffee, is there? Bit redundant, really, given what you do for a living.'

'And also pointless if you were thinking of a quick shag. Do yourself a favour, eh? Go to bed and make tomorrow a new day.'

'You should be a priest, you should. Thanks for the ride.'

Behind her, a different collection of kids from the morning zombies, wearing different uniforms, spilled down from the station platform. There were only a few, and their brightly coloured blazers screamed *private school*. No state school would make parents buy anything so expensive as that. Bridget drove carefully out of Station Square, giving due allowance for the tendency of teenage boys to push each other in front of moving vehicles, then headed down the hill.

Chapter 29

Back at the Mill, Kat was waiting impatiently for news, even though she looked disappointed when Bridget walked in. 'You were quick. Too quick,' said the young barista.

'Too quick for what?'

'To go back to his place. I would have covered for you.'

Really? That was her biggest concern?

'You're joking aren't you?'

'No! He must be the same age as you, so what's wrong with that?'

'If age is your main criteria, why aren't you shagging Curtis the tractor mechanic? You even went to school with him, didn't you?'

'Because he still has the same mental age that he did at puberty. Boys are such losers.'

'Not gonna argue with that.' Bridget couldn't help sighing more loudly than she'd intended.

Kat noticed and moved a step closer, lowering her voice. 'So if you weren't after his body, what were you doing? Where did you go?'

'If Lucy was here, I'd tell her.'

'Do you think she's okay? Have you heard from her since this morning?'

'Yeah. She's fine, apart from the fact that they can't have the funeral for ages. They need to book a mini-digger or something. She'll probably come back on Sunday.'

They had one customer left, a man who'd been looking at his phone. He got up, brought his empty cup to the counter and wished them a good weekend.

'I'll do it,' said Kat. She grabbed the pillar sign that said *Closed* and plonked it in the middle of the archway. When she came back, she looked at Bridget in a way that the older, shorter, stouter woman found disconcerting, as if her duckling had suddenly grown into a creature from a low budget sci-fi series on a distant TV channel. 'Why won't you talk to me about it? We've seen more of each other this week than I used to see of Feargal. He was always off somewhere, doing cash jobs and stuff. If you can't trust me now …?'

'Of course I trust you! It was you who told me that you weren't interested in finding out what happened to Millie.'

'That was Tuesday. This is Friday. That was before we knew that Lucy was innocent.'

Bridget stepped forwards, and it was Kat's turn to be intimidated. 'Lucy was *always* innocent.'

'It's alright for you. You'll be off in a couple of weeks and I could be serving coffee to a killer!'

Bridget was only thirty-six, but she couldn't help wondering if all young people were drama queens. 'I'm not going anywhere in the near future. Are you really interested?'

'I am. I might know something.'

'Let's finish clearing up first. Not that there's much to do. You've done well.'

They worked quickly and in silence to put the café to bed, apart from making two last drinks, which Kat was about to take into the kitchen.

'Let's go by the window,' said Bridget. 'Too easy to sneak up and listen outside the kitchen. And I like watching the wheel going round.' She grabbed the last two slices of a particularly light lemon drizzle cake and followed Kat to the table with the best view. 'Still no sign of Coffin Joe.'

'Oh. You missed him. He was in the other day while you were out. He's hard at work on something for Millie, but the vicar still hasn't been able to track down Millie's Canadian relatives, so no progress on her funeral, either.'

'Canada's a big place. Right. This is where I'm up to: I know that Millie was poisoned with a cappuccino from her own machine. She probably made it herself.'

Katarina's cup was filled to the brim with foamed milky chocolate and decorated with a smiley face in cocoa powder. It was also halfway to her lips. She stared at the drink with alarm and said, 'How do you know that?' She put the cup down and sat back.

'It had to have some bitterness in it for starters, hence the coffee. Millie knew how to use that machine on her worktop, and no way would she have burnt the milk. That means there was no chance of the amygdalin breaking down, since the perfect temperature for a cappuccino is too cool to start this process, and because she always used that disgusting unpasteurised stuff, all the killer had to do was make sure her flask of Mike's Magic Milk was topped up with a nice lethal dose. She had some flapjack with her coffee, and that delayed the digestion until the poor woman was in the tent.'

Katarina shivered. 'That's so … creepy. And scary. She cooked up her own death warrant.' She shook her head. 'When you put it like that, it's so … cold. Calculated.'

'It is. It was. Look, Kat, I have a good idea who did it, but I'm not going to say. Yet.'

'Why not! You can't do that to me.'

'I don't want to risk saying something unless I'm absolutely sure. If I *am* wrong, then we'd have two lives ruined and a killer still hanging around.'

'Why aren't you sure?'

'Because I can't figure out why they brought the poison into the tent to plant on Lucy, and I can't figure out how they got the raw materials.'

'Can you buy this stuff on the internet? On the dark web or something.'

'No. Well, you can probably buy hydrogen cyanide if you're barmy, but no. This was made in the village, using locally sourced organic cherry stones. If only it wasn't pick-your-own, I might stand a chance of narrowing it down.'

'But it isn't PYO.'

'You said …'

'Soft fruit, yeah. Totally. Not cherries. The trees are huge, and you need a ladder. Or an actual cherry picker. When they're in season, like now, a couple of the lads go up and pick them, then Mike sells them in punnets.' Kat had forgotten about the possibility of poisonous milk, and happily slurped her hot chocolate. 'In fact, Perry's boys do a lot of it. It's just round the back from their cottage.'

Bridget sat back, stunned. Kat started to say something, but Bridget interrupted. 'Give us a sec, yeah?'

Bridget rubbed her hands on her jeans and stared out of the window. The millwheel kept turning, water pouring in and out. One bucket had been repaired recently, and the wood was fresh and easy to spot. Every time it reappeared at the top, it reminded Bridget that she was going nowhere with this "investigation", just turning round and round. She thought she'd go mad with it, and then she thought she was hallucinating, because the wheel started to slow down. She was about to tell Kat that she was giving up when the wheel didn't just slow down, it stopped.

'What's happened to the wheel?' she asked.

'Joe turns it off at the weekend. It needs someone to watch the sluice gates or something, and he's not always here.'

Bridget tried not to think about a coffin maker lurking under the floor *all the time* and suppressed the image with a shudder. How did she even know that Coffin Joe existed ...? Because of the wheel. And the coffins making up Perry's workstation at the Bake Off. Like the molehills in the fields – all of them proved that there was *something* there.

So *think,* girl. It had been the mantra from her A Level chemistry teacher, and Miss Akinya had been the last person who'd called her a girl without getting her back up. *When you have evidence of an event, look at the inputs and the rules. If they don't explain the event, either you've missed an input or you've discovered a new law of science, and it says* Gorrigan *on your folder, not* Einstein.

There was one more place Bridget needed to look before she risked upsetting *everyone* in Byford.

Bridget took a deep breath and said, 'Okay, Kat, it's time to put on your big girl pants and call Bradley Nicol.'

The frightened duckling was back. 'No. No chance. Never. Why?'

'Tell him you need the pictures he took at the Bake Off. He was everywhere with that camera, so there must be loads. Tell him you only need pictures of Millie's workstation, the earlier the better. And tell him there might be a story in it. You can do it.'

'That's if he picks up. He might not want to talk to *anyone* from here after what you said to him the other day.'

'He'll pick up. Message him first if you like and tell that him you offered to call because the alternative was me stalking him.'

She didn't say yes, but she didn't say no either. Bridget forced the issue. 'I don't want to witness this, so I'll go get my laptop while you call him. We're gonna need a bigger screen to crack this case.'

She got up and strode into the kitchen, then ducked out of sight. She counted slowly to a hundred, then picked up her computer. The delay had worked – not enough to get Kat to *call* rather than message, but the result was the same. Better, even, because he'd shared a link to cloud storage which had *all* the pictures from last Saturday. Bridget moved her chair round so that Kat could see the screen and got clicking.

After five minutes, Bridget said, 'Do you think he has a backup, because I would *so* like to delete these pictures of me.'

'Erm. Yeah. Why *did* you wear that dress?'

'It looked suitable for the countryside, it was my size and it had long sleeves to cover these.' To take away thoughts of *that* dress, she held up her arms and rotated her forearms to display the ink. 'Didn't want these to be what people took away from seeing me for the first time.'

Katarina did not take the hint. She peered at the screen, then at Bridget's arms. 'Wrong call. You shouldn't have worn a black vest underneath, either.'

'Let's find one of Millie, shall we?'

They soon did, a picture taken before Bridget had arrived. Villagers were unpacking crates and putting Millie's ingredients and pre-made bakes onto her workstation. It confirmed part of what Bridget suspected, but she needed to see it in detail. Kat swiped through more pictures. 'There,' said Bridget. 'Look at the flapjack. No wonder Millie asked Debs to go and get more mixture.'

'Burnt round the edges and raw in the middle. Yeuch. Seen enough?'

'Yes. Drink up, girl. You're coming with me.'

'What? Why? Where are we going?'

'To see Magic Mike. He didn't kill Millie, but he might just help me prove who did.'

Katarina fastened her seat belt, then fussed with the seat adjuster to give herself more room. 'You know that Mike doesn't keep records and stuff for his fruit business. Strictly cash only. He got a one-star review for that.'

Bridget hesitated with her fingers by the ignition key, then gripped it and started the engine. 'That helps, I think.' She was back at the Meadow farmyard in two minutes, and this time she parked near the unpretentious, four-square farmhouse. She was heading for the door when she noticed that Kat had gone off to the side. 'Where are you going?'

'Round the back. Farmers never answer their front door.'

Bridget ran to catch up and intercepted her colleague before she could walk straight through the open porch. The back of Meadow Farmhouse had a sort of professional neglect to it: there was a decent-sized garden, mostly lawn and shrubs with a few tulips fading away. Nothing was in ruins, but nothing looked like it was particularly *loved* either, not like you'd expect if generations of farmers had been tending it. The only thing that looked *loved* was the patio furniture and the big gas barbecue. That positively gleamed.

'Hello?' she shouted. 'It's Bridget from Caffè Milano.'

'Come in,' came a voice, and Bridget followed it.

The kitchen wouldn't be appearing in any interiors magazines, that was for certain. Yes, it had a big table, but the units were tired and the cooker might have been decades old; not so the microwave: like the grill outside, it looked bang up to date.

Mike Mason had stood up to say hello, and the first person he greeted was Kat. He said *Hi* in a familiar way that spoke of years of acquaintance, then focused on Bridget. 'This is unexpected. Is everything okay?'

'Have you got a second?' said Bridget.

'Yes please. All distractions welcome.' He pointed to papers spread all over the table. 'I hate VAT with a passion. I only ever do it on Fridays, and I'm not allowed to go to the pub until I'm finished. You have to incentivise yourself.'

'You do. I feel your pain, Mike.'

'Sit down. Please. Is there any point putting the kettle on?'

The girls sat, and Bridget said, 'No thanks. We both tend to stop with the caffeine after work.'

He sat, too, and carefully moved piles of invoices and bank statements. There must be a computer somewhere, reasoned Bridget, because no business could survive on paper any more. She'd only seen Mike briefly at the Bake Off and on his flying visit to the Spinning Room; close up, he was older than she'd thought, somewhere between Feargal and Perry, so late thirties. He was dressed for hard work, and his face was lined from doing it outdoors. The creases moved around a lot when he spoke, giving Magic Mike a very mobile face.

'Nice to see you again,' he said. 'Sorry I had to run the other day – I'm way too busy in the week. I'll see you tomorrow, and if you take orders, put a couple of croissants aside for me.'

'See?' said Kat. 'I told you we needed more at the weekends.'

'No problem,' said Bridget. 'They'll be waiting.' She paused. 'Don't take this the wrong way, but have the police been to see you?'

He sat back on the wooden chair, and it creaked alarmingly. 'Amos said you'd become Byford's Miss Marple.'

Bridget was surprised no one had said it before: it was the obvious reference. Maybe it's because all the people she'd spoken to were either too young to have heard of the legendary sleuth (like Kat), or they were too close to Millie Easterby for things to be quite so casual. 'Have you ever seen or read any Agatha Christie?' she asked.

'Can't say as I have. Mum used to watch them occasionally. Probably still does when she's relaxing.'

'So there's no point telling you that I hate knitting and gardening is there?'

He laughed, and the lines on his face moved away from his mouth like ripples in a pond. 'You shouldn't judge books by their cover, but no, knitting is not what I thought of when you first appeared in my life.'

Bridget forced herself to grin. *Please tell me he's not flirting with me,* she thought. *That would make every man on Kat's list who I've met thinks it's okay to act this way.* The grin collapsed. 'Why was Amos talking about me?'

'He doesn't get out much. Very self-contained is Amos, unlike Louis. Amos is a good listener, though. Very dry sense of humour, too. Apparently you've upset Louis because you haven't brought him any tea or biscuits, or even been to see the gallery. He's in a huff and blames it on you spending all your time stirring up trouble.'

Bridget turned to Kat. 'Did you know that?'

'No, but I did wonder where he's been.'

'How do you cope with everyone talking about you?' she asked both of them, and both of them shrugged. 'Police, Mike?'

'Yesterday evening. Wanted to know about the Easterby cherries.'

'Who came?'

'Vicky Higham. She comes in the White Hart quite a bit.'

'And?'

'I think she's got a boyfriend. Bit too young for me anyway.'

Bridget's hands formed into fists, and she was on the verge of praying for strength. 'What. Did. She. Ask?'

'To see my records. Most of the crop goes straight to a place that packages them for supermarkets. When I told her I sold the rest for cash only, and that I don't have CCTV on the bench where I sell it, you'd think I'd killed her teddy bear. She almost cried.'

'Did she tell you why she was asking?'

'Not as such. I guessed, though.'

'Did she ask about any specific people?'

'Yes she did. Asked if I remembered selling quantities to Deb Giddings, Dom and Anya Calvert, Perry and Ferg. Oh, and Nathan Frost for some reason. The answer was yes to all of them except Perry and Nathan. The cherries are too expensive and too fragile to leave an honesty box, so I'd know, wouldn't I?'

'Did no one else sell them? Amos, for example.'

'Only occasionally, and Amos is nothing if not precise. When he covered for me, he'd show me the money and tell me if anyone local bought them. Other than the odd lunch hour, I sold every cherry myself. I also watched Perry's lads doing the picking, and they didn't walk off with any.'

Kat fidgeted in her seat. 'That sounds like a total dead-end, then.'

'No. It sounds perfect.' She stood up. 'Do I need wellingtons to get safely to the cherry orchard?'

'Now? Why?'

'I'll explain when we get there.'

He looked at her feet. 'You'll be fine.'

Chapter 30

Bridget stopped dead when she saw the concrete track that led down the gentle slope towards the river. The cows had just walked up it on their way to the milking parlour and it was covered in what you'd expect. 'You have to be kidding me,' she said.

'What's wrong?' said Mike.

'I thought you said I wouldn't need wellingtons. Look at that lot.'

'Walk next to the fence, then. The girls avoid the barbed wire for obvious reasons.'

He was right. If she kept her balance, there was a clean and dry strip about a foot wide that ran down the edge of the track. She sighed and set off at a pace, hoping desperately that she wouldn't bang her hip into the fence and fall over.

The concrete path turned and headed towards the ford, and Mike led them away from it and into a sort of mini valley on the left that was protected from the winds by a stand of trees on a rise.

At least that's what he told her: Bridget had no idea where the prevailing winds might come from. 'Perfect spot,' he said.

The Japanese are well known for their obsession with *Sakura,* the flowering cherry. No one was going to get obsessed by these trees, mainly because you couldn't see them: they were inside a huge wood and polythene hangar.

'What's that for?' she asked. 'If this is a perfect spot, why put them in there?'

'Birds. It's a perfect spot because no one can complain about me spoiling the view. If I didn't cover the trees, I wouldn't have a crop worth cultivating. Have a look inside.'

He lifted a flap of plastic and pinned it up. The temperature inside was closer to summer, and the air was ripe with the sweet smells of growing things and a bitter edge of decay. Kat was right about needing ladders, though: the lowest branches were a good ten feet off the ground.

'I've let things go this week,' said Mike. 'What with one thing and another. It's like everything's been paralysed with what happened to Millie. I'll have to see if Perry's lads are playing rugby tomorrow.'

'Do you have thefts?' asked Bridget.

'No. If I left the ladders up here, I probably would, but they're locked away.'

'Good. Show me what happens to the waste, because there's nothing you can do with rotting fruit if it's got stones in it.'

Understanding dawned on Mike's face. 'The barrel! The lads swore blind it wasn't them.'

Fear gripped Bridget's chest. She was *so* close. 'Show me.'

Mike strode through the grass towards the back of the tent. With no cows to eat it, the grass was thick and going to seed. Bridget struggled to catch up, and at the end of the orchard she found him next to a giant blue barrel sitting on a pile of wooden pallets. On the side, faded printing said that the barrel had originally contained something that was toxic in large doses – a bit like the cherry stones for which it had been repurposed.

Bridget had to look up to see the top of the barrel: even a tall man would have trouble tipping anything into this monstrosity. She started running through what must have happened, speaking aloud to clarify her thoughts.

'You pick the fruit – with ladders. You sort it. You put the waste in one bucket and use your ladder to climb up and chuck it into the barrel.' She turned to Mike. 'Let me guess: one day a couple of weeks ago, it was on its side when you came in.'

He had followed her logic and carried on. 'And I blamed the boys. We'd harvested for an hour the night before, and I left them to clear up with just the short steps while I took the big ladders back down. When I came to collect the little steps, I never went to the end of the hangar, so I didn't see for myself.'

He shook his head in frustration at what he'd missed. 'The next morning, the barrel was on its side, and the lads swore blind it was upright when they left it … and there wasn't much mess, either. Come to think of it, there should have been a lot more. Yeah, someone definitely stole the waste fruit.'

Kat joined in. 'Whoever came to steal the waste didn't know it would be out of reach in a barrel! They had to tip it over to get the mush out.'

Bridget already had her phone out. 'Show me your phone, Mike. I need your number.' He did as she asked and held up the screen. 'I'm gonna text you Liz Swindlehurst's contact details. Call her and tell her what you told me. Tell her that there's bound to be forensic evidence on that barrel somewhere, because it's been protected from the rain by the tent. Brilliant. There you go.'

'Of course I'll call her, but why don't you do it?' said Mike.

'Because Kat and I are going to follow the killer's footsteps. Come on, girl.'

Bridget didn't wait for any more questions and set off through the tent and back to the path. When she got there, she stopped and surveyed the Cowan valley and the village of Byford, all laid out before her.

They weren't on a huge hill, just enough of a rise to allow you to see the skyline and the main features. To her right were the metal sheds of Meadow Farm, then the imposing bulk of Ford Mill standing behind the cottages. She couldn't see the river or the bridge, but on the other side, she could clearly see the green, the village shop and then, jutting out into a curve in the river, the unfenced back of the new St Peter's School campus.

This had started with a death in a tent over the river, and she had seen the answer in the cherry tent behind her. She hadn't realised that she was moving until Kat said, 'Where are we going?'

Bridget had rejoined the concrete path which led to a huge meadow by the river and carried on through it to the ford, down from the bridge. The meadow would be a natural flood plain in winter, and the concrete was probably laid on top of a track first used before the Romans came along. There was no cow muck here, so Bridget could stride along the path.

'Do you know who did it?' said Kat. 'Are you certain?'

'Yes. And we're going to look for more evidence.'

'Who was it?'

'One more link in the chain, Kat.'

'Where are you … Oh My God!'

The River Cowan is not the Thames. It's not even the Kent or the Lune. It comes from hills quite close to the coast, and is both quick to rise and quick to fall. Two days of dry weather had dropped the level to where Bridget could see the underwater path through the ford. She stepped into the water and took two steps before she realised how stupid she'd been. Her Doc Martens were great in the rain, but no use for fording a river.

'Ow! It's bloody freezing!' she exclaimed, turning round in shock.

Kat stood on the apron with a look of horror on her face. 'What did you expect?'

'Sod it,' said Bridget and turned back. She set her sights on the other side and waded the few metres to sanctuary. 'Are you coming?'

'I want new Converse if I do.'

'Whatever.'

She turned west and left her duckling to get her feet wet or get left behind.

'Ow! Ow! Ow! I hate you.'

There was a path along the north side of the river, and a much steeper slope that protected the village from flooding. Bridget squelched along the footpath with a grimace, and Kat caught up with her.

'If Mum or Dad was watching, I may have to kill you. If we're going to the shop, I *will* kill you.'

'We're going back to school, kid. Ah, here we are.'

A path led down from the school playing fields, and Bridget did her best to get up it without sliding back in a heap. With a puff and a heave, she got to the top and paused to recover her breath.

'Is this safe?' she panted, pointing to the half-sized football pitch. 'This close to the river?'

Kat was depressingly unwinded. 'The playground's fenced, and there had to be two adults when we came out. I used to pray that no one would turn up to help, then I wouldn't have to do PE outside.'

'Why not fence in the playing fields?'

'Dunno. Dad said that it's something to do with the status of the land and the lease.'

Bridget tracked the view again, this time turning full circle. Across the river were higher pastures above the flood plain, small woods and an outcrop of rock, steep on one side and shallower on the other. It was what sheltered Mike Mason's cherry trees.

'You callous bastard,' said Bridget, directing her words to the open view. Her phone rang, and it was DS Liz Swindlehurst. 'Hi, did Mike call you?' Bridget asked.

'He did. Luckily, we were having a late meeting, so I hadn't gone home. Where are you? I'm on my way up to Byford.'

'At the school, and I'm going in. Round the back. If I can. Is Tracey coming?'

'The Commander said no, not until I'd seen it myself. We're running out of money. Why are you going into the school?'

'Come and see for yourself.'

Bridget disconnected and, now that her chest was no longer heaving quite so badly, she set off across the football pitch, feet still squelching (and now *very* cold). 'Did you watch *Breaking Bad*?' she asked.

'Not my thing,' said Kat. 'It was that teacher who made meth, wasn't it … You don't think Mr Frost made the amygdalin?'

'Where better than the school kitchens? No one can see them. Not a single property overlooks them. Perfect. Looks like we're just in time.'

The school playground was a riot of primary colours. They brightened up the play equipment, they shone out from the walls and they were ingrained in the soft-impact flooring. One corner even had a stepped series of raised planters painted in rainbow stripes and holding a mixture of bright flowers and earnest vegetables. It all helped you forget the high fence and the sturdy gate.

'Why is it unlocked?' said Kat.

'Because he didn't want to be seen, and he's in there now, I'll bet. Where's the kitchens?'

'Over there, round the corner. You're right – they're on the opposite side to my bedroom. No one can see them.'

The school kitchen had an outside door. Bridget went through it, and there he was: Millicent Easterby's killer.

'Mr Frost! What are you doing?' said Kat, utterly appalled that the ultimate authority figure of her childhood – a teacher – could be the one responsible for a violent death.

The kitchens of St Peter's School were small, much smaller than Caffè Milano's at Ford Mill. After all, there weren't many to feed here, and most of the food was cooked off-site and delivered chilled. They were big enough, though.

'You're trespassing,' said Nathan Frost.

'And you're trying to cover your tracks,' said Bridget. She turned to Kat. 'Look – he's got stepladders. Properly prepared today. He's going to climb up there and take the extractor apart. There will be trace evidence in the filters.'

'I'm fixing a light,' said Frost. 'What are you talking about?'

'Plausible, isn't he?'

'Ms Gorrigan, you are trespassing. Please leave now.'

'Or what? The police are on their way to seal the premises.'

'No they're not. I am going to have to take action if you don't leave.'

Bridget walked over to the five-ring burner and hoisted herself on top of it. 'Go ahead and make my day. Kat, go and make sure Liz knows where we are.'

'I'm not leaving you in here.'

'He won't touch me, and if he does, he'll discover that I can do a great impression of an immovable object. Go on.'

Kat cast a last glance at the teacher and ran out of the door. There was silence for a moment, and Bridget was seriously regretting what she'd done: the pot-holding framework was digging into her backside *most* uncomfortably. She was also going to regret everything else if she was wrong about Nathan Frost.

The headteacher looked around, shrugged his shoulders and went to move the steps and the cleaning equipment he'd brought along with him. Bridget took a quick photograph and grinned. 'You don't need that stuff to change a lightbulb. Now I've got a picture of it.'

'But you do need it to clean the fridge,' said Frost. 'Which was going to be my next job.'

'Such dedication.'

'Only way to run a small school. Our budget is tiny.'

Footsteps thumped outside, and the reassuring bulk of Liz filled the doorway. 'What's going on?' asked the detective.

With great relief, Bridget hopped off the cooker. Or tried to – the bars caught in her back pocket, and there was a tearing noise. Today was definitely Friday the Thirteenth. 'Mr Frost here was about to remove evidence. If you check the filter, there will be traces of the diethyl ether he used to extract the amygdalin. And other things that shouldn't be there in a school kitchen.'

'Are you serious?'

'Yes. I'll pay for the tests myself if I have to.'

Liz turned to Frost. 'If you don't mind, sir?'

The teacher's back went stiff. 'It's school policy not to allow police searches without a warrant.'

'My arse it is,' said Bridget. 'I'll wait here while you go up the road and see Colonel Shepherd. He'll sign you a warrant. No, hang on, I've got a better idea. You stay here, Liz, and I'll go and see the chair of governors. She'll give permission.'

Liz didn't need it pointed out to her. She could see the gear that Frost had brought with him. 'Will you be long?'

'Dunno.'

'Take as long as you like,' said Frost. 'I have better things to do.' With that, he carried on packing up and left the kitchen.

'Off you go,' said Liz. 'What have you done to your shoes?'

'Crossed the Rubicon, obviously.'

Kat had been peering over Liz's shoulder, and Bridget said, 'Run home and get a car. I am not walking through the village with my backside hanging out of my jeans and wet feet.'

'Erm, sorry, Boss. Dad's out in the only car I'm insured to drive. I know. Hang on.'

Kat vanished, and Bridget squelched out of the kitchen and turned to walk up the drive. On the way, she sent Deborah a message: *Coming over. Will have to remove my shoes. I have bad news. Sorry.*

When Bridget got near the road, Kat slipped back through a gap in the fence which separated school and shop. She ran over to Bridget, drops of water spraying out of her shoes, and said, 'Here. This should fit. It's Dad's.'

She held out a waxed jacket. A much-abused wax jacket only one rung above the one that Conrad Clarke wore to walk his dog.

'No,' Bridget told her duckling.

'Yes. No one wants to see your pants, Boss, big girl or … otherwise.'

Bridget snatched the coat and shoved her arms through the sleeves.

'Perfect!' said Kat with a way too happy smile. 'You fit right in now.'

Bridget channelled the god of the underworld into a death stare.

'Orange sauce.'

'Eh?'

Bridget shoved her hands in the pockets and squelched off to see the vicar.

Chapter 31

The vicar met them on the doorstep, and was still adjusting her dog collar after a quick change. Presumably if things got really serious, she'd swap the lounge pants for something more formal. 'What's going on?'

'The police need your permission to search the school. I believe there's evidence in there. And so do they – Liz is guarding it to stop Nathan Frost destroying it.'

'Nathan! I don't believe you.'

'One of us is finished in Byford, Deborah: him or me. If you give permission, we'll know for certain.'

'I'll go down now.'

Bridget placed a call. 'No need. I've set it to record what you say. Just give permission. That's all they need. Hello, Liz? I've got the chair of governors here …'

Deborah didn't waste time. She gave the police what they needed and passed the phone back. Meanwhile, Bridget had been unlacing her boots. Or trying to, because the water had done nothing for her knots. In the end, Katarina had to pull them off, and then Deborah showed them into the kitchen. After commenting that the black paint on Bridget's toenails was *very neat*.

'I'm afraid that the diocese doesn't like spending money on clergy property. They've told me I'm welcome to update it myself … Tea?'

'Please.'

They waited in silence while the kettle boiled. The kitchen did look well past its sell-by date, and one of the doors was sagging badly. It was clean, though, and there was a decent wooden table to sit round. Bridget guessed that the vicar only brought those she really trusted in here.

'Why?' said Deborah. 'How is also important, but why?'

'Did you know they were in a relationship?'

Sourness and guilt fought for supremacy on the vicar's face. 'Don't ask, don't tell. I was fairly certain, yes, but if I'd known officially, I'd have had to take action. It wasn't against the rules, but it would have made it very awkward for everyone if it became public. It must have been going on for a while before I had my suspicions, and I decided to wait it out. Either they'd grow together, or I could be there to support Millie.'

The guilt won out, and Deborah looked imploringly at Bridget. 'Is that why he did it? Was she going to leave him?'

'I think it was more than that, Deborah. I think he could have stood that: after all, if no one else ever knew … No, I think it was the playing fields.'

'What do you mean?'

'Ask Perry if you don't believe me, but Millie was planning to sell the *whole* property to Edwin Duke, including the playing fields, and sell it with no strings attached.'

'She wouldn't have done that!'

'I'm afraid she would. Edwin could have built houses on that site quite easily: it's above the flood plain and within the village envelope. The view is tremendous. Or he might just have wanted to have the school and Dom Calvert over a barrel. We'll never know.'

While the vicar digested the news, Bridget helped herself to a couple of biscuits. That was a lot to take in for Deborah. 'How did he do it?' she finally asked.

'He knew Millie would have a lot of visitors that day. He knew there would be plenty of other people who *could* have administered the poison. He had one advantage over them, though: he knew about the CCTV at the shop. He came round the path from the bridge and through the back. He says he was only there for a short time, but he was there for ages.'

'How will the police ever prove that?'

'Show her the flapjack picture, Kat.'

'Is that what you wanted it for?' asked the girl. 'It's not proof of anything.'

'Show her anyway.' Kat found the picture on her phone, and Bridget continued. 'Brad Nicol took these. Millie has been making this flapjack for years. She wouldn't have made something like *that*.'

Deborah had to put reading glasses on to study the phone. 'You're right. Millie was far too … She had much higher standards. No wonder she sent me back to get more mixture and was reluctant to show me why.' She made a circular motion with her hand in front of the phone. 'If someone else *had* made it and wrapped it, and this was the first time she'd seen it … Yes. I can see her rejecting it.'

'He was there a long time,' continued Bridget. 'Helping out. Baking flapjack. Tidying up. Putting poison in the raw milk.'

'I thought the police had tested everything in the house?'

'He emptied one flask and put it in the dishwasher. When they double check, they'll find Feargal's fingerprints on the flask in the fridge, and Nathan has already said he took a *full* flask with him. They'll also check the other rooms. He would have been hiding out of the way when visitors called. They had to ring the bell from on the road, remember?'

'Won't his fingerprints … and DNA, I suppose … won't that be all over the house if they were in a relationship?'

'Yes, but Millie spent all morning in the kitchen. His fingerprints will be on top and in places like the hall. I'll bet he was leaning on the banisters. Not only that, the police have kept all her equipment from the tent. There will be lots of evidence that he was in School House for more than a quick visit.'

The plate of biscuits was empty now. 'Excuse me,' said Deborah. 'This calls for emergency measures.'

She jumped up like she needed to move, to do something rather than sit and think. She opened a cupboard and reached on tiptoes to the top shelf, then returned with a box of Jaffa Cakes. 'What about the bottle of poison in Lucy's handbag?'

'He couldn't afford to put the amygdalin in the milk until he was sure he could manipulate Millie into drinking it. There were simply too many visitors, and his own plan of spreading the blame to someone in the tent meant that he had to walk out of School House with it. He may even have planned to put it somewhere else until he saw Brad's camera. After that, her collapse was the only chance he had to get rid of it.'

There was a moment's silence, broken by Kat. 'Is that all you've got?'

'You what?' responded Bridget.

'I did do one year at Uni, and we did loads on *burden of proof.* A good barrister will easily cast doubt on what you've said, even if all the forensic evidence is where you think it will be.'

'Excuse me one minute,' said Deborah, who rose and left without another word.

Bridget argued with Kat for a couple of minutes, and her duckling was adamant. 'The Crown won't have enough.'

'Yes they will,' said Deborah from the doorway. 'These have got an elasticated waist, and the socks are clean.' The vicar was now wearing black trousers and held out the lounge pants and a pair of pink fluffy socks to Bridget.

'Thanks,' said Bridget, taking the clothes. 'Why do you think there will be enough evidence?'

'Because I'm going to see him now, while the police are collecting their samples.'

'You can't go and see him on your own!' said Kat.

'I've just seen him come back from the upstairs window. I'm going to give him a chance to explain himself if he's innocent or to confess if he's guilty.'

'I'll come with you,' said Bridget.

'No, thank you. This is my village and my school. He certainly won't talk with you there.'

'He's been pretty cold so far,' said Bridget. 'What makes you think he'll fall over when Liz has already had a go. No offence, Deborah, but I know who I'd find more intimidating.'

Deborah picked up her coat from the back of a chair and checked her phone. 'As I said, this is my village and my school. He may have an explanation for everything you've said, but if he hasn't …' She let her words hang in the air and left them in her kitchen. 'Close the door behind you when you leave,' she shouted from the hall.

They were still staring at the door when Bridget's phone rang. It was Lucy. Bridget answered and put it on speaker.

'What's going on?' said Lucy. 'Tom's just had Ross on the phone saying you've gone all Terminator.'

'Don't worry, boss,' said Kat in a loud voice. 'We were never in danger.'

'Sod that,' said Lucy. 'I want to know why you didn't wait until I got back!'

Word got round. Word *always* gets round in a village. A steady stream of people who'd not set foot in Caffè Milano before came in during the next day to find out from the horse's mouth what was going on. By the middle of the afternoon, Bridget had to send Lucy out for more cakes and pastries, and Kat was complaining that her overnight delivery of new Converse were pinching her feet.

The most bizarre moment occurred just before lunch, when Anya and Fliss swept in together. Bridget leaned over the counter, and she could see two toddlers lurking by the arch. Grace, whom she'd met on that first day, was pointing her finger at Bridget and whispering something in the ear of the girl who must be Violet, Fliss's daughter. Both wore pink leotards, which told Bridget where they'd come from but not why their mothers were here. Before she considered the Valkyrie and the Pixie, Bridget noted that Grace seemed to be very much in charge of the little gang. If you can make a gang from a pair of three-year-olds. On reflection, you absolutely could.

Fliss finished talking to a scared-looking man, and then the Queen Bees of Byford came up to the counter.

'Hiya,' said Bridget. 'What can I get you?'

'Some other time,' said Fliss. 'We both have hungry children to feed, but we wanted to say thank you.'

'Yes,' added Anya. She had a rugged backpack, and slipped it off her shoulder. 'For what you did about Millie. We all know that it was you who … forced the issue. We wanted to give you this.'

Ooh! Was Bridget going to get a brown envelope stuffed with twenties? That would go down a treat.

Anya opened her backpack and took out … Oh. Bridget had not expected to see *that* again.

'Your business was very generous with the sponsorship, and this is all that's left.'

Anya held out the Bake Off trophy, the wooden spoon embedded in a varnished plinth.

'Holly from upstairs made it,' added Fliss, as if that made it suddenly desirable.

Bridget had no choice but to accept the trophy, and was clearly expected to be grateful. 'Thank you. I think. Will there be another one next year?'

The Pixie looked up and the Valkyrie looked down. 'Too early to think about that,' said Anya decisively. She raised her head. 'Come on,

Grace. Let's go.'

Bridget had a grade A in A level physics. She understood the Standard Model of the universe. She had wrapped her head around the strong force and the weak force and how they governed interactions at the subatomic level. What she struggled with was the forces driving Anya and Fliss together, when they clearly didn't like each other. Whatever it was, a different force now drove them apart, splitting them and sending them in different directions, their little electrons coming into orbit and circling their mothers.

'What was that about?' asked Lucy, emerging from the kitchen with some prepped salads.

'Yours, I think,' said Bridget, placing the trophy on the back counter.

'Oh no,' said Lucy. 'That's most definitely yours. Budge up, I need to get in the chiller.'

Tom Morton arrived half an hour before closing, and he had that *bearing up* look on him that English men adopt now that the complete *stiff upper lip* is discouraged. Lucy fussed him into a quiet corner and Bridget took him a pot of strong tea. 'I'm sorry about your granddad,' she said. 'It's never easy, is it?'

'Thank you. No, it isn't. I think I'm more tired than anything. I only stopped here because I have to go into work.'

'What's up?' said Lucy.

'I was heading for Garstang until Ross called. Nathan Frost made a statement admitting murder this morning, then No-Commented his way through the interview. Ross wants me to look over the files before they pass them to the CPS.'

'Why?' asked Kat, who had abandoned the counter to join in.

'In case he retracts the confession later. Ross wants to be certain that there's enough supporting evidence for the CPS to charge him. I came here because I wanted to see a friendly face before I disappear into the bunker.'

Bridget grabbed Kat's arm and steered her away to leave Tom with Lucy. When she turned round, Perry Lockwood was waiting at the counter. For some reason, Kat detoured and went into the kitchen.

'You've certainly had a large impact in a short time,' said Perry. 'Are you still serving?'

'Of course. Coming up.'

Kat was still missing when Bridget slid Perry's coffee over the counter. He made no move to go and sit down after he'd handed over the money. Instead, he picked up a canvas tote and placed it in front of Bridget. The bag was one she recognised – a free sample from a merchandising company with *Your Logo Here* in big letters. Lucy had picked up mountains of stuff like that when she was creating the Caffè Milano brand.

'It seems you have an admirer,' said Perry, waggling his eyebrows. 'Or should I say *another* one?'

'The only male admirer I'm interested in is me dad,' she said with as much finality as she could.

'Oh. Right. Well, I'm sure it's well intentioned. Here.'

He lifted what looked like a snow globe from the tote bag. It was under a snow globe dome – a big one on a dark wooden base. And what in the Devil's name was *that* …? Bridget picked it up and peered through the glass. 'Is that *me*?'

'Who else?'

The bell jar contained a perfect replica of the coffee shop counter, with an equally perfect replica of the coffee machine sitting on top of it. The replica of the barista behind was less perfect, but definitely Bridget, from the black hair, uniform shirt and squishy hips right down to the ink on her arms. 'Bloody hell, Perry. Who did this?' She looked up and was half afraid that it had been the man himself, but no: he was shaking his head.

'Does your customer look familiar?' he asked with a smile.

She peered again. 'Why am I making coffee for a strawberry with legs?' And then it dawned on her. 'Space Fruit! Did Anthony make this?'

'He did. Hayley came in to sign the lease on the studio this morning and brought this with her.'

'Right. I don't know what to say.'

'I can pass on your thanks or give you his number. It is exquisite.'

'Erm. Right. Pass on my thanks.' She couldn't stop revolving the globe and admiring the details. Except for the face. Her head was bowed and she couldn't tell whether he'd caught her likeness or not. 'What a hobby. He should do this professionally. I take it he doesn't star in the porno movies they're gonna be making.'

Perry snorted. 'I could murder Fliss sometimes. Sorry. Wrong thing to say. I had no idea that being her PR fixer was part of the job. She says something outrageous in that sweet voice of hers, and the next thing you know, Edwin is sending me round to deny it.' He sighed. 'Anthony is a model maker. He designed and made the models for the Space Fruit merchandise, and made a packet from them.'

'Figures.'

'Mmm. Their business is going to be selling miniature model components and tools. Anthony is going to focus on model railways and there's a third member of the team – Donna Ramsey. She's a big noise in doll's houses. Apparently. Hayley is the face of the channel, with Anthony and Donna doing the demonstrations.'

Bridget finally put the dome down. 'Wow. Why here?'

'You know Laura and Shannon?'

'Turn the Paige. Yeah, of course. Not that they come down here much.'

'Oh?'

'Kat's always taking stuff up to them. She's a bit of an acolyte.' She frowned. 'In fact, I'm not entirely sure whether we're being paid for the coffee in cash or kind yet. Either way, they owe us a fair bit.'

'That doesn't sound like you, Bridget,' he observed. 'Mike Mason says you're very hot on freebies.'

She snorted. 'Now there's a chancer. So what have Laura Paige and Shannon Turner got to do with Anthony and Hayley?'

'Hayley is Laura's sister, and Shannon used to work with Tony, apparently, and Laura tipped Hayley off about the empty studio. Mini Magic Models get the virtual keys on Monday, but I've no idea when they'll start broadcasting.'

He took a sip of coffee and shook his head. 'There's more. You know what, Bridget, I think I must be losing my touch.'

'How come?'

'I let you lot have the kitchens for nothing, and then Tony insists that we make some space for CARM at a peppercorn rent.'

'Who's Calm? Some alternative therapy lot?'

'You'll see. I'm sure you'll be ... transported when you meet them.' He suddenly realised that a young couple were waiting patiently behind him. 'Have you got a second?'

'Kat! Needed!'

Bridget stepped away from the counter, putting the gift in a prominent position on the back counter. She moved to a window and Perry came over to stand next to her.

'Feargal paid me a visit last night,' he began. 'Quite late.'

'Was he still drunk after your boozy lunch?'

'He was never *that* drunk, but he had sobered up a lot when he came back. When we spoke yesterday, I had to tell him that he couldn't have a month rent-free – he could have a week or sign the tenancy agreement. He thought it over and he'll be gone by next Friday. He's got a job working as relief manager for a pub chain in Birmingham. It'll be summer holiday season soon.'

'Shame. I hope he'll come here to say goodbye.'

'And to thank you for clearing his name, I'm sure. He'll be coming back for Millie's funeral as well, obviously. Now that he's allowed to be the grieving ex-husband, of course.'

There was a trace of bitterness there, enough to make Bridget wonder what nerve had been touched.

Perry continued, 'Duke has invited him to stay at the Lodge for the funeral as we don't know when it will be, and come next week, I'll have a different problem.'

'What's that?'

'Did you see the rest of Number Four, or just the kitchen?'

'Just the kitchen.'

'That's being replaced, starting after Ferg leaves. The rest has already been renovated. That's one of the reasons we let him stay: to keep an eye on the place during refurbishment. It's in much better condition than the Cairndale flat.'

'How do you know that?'

'I asked Andrea at Carter's. Do you fancy it? It would be handy for the Mill, especially in winter. You could get the Cairndale flat done up while you're here, then make a decision.'

'I am not living in this village!'

'Why not? Fliss has already dubbed you *Our very own Dark Angel*. You'd fit right in.'

'*Dark Angel* me foot. You made that up.'

'No I didn't. You credit me with too much imagination. Fliss is also very keen for you to move in.'

Was Perry saying that he wanted to see more of her? '*Also* keen?'

'Sorry.'

It was the word he'd said to her more often than any other. *Sorry.* Before she could try to prise him out of his shell, he surprised her.

'Sorry, I meant that Fliss is keen for you to move in so that you'll get bored on Wednesday nights and join the quiz team. Fliss says you can even choose the name.' He looked down at her jeans, something that hadn't happened for a long time. 'Once you've finished plucking your legs with the tweezers, that is.'

It was Bridget's turn to flounder.

'At least think about it,' said Perry, taking a step back. 'I'll see you on Monday, no doubt.'

Bridget took his empty cup and looked around the Spinning Room. It was exactly a week since Millie Easterby had collapsed in front of her and died on the floor of the Bake Off tent. She thought of all the people she'd met since then, and how they'd responded to her, including the Mill's new tenants in the studio.

Behind the shiny new coffee machine, the mini model of her worked hard under its glass dome, and next to the dome, the Bake Off trophy stood as a reminder of what she'd achieved. A few seconds later, she had her third *moment.*

Coming here had been a challenge. It had made her reassess an awful lot of things about herself and about her responses to people. Perhaps she was more suited to village life than she realised. And perhaps Byford was ready for a resident Goth, to go with the many other peculiar residents. It was definitely something to think about.

Bridget, Lucy and Kat's stories continue in An Extra Shot of Murder.
If you want to know how Lucy met Tom, you can find out in A Serpent in Paradise *by Mark Hayden.*

And you can read about how the first branch of Caffè Milano came to be opened and how Bridget met Lucy in the sequel, Another Place to Die, *also by Mark Hayden.*

Also available from Paw Press

Extra Shot of Murder –
The Second Caffè Milano English Village Mystery

By
Ruth Ward

All Change for Byford and Beyond.
Bridget is loving life. She loves her job, her new house, and she quite fancies the guy on the top floor with magic hands. Things are looking up for the Goth girl from Garston.
As dawn breaks over the Cowan Valley, Bridget takes a coffee to the studio where Tony Carson and his partners are ready to launch their business channel. Instead of a new start, she finds that Tony has come to a terrible end.

Murder with an Extra Shot

After her last entanglement with violent death, Bridget vows to stay well away until things go from bad to worse and she has to quit the café. With nothing left to lose, she decides to look into Tony's murder before the killer disappears into the background.
When Bridget is backed into a corner, there is only one thing that will help her – she needs to find her A Game.

***

If you're enjoying the Byford stories, why not join Ruth's elite group of supporters:

The Friends of Ford Mill

Visit the Paw Press website and sign up for the mailing list, or search **Facebook** for the Friends of Ford Mill Group.
Either way, you're guaranteed to be kept up with news from Paw Press.

A Note from Ruth

Thank you for reading my book, and I hope you enjoyed it. If you *really* enjoyed it, there's a sequel called *Extra Shot of Murder*. No pressure. Just saying…

What you've just read is the second, slightly longer version of a book first published in 2022 and written for charity. It featured characters from Mark Hayden's King's Watch universe, and I'm grateful that my brother let me borrow them. Thanks to the generosity of my his readers, the charity edition raised thousands of pounds.

One year later, he suggested that I should continue the series – that the world needed more Bridget and Lucy and that writing another book would keep me out of trouble. I couldn't possibly comment.

To make *MWiT* work as the start of a series, I re-wrote it and introduced some of the characters who appear in *Extra Shot*. Otherwise, it's the same – same story, same victim, same murderer, and I need to make the same acknowledgements that I did first time around.

If you're looking for the town of Cairndale or the village of Byford, you can find plenty like them in North Lancashire and South Westmorland. What you won't find is their exact match. To create the setting, the very real (and very nice) towns of Carnforth and Milnthorpe were razed to the ground and Cairndale was built on their ruins. This was mostly done to protect the guilty, and any resemblance to living people is entirely coincidental.

When it comes to *actual* living people, there are a lot to whom I owe a big debt. First and foremost are Rachel Lawston, Katie Birks and Kirsty Parkinson.

Rachel has designed all of Mark Hayden's covers, and she took pity on me. Not only did she do the first version of the cover as a gift, she also produced my profile picture (which is a portrait of her own cat, Professor Moriarti, and not *my* cat, Wombat. Just wanted to clear that up).

Katie Birks has played a crucial role, and she has been a model of patience. When I wrote the second edition, she took over cover duties and tweaked Rachel's work to what you saw on the front. She also handles the website for Paw Press, and that deserves a medal.

Also crucial to the second edition is Kirsty Parkinson, who bravely took on the editing and hammered out all sorts of bugs, errors and infelicities. All remaining imperfections are entirely my fault.

If you found the map useful (not always the case with eBooks), then I'm thrilled, because Josh Hinge put a lot of effort into turning my scribble into something worth looking at. Bless you, Josh.

Thanks to Lucy Campbell, Paula Berman, Lore Deus, Ian Forsdike and Sheila Joss, all of whom read the first draft and gave me feedback.

And finally, thanks go to Mrs Hayden. Not only did she read the first draft for me, she allowed Mark time off to work on the project. Greater love hath no woman…

If you *do* read *Extra Shot of Murder*, I promise that the Author's Note will be a lot shorter.

Until then,

Thanks for making it this far,

Ruth Ward.

Printed in Great Britain
by Amazon

55373645R00138